THE
ESCAPE
OF
LIGHT

Turner Publishing Company
Nashville, Tennessee
www.turnerpublishing.com

The Escape of Light
Copyright © 2019 Fred Venturini. All rights reserved.

Cover design: Lauren Peters-Collaer
Book design: Karen Sheets de Gracia

Library of Congress Cataloging-in-Publication Data
Names: Venturini, Fred, author.
Title: The escape of light / by Fred Venturini.
Description: [Nashville] : Turner Publishing Company, [2019] | Summary:
    "Teenage burn survivor Wilder Tate faces the challenges of high school but
    in the aftermath of tragedy he discovers the capacity to forgive and
    empathize—learning the importance of healing from the inside out"
    —Provided by publisher. |
Identifiers: LCCN 2019006652 (print) | LCCN 2019009177 (ebook) |
    ISBN 9781684423941 (epub) | ISBN 9781684423927 (pbk.) | ISBN 9781684423934
    (hardcover)
Subjects: | CYAC: Burns and scalds—Fiction. | Disfigured persons—Fiction. |
    High schools—Fiction. | Schools—Fiction. | Forgiveness—Fiction.
Classification: LCC PZ7.1.V447 (ebook) | LCC PZ7.1.V447 Esc 2019 (print) |
    DDC [Fic]—dc23
LC record available at https://lccn.loc.gov/2019006652

Printed in the United States of America

19 20 21 22   10 9 8 7 6 5 4 3 2 1

THE
ESCAPE
OF
LIGHT

—

FRED VENTURINI

TURNER
PUBLISHING COMPANY

THE BOY

I don't know when I became separated from the boy.

I was Wilder Tate, A-student, basketball junkie, unfortunate victim.

The boy was Wilder Tate, eternally ten years old and too dumb to know the consequences of each step he took and each word he said on March 23, 2010, The Day That It Happened.

The worst injury the boy had experienced up until that day was a set of puncture holes in his ass cheek, incurred when he tried to imitate Elmer Fudd by stepping on the head of a rake, allowing the handle to fly up in his face. The boy wanted to make his mother laugh, but instead, he stumbled ass-first onto the tines. The holes required stitches, and he learned the hard way that cartoons are not real.

March came that year and locked away the sun for the whole damn month. The boy's father had been dead for two years, and his mother was at work. His grandparents lived two houses away, and that's where he stayed after school until his mother got home.

His grandparents were always seated at the kitchen table, the smoke of Viceroys clouding at the ceiling, which had turned a shade of yellow long ago. Their TV had dials instead of buttons, and when the local news ended, they clicked it over to cable news.

His grandmother let him eat Rice Chex for lunch, the hollow squares anchored to the bottom of the bowl by heaps of sugar. His grandfather helped him with his homework, and when it was done they'd work puzzles together, or he'd read one of his grandmother's old Stephen King paperbacks. Even with his eyes watering from the cigarette smoke, the boy always stayed for a few more puzzle pieces after his mother called him home.

But on the day he was burned, he was too stupid to walk straight to his grandparents' house after getting off the bus. He heard a noise in the crumbling garage behind his house and knew it had to be Randy Meadows, a snake of a kid, thirteen years old and already a torturer of animals, a known thief, a pyromaniac with a love for huffing gasoline.

Still, the boy wandered into the garage and saw Randy siphoning fuel out of a rusty push mower, collecting it in a dog bowl, intending to take it along and inhale the fumes where it was safer to get high.

The boy surprised Randy. They weren't friends anymore, having fought just a week earlier near the city shed.

During that confrontation, the boy thought his odds long if he chose to fight back. He was only ten, and Randy wasn't just thirteen but the kind of thirteen where you're already needing a shave and can buy cigarettes without getting carded. But when Randy shoved him down the rock pile again and again during a quickly escalating game of King of the Mountain, the boy took the first punch, and they fought, and now he was entering his own garage, his home turf, ready for another fight.

Instead, he ended up covered in blazing gasoline. The garage turned into a sunspot. Blind and burning, he whipped himself onto the ground and rolled.

When the flash subsided, he was smoking and muddy. He cried out for help, but Randy was gone.

The burns seeped fluid as he crawled to the door. The boy's torso was charred, and the tips of the flames had licked his neck, turning it pink and slick. He dragged himself through the gravel of the driveway, and by the time he made it to the road, he was shivering. His muscles cramped shut. Rocks and dirt clung to the wetness of his smoldering wounds.

The boy should have died right then and there, but for some reason, he kept on.

———

Nothing could be salvaged but my Timex watch.

The remains of my Chicago Bulls T-shirt were stuck to my burns, the edges curled up and black. My jeans felt baked and stiff. The double-knots in my favorite pair of Nikes were a congealed ball of melted plastic.

The nurses went to work with bandage scissors, working the silver jaws through my laces, through the denim, trimming away the pieces of my T-shirt that weren't fused to my body.

A nurse slipped the scissors under the plastic band of my Timex.

"Wait," I said. "Don't cut it. Please."

My father bought that Timex, the last birthday gift he gave me before the heart attack. I never took it off, not even when I showered.

Even though the watch was covered in soot, it still worked.

"Takes a licking and keeps on ticking," I said, trying to smile, and the nurse put the scissors down.

I kept the watch, thinking that the memory of my father could overwhelm how it reminded me of the day I got burned, but it didn't. I left it in a dresser drawer and didn't see it again for over seven years.

———

During my hospital stay, the window was my clock and only two times existed, light and dark. I'd wake up, my mind greasy with drugs, my body sticky with wet gauze as it clung to my worst burns. A nurse hovered over me, waiting for the eschar to ripen. Always a different nurse, depending on how the shifts fell. They scrubbed the burns clean and changed my dressing four times a day.

Scrubbing a fresh burn to retain its rawness is a torture Satan himself may find too extreme. I thrashed hard enough to break the footing of the nurses holding me, the squeak of their sneakers lost in my screaming. Eventually, the nurses started to come in threes—one to pin down my legs and another to hold my arms, leaving the last one to do the actual work.

Out of all the nurses, the one I remember is Sandy. It was just seven years ago, and I don't remember what she looked like. I don't remember a lot of things I should. I guess it's true that a childhood trauma punches random holes in your memory.

What you don't forget is how doctors recite how hypertrophic scarring works, how your own collagen turns against you, thickening the scars, making it clear you'll never look the same.

You don't forget how Sandy tells you you're hurt so bad, you're burned so deep that there is no skin left to heal itself, so they have to shave and scrub the site clean so that skin grafts can be applied.

You don't forget the cop in street clothes asking you what happened, taking notes with such intensity he glances at your mummified face only once or twice, and you tell him that Randy Meadows had broken into your garage and siphoned some gasoline because he loved to huff. You smelled the fumes and knew you should run away because just a week before, you beat his ass near the city shed where the neighborhood kids sometimes played King of the Mountain, and kids like Randy always wanted revenge—but you didn't run away, and he shoved you into the bowl of gasoline.

The fumes smelled almost pretty, they bent your vision, and you could barely see him as he sparked a book of matches, and then there was nothing but white light and a little voice telling you to stop, drop, and roll.

"So, he came after you," the cop said. "You ran. He shoved you into the gas, and then, he lit you on fire?" I nodded, but I could tell that as much as the cop pitied me, he didn't believe my story.

When the interview was finished, he said, "You're a brave boy," mostly as punctuation. He smiled without looking me in the eyes before he walked away.

Brave boy? The thought filled me with rage and shame, and that's when I left him behind, I think. I just handed a different Wilder the truth, as if he were strong enough to carry it, and left him at the bus stop, listening to the rustle of activity in his garage, wondering if he should investigate or just run down to his grandparents' house.

———

For the grafts, I got to choose the harvest location—my thigh or my ass. I chose my thigh so I wouldn't have to sit on a surgical site while I recovered. They took two long strips of healthy tissue, starting from the top of my knee, ending just below my hip. The wounds that the grafts left on my leg wouldn't stop weeping. When the strip-mined leg soaked through the gauze, they wrapped it with more gauze until my thigh looked like a paper towel roll.

One day Sandy gave me bandage scissors. She said I had all day to remove the dressings myself, because that evening, they were coming off no matter what.

The nurses were not cruel, but they needed to trick me sometimes because I was afraid of the pain. One day, I had a dressing stuck to my face and it wouldn't come off. I screamed every time Sandy pulled at the edges. She suggested a hot bath to let the steam loosen the dressing.

She knelt next to me, whispering, easing me into relaxation. "Close your eyes," she said, and I did, tilting my head back. She tore the bandage off when I wasn't looking. I thrashed and kicked in the water. I called her horrible names.

Sandy still threw me a going-away party when I was close to being discharged. I got popcorn, balloons, and a chance to pick out some horror movie favorites to watch. Even some of the off-duty nurses came in special, just to see me off. Much to my mother's embarrassment, we watched *Halloween II*. I'd seen that one before, but since Michael Myers was loose in a hospital for most of the movie, I figured that one would freak them out.

I forgot that he got lit on fire at the end, and when it happened, I knew what he was going through, but I didn't feel sorry for him. Michael Myers was a dick.

———

After weeks in the hospital, after the whirlpool baths, the drugs, the skin graft surgeries, the visits, the cards, the crying, after the psychologist cleared me, after the going-away party, I finally returned home.

When Mom declared herself responsible for changing my dressings, I concealed a healthy eye roll because JoAnn "Jo" Tate had both a weak stomach and a soul made of cotton candy.

Just the year before, a mama sparrow nested in the wreath she hung outside in the spring. The wind knocked it over, killing half the hatchlings.

She discovered the disaster at night because she always checked the nest before bedtime. Within seconds, she was out there in a nightgown, wearing oven mitts while she settled the nest back into place. I told her that she didn't need the gloves, that mother birds deserting their nestlings after human touch was just a myth, it's right there on the internet, but she said "better safe than sorry" as she cupped the babies in the same silicon gloves she used to pluck frozen pizzas from the oven.

The entire time, she ignored the hatchlings that were dashed on the planks of the porch. When she was satisfied with the stability of the nest, she took the gloves off and threw them in the wash. Then, she stood in the kitchen and started to cry.

"I knew I should have put a nail in the bottom of that wreath."

"You couldn't have known a bird would build a nest there," I said.

"Can you clean up the mess out there?" she asked.

"Can I wait until tomorrow morning?"

"I want to bury them in the morning," she said. "Clean it up and put the bag out back for me, near the garden. Put a brick on it so it doesn't blow away."

So I scooped the dead nestlings into a black garbage bag so she wouldn't see them.

Then I scoured the garage for the longest nail I could find and tapped it into the bottom half of the wreath before I went inside. She was already on the phone with my grandmother, tearfully confessing her sins against the local sparrow population.

So, yeah, I couldn't imagine my mother ripping away gauze pads soaked with burn sap with the same ruthlessness as Sandy the nurse.

Her first and only attempt to remove my dressing went about as I expected. She picked at the corner of the gauze, and I hissed.

"Am I hurting you?" she asked.

"It's fine."

"I can go slower than the nurses. We have time."

She didn't have the time, not really, because the money Dad left us wouldn't last forever, and when you're a waitress you don't get paid sick leave to care for your children.

"Aren't you the one who taught me that you just yank the Band-Aid off?" I asked.

"This isn't a Band-Aid," she said and pulled a little more, watching me closely. I grimaced. I couldn't help it.

"Lollygagging just makes it worse."

"I guess I love you too much to do the job right," she said.

Removing the old dressing, assisting me in the shower, and then helping me apply new bandages took all morning, most of it spent on her worrying that she was hurting me.

So I fired her and started tearing off the bandages myself.

———

The right side of my face is disfigured, with second-degree burn scars running just below my eye all the way down to my collarbone.

A T-shirt covers up most of the third-degree burns. The scars on my right tricep look like lingering road rash, something I can explain away as the product of a cool motorcycle accident, even though I've never touched a motorcycle. My upper arm, chest, and the right side of my abdomen are smothered with hypertrophic scarring. Grafted skin created webbed valleys of a calmer color in the red mess, patches of repair so minimal and haphazard I imagined the operating surgeon was the kind of guy who used a lot of duct tape around the house.

I tried forcing myself to feel normal, but there was always the boy at the bus stop, that ten-year-old Wilder with no scars, waiting for me to answer him, to tell him what to do. I wanted to leave him there forever, stuck in a black hole where nothing could escape and time did not exist. I never wanted to talk to him again, or else he might whisper the truth.

I tried to move on. I tried to forget, but scars on your face have a way of constantly reminding you that they're still there—not in the mirror, but in the eyes of other people.

For family and friends, seeing the burned kid that I became instead of the normal one they remembered was jarring. You can be born ugly and everything is just dandy—they've never known you any other way. But when you're a cute kid who's suddenly transformed against his will, they can't hide their sadness or their horror no matter how hard they try.

They would say, "It's not your fault." They told me, "You're so brave." They insisted, "You can't blame yourself for what happened."

They make it so, so easy to be a burn victim. And why not? It is easy to be a burn victim—get set on fire, and you meet every qualification.

But becoming a burn survivor? That one took me a hell of a lot longer.

PART ONE
ASHES

SWING SET HERO

On my first day at Herrick Community High School, all the friendships I built in grade school were stripped away, and I was back at ground zero.

In grade school, I stayed with the same group of kids all the way through eighth grade, but after junior-high graduation, we got scattered. The Catholic kids went to the Catholic high school, the one that charges tuition and beats the crap out of everyone at sports. Mater Dei. I think every Catholic high school is named Mater Dei. It's like the John Smith of Catholic high school names. Anyway, they always win the regional basketball tournament, and the kids that went there wore Mater Dei stuff everywhere.

Most of the other students went to North Central High School, a regional school that swallows up all the junior-high kids from towns so small they can't sustain their own high schools.

Out of my eighth-grade class of twenty-four students, seven went to Mater Dei, fifteen went to North Central, and I was one of the unlucky ones who had to bus into Herrick Community High School, just because I lived beyond some invisible township line.

Mom and I lived at the end of a long, dead-end road. She always got a kick out of calling it a poor man's cul-de-sac. We lived in Roselake, and I attended Roselake Grade School, and Roselake kids got sucked up into North Central.

Only I didn't actually live in Roselake. Which is fine with me, because fuck Roselake, the closest actual lake is like twenty-five miles away. Somewhere along that dead-end road, Roselake ended and Herrick township began, thanks to some annexation deal that I was too young to understand at the time. I just knew our address changed, Mom assured me I'd stay at Roselake Grade School, and I forgot all about it until high school enrollment came around.

So I was alone. Well, except for Preston.

Preston Brenner didn't live all that close, but his house was another rural address annexed to Herrick. While we never clashed during our grade school and middle school years, we weren't friends. I was the burned kid, and he was the exact kind of guy you'd expect a Preston to be, the guy that wears his letter jacket everywhere even though he can't dribble for shit and never met a shot he couldn't brick.

Being so far away, I was one of the bus's first pickups, so I had plenty of time to let the first-day dread fester.

With the bus empty, I was free to sit anywhere. More importantly, I could choose the orientation of my disfigured face. I could sit scars-in, concealing them, hoping that someone would sit next to me and strike up a conversation, or I could sit scars-out and all but guarantee the seat to myself for the whole trip.

I always maintained an awareness of my scars' current state of visibility. With the damage confined to the right side of my face, I could easily sit in a restaurant booth and hide it against the window. I could sit with my chin in my right hand, concealing almost all of the destroyed tissue while looking thoughtful. If I was walking through a crowd, I could pretend to scratch my right ear, allowing my hand to mostly veil the disfigurement.

Sit scars-out.

Why?

Don't be guilty of false advertising just to lure someone into sitting next to you.

Inner voices are always assholes, but you take the cake.

I've had a lot of practice.

So of course I sat scars-out. Two stops later, Preston got on the bus, the thin wire of his Apple earbuds dangling in front of his polo shirt. I thought he might have been going for total sensory insulation, trying to give himself an excuse not to talk to anyone, including me.

He surprised me, though, making eye contact, offering a half-smile, and instead of waving, he gave me this little salute, touching two fingers just above his eye.

I waved back. He slid into an empty bench right next to me and plucked out his earbuds.

"Are you another lucky winner of the Herrick Community High School's screwed-up boundary-line sweepstakes?"

The answer seemed obvious enough. Was he making fun of me?

"Too bad Howie wasn't around to join us," I said.

Preston's best friend was Howie Malone. Howie was a solid dude. He was the first one to see me in the hallway when I returned to fifth grade after the burn hospitalization. He got the class to kick in and buy me the new *Final Fantasy* game, knowing I'd love it (he was right) and knowing I'd probably enjoy spending a solid month glued to my PlayStation (also correct). His father took a job on the West Coast before our eighth-grade year, so Preston had been a best-friend free agent for an entire school year.

"Man, Howie can eat a dick," he said.

"I thought you guys were tight?"

"When he moved we were going to keep in touch. Dude ghosted me. Fuck him."

"Weird," I said. "Howie was nice to me."

"Friendship is just weak, man. Growing up is mostly shedding friends," he said.

He had a point. I'd say that 99 percent of friendships cannot survive one simple, filtering element, and that's convenience. When you're from a small town and have a small school, it's easy to be friends with everyone. You're all close, you spend all day together, but once that convenience is removed? Once you change schools or move away or grow up and go to college and get a job? How many friendships filter through all that inconvenience?

"You've already been through the school-change thing, what's it like?" he asked.

"That was in second grade," I said.

Preston was a kindergarten-through-eighth-grade legacy student at Roselake Grade School. I showed up in second grade, after my father died. Mom couldn't stay in our house anymore. Dad was in the walls, like smoke.

"Second grade or not, you've changed schools one more time than me. Any tips?" Preston asked.

"Yeah," I said. "Try to blend in."

He laughed.

I barely remembered Sesser, the town where we used to live, or St. Francis Academy, the Catholic school I attended until we moved. I don't remember names of kids I once played with every day. No friendships survived. Twenty miles away? Three towns away? Might as well be on a Martian space station.

I do remember the blonde girl from the swing set, and I wish I remembered her name. That was back in the Sesser days. I liked her. You always remember feelings because feelings are what anchor our memories. Perhaps you remember that first baseball game or concert, but it's the awe that etches its place in your history.

Like is such a shitty word to use, but you don't fall in love in first grade. Not in a real way. I don't know when you're equipped with that ability, but it sure isn't when you need your mom to cut up your hot dogs. Maybe yearn is the right word, the wanting of something that you can't understand, something that may not even exist to you yet.

So I yearned for the blonde girl, and now that I look back on one of my few memories from first grade, I think she might have liked me, too, because she would always ask me to save her while I was swinging.

Time and time again, she'd get a boy to chase her and draw her pursuer to my swing set, begging for me to rescue her.

"Wilder, save me!" she'd cry through a mouthful of giggles. "Save me!"

Did I save her? I don't remember. I'd like to think I saved her a time or two. Maybe she would have remembered me and heard about my burns and reached out. Maybe she just forgot me the day I left that Catholic school and didn't share the yearning that timestamped the whole experience for me.

She'll always be my first crush, nameless and distant. I moved away from Sesser, and the yearning remains, but I'm okay with never seeing her. If the swing set girl remembers me at all, it's as a first-grade kid with a normal face doing his best hero impersonation, and that boy has been gone a long, long time.

———

Herrick High School was a squat building made from faded bricks. When I got off the bus, I had to take a detour around some orange cones on the sidewalk, where a piece of concrete had heaved into a tripping hazard. The classroom windows were rectangular and tinted, and the caulk had fallen away from the seams like a ripened scab.

I kept my head down until I passed the gymnasium entrance, but not before glancing inside. The gym floor was gleaming perfection, each strip of hardwood buried in shimmering lacquer. As a junior-high player, I'd seen plenty of schools that relished their gyms above all else. Many schools had ancient tile in the hallways and shoddy asphalt in the parking lots, but their gyms had new rims, white nets, and a tight, hardwood floor.

Herrick's gym was the most beautiful one yet. Sure, the floor was perfect, but the baskets had oversized backboards made of tempered glass. The rims were the expensive kind, the breakaway versions that could tolerate a dunk. I loved those rims since they always gave a softer touch on long-range shots, making it easier to get a shooter's bounce. The cushioned impact zones on each side of the floor were new, decorated with stripes of green and gold.

The logo on center court was a Griffin, a mythical beast with the body of a lion and the head of an eagle. At Roselake, our team was the Eagles, so this wasn't a bad upgrade. In fact, it was kind of a fitting evolution. Maybe even a sign, since I had reservations about trying out for the high school basketball team. I loved basketball, don't get me wrong, but sitting on the bench during an entire freshman season was no way to get my fix. Judging by the look of the gym, the pressure might be even higher than expected in Herrick. Basketball games were church in a lot of local schools, but this place looked like the Vatican.

I stepped inside, hoping to get a closer look at the logo. The Griffin sat on its back legs, its tail curled in such a way that you could tell it was about to leap at something. Its eagle head had tiny eyes, giving it an angry squint, and the front legs, which were talons, were raised up in a fighting stance.

Hence the name, the Herrick Fighting Griffins, but if you ask me, they don't make Griffins of any other variety.

I didn't want to get caught fantasizing about basketball, so I slipped back into the hallway, which was packed with enough students to fill ten Roselakes, all of them far too concerned with smartphones or old friends or figuring out their new locker combinations to notice my scars.

I helped keep it that way by keeping my hoodie up as I pressed through to my locker. Entering the combination only took two tries to get right. I dumped my supplies inside, leaving it to organize later. I didn't want to be late for my first class, and I still had to find it.

The room numbers were out of order. I passed room four, and the next one on the right was room nine, a pattern that made no sense. I backtracked and found room seven.

"What room you looking for?" The voice was so close, I flinched. A brown-haired girl stood behind me, clutching her books against a denim jacket.

"Five," I said.

"English," she said. "Me too. Follow me."

"I can't," I said, not even knowing why I couldn't. So I made up a reason. "I forgot something in my locker."

She shrugged. "Room five is upstairs, second door on the left."

"Why are all the numbers out of order?"

"Renovations a long time ago," she said. "Changing them now would just confuse everyone." Sounded like a joke, but she didn't laugh.

"Well, thanks," I said.

"Cool scars," she said and headed up the stairs.

I pretended to look for something in my locker for a slow count of ten, then headed upstairs.

The English teacher was Miss Harrington. She was a younger teacher, the kind of person you would trust to help you pick out a couple of shirts at a clothing store. She wore tall boots over her jeans and an oragamied scarf even though the forecast was for a high of seventy-five that day. The mornings remained cold, so jackets and hoodies were hanging on the backs of chairs.

The class was mostly freshmen, with a few sophomores mixed in, hoping to shore up their English credits. Miss Harrington took attendance by calling out everyone by name and having an icebreaker chat with them.

"So, Wilder Tate?" she said, and I raised my hand. "What was the best day of your summer vacation?"

She never asked the same question twice, and I was lucky to get that softball instead of the tougher fare such as "What is your personal motto?" or "If you were an animal what would you be, and why?" which had a job interview flavor to them.

"My birthday. I got an indoor basketball hoop, the kind you hang on your closet door," I said.

I noticed that her eyes kept breaking away, just slightly, to get a better look at the decimated side of my face. I wish people wouldn't hide that they're looking. Nibbling glances like that, it gets old fast. Just give my face a stare, get your fill, and move on with your life.

"Is basketball your favorite sport?" Miss Harrington said.

"I enjoy curling much more, but that doesn't work out so well in the Illinois humidity."

The joke earned a few weak laughs and a smile from Miss Harrington. A kid who had already introduced himself—Jackson Kuhn—blurted out, "What happened to your face? Were you really set on fire?"

Way to rip the Band-Aid off the situation, Jackson.

"Don't be rude," Miss Harrington said. "You don't have to answer that, Wilder. I'm sorry."

"It's not rude," Jackson said. "A lot of us are thinking it, but everyone else is too afraid to ask. I'm just asking."

"Hey, Jackson," a voice said. I turned around and saw a girl with freckles and red hair tied into a simple ponytail. I never saw her walk into class, and I definitely would have noticed.

"Why do you insist on being called Jackson instead of Jack?" she said. "It's weird. A lot of us are thinking it, but they're too afraid to ask. I'm just asking."

The class laughed, and Miss Harrington stifled a chuckle with the back of her hand.

"It's just, like, it's just my name—it's what my parents call me," Jackson said, and I suddenly felt sorry for him. I got the feeling he might have even liked the redheaded girl.

"Oh? So it's not your fault?" she said.

Miss Harrington regained control of the class. "Lane McKenzie?"

A girl sitting in the back of the room raised her hand—the same one who told me where to find room five and that my scars were cool.

"What's your favorite hobby?"

"Sleeping!" Jackson said. Half the class cracked up, but I didn't get the joke. Miss Harrington seethed. "That's two hours of detention," she announced, putting a tourniquet on the laughter. "Minimum. We'll meet with Principal Turner after class and see if we can't get that upgraded to a suspension."

"It was just a stupid joke!" he pleaded.

I couldn't see Lane's face from my side of the classroom. Her brown hair was frizzy and didn't look like it got much in the way of fruity shampoos, expensive conditioners, and precision styling.

"May I be excused for a moment?" Lane asked, her voice as timid as her posture.

"Of course," Miss Harrington said.

She fumbled her books as she tried to gather them into her backpack. The English text smacked against the tile, and someone snorted, trying to hold in a laugh. Everyone was quiet as she knelt down to recover the book, a silence so heavy and toxic I was afraid to breathe. She stood and took a wobbling breath that everyone could hear. I expected her to cry. She didn't, and hurried out of the room.

Miss Harrington regrouped and read the next name. "Jenna Weaver?" The freckled girl who had come to my aid raised her hand.

"What is your favorite subject at school?" Miss Harrington asked.

"Why English, of course," she said, angling her words just enough to get a laugh. "Unless cheerleading is a subject. Then I'd like to change my answer."

And just like that, my favorite subject at school became Jenna Weaver.

DEFENSE

All the way up through eighth grade, I'd skip the cafeteria line and sit alone. I'd grab a bag of chips and a soda from the vending machines, scarf them down, and make sure I was the first one into the gymnasium to shoot baskets until the bell rang.

I didn't fear exclusion or bullying. Instead, I feared inclusion I couldn't trust, friends and conversations that occurred not because of who I was but because of what had happened to me.

Basketball saved me from all that and more. I wore a T-shirt underneath my jersey, which covered the scar tissue on my arm. My face was still visible, but the game has a flow, and when I give up to its tide, the scars are gone. I got high fives because I did my job—the ball goes in the hoop because I helped with spacing, or a screen, or drilled the shot myself.

When the buzzer sounds, we won or we lost, and the score is all that matters in the locker room.

Then, the uniforms are piled into a laundry basket, and the boys herd into the showers. I was always the last one to take off my jersey, stalling until everyone else was at their lockers in street clothes, combing their shampoo-slick hair.

I'd finally sneak into the shower room with my clothes on, cranking up three faucets hot enough to turn the place as misty and humid as a rainforest. I'd strip off my boxers and T-shirt under the cover of steam, and only then did my scars return.

I skipped the cafeteria lunch and opted for vending-machine cuisine. They even had my old standby—cheddar and sour cream Ruffles. Now that I was a freshman, I had brought along enough money for two bags and a Coke to wash it down. Forgive me, but screw Pepsi. Honestly.

A hand landed on my shoulder, and I flinched so hard, the quarters in my sweaty palm rattled onto the tile, some rolling under the machine.

"The wild man!" Preston said. He knelt down to help gather the loose coins. "Have you ever in your life eaten a hot lunch at school?"

"I swore I'd never make that mistake again," I said.

"True dat," he said, the slang never quite fitting him, just as sports never quite fit him. He was athletic and strong, but that was the problem—lifting weights made him too wide and slow. I could be slippery on the court, where he was just stiff. He wasn't fluid enough to slide through a gap in the defense or let a shot go with an oiled release.

"I found us a shortcut through the trials of the nobody freshman," he said. "On day one, no less. What do you think of sitting with the captain of the basketball team during lunch?"

My mother was already pestering me to go out for the high school team, but playing in the rec center's open league on Wednesday nights appealed a hell of a lot more.

"Man, that sounds great," I lied, "but I figured I'd just eat these chips and—"

"Maybe I said it the wrong way," Preston said. "I don't have the 'in' with the basketball guys—you do. They've heard of you."

"Of course," I said. My burns made for a story too juicy to remain in the confines of just one small town.

"Not the burns," he said, "the Trinity Lutheran game."

The Trinity Lutheran Saints were a junior-high team that had gone undefeated for the better part of two seasons, including a Class A junior-high state championship. If you didn't remember they were state champs, helpful reminders were everywhere—on the school reader board, the banners in the gym, and a sign posted on the edge of town. Not a cheap or homemade sign, either—I'm talking one of the official, white-letters-on-green-metal signs commissioned by the state that went right under their population number.

We were the team that finally broke their streak, in their gym no less. I didn't know that I had made ten three-pointers in a row until the end of the third quarter during a time-out, when the referee asked the other referee if the burned kid had even missed. They checked with the scorer, and I have to admit, I listened in—bad move. I missed my next three attempts in the fourth quarter, but we held off the Saints for a five-point win.

Our upset win made the front page of not one but two local newspapers. Sounds impressive, but I lived in a part of Southern Illinois where the city council meetings usually made the front page. Headline news was a low bar, but Mom still cut out the articles and left them on the fridge until the edges curled.

My "signature" game simply highlighted my weaknesses. Three-pointers aside, my offensive game was shaky. I couldn't ball-handle for crap, and I was horrible at finishing around the basket. I couldn't make free throws consistently. I'd often embarrass myself in the pregame layup line, opting to pull up for three-pointers instead. Our middle school coach, Norman Watkins, liked to say that I had a better three-point percentage than layup percentage. Sounded like a joke, but it was true. Layups wouldn't come easy for me until I could jump, and sadly, my vertical leap was more like a vertical hop. Height wouldn't save me. I was destined to be six feet tall, max, when my growth spurt finally decided to come around.

Defense was my strength. Even when we were in a zone scheme, I always got a man-to-man assignment to shut down the other team's best player, and more times than not, I delivered. I couldn't leap, but I was quick and took enough pride in defense to push myself harder than just about anyone on the court.

"The Trinity Lutheran game was a fluke," I said. It was my turn at the vending machine, but I didn't recover enough quarters for even one bag of chips.

Preston held up two dollars.

"Chips are on me, just eat them slow and chill. Give us enough time to break the ice. Deal?"

I looked back at the machine. "I'm going to be short on the Coke."
He held up a third dollar, and we had a deal.

———————

Theo Lang walked across the cafeteria, leading a pack of high school jocks
to their regular lunch table, each one of his followers taller than him.

"How the hell is a dude that short the captain?" I said. Team captaincies
are usually formal titles where seniority trumps talent. However, Theo
had been the captain since last year, his sophomore campaign. Either the
seniors were a dumpster fire or Theo blended straight A's and charisma
with his scoring title, giving the coach no choice but to tap him as the
team's leader and role model. All the more impressive considering he
wasn't even six feet tall.

"Never underestimate the undersized point guard," Preston said with
a cheek full of sloppy joe. I had just reached the tragic and dusty bottom
of my Ruffles bag. He waved at Theo, getting his attention, then pointed
at me.

How did this happen? I let Preston deliver me as an offering to the
most influential non-senior in school.

Theo straddled the cafeteria bench so he could face me—thankfully,
he was facing my good side. He offered a handshake, and I could almost
feel his friendliness meter getting forced up to salesman levels of intensity.

I returned the handshake. At least he wasn't one of those bros who
took a handshake as an invitation to show off granite-crushing grip
strength.

"So, you're the Doberman," Theo said.

"Haven't heard that one," I said.

"Like all good nicknames, it's earned through reputation," Theo said.
"Defense, dude. Word is it's like you're on crack out there when you're
guarding a guy."

"And he can shoot the trey," Preston said.

"You don't need to recruit me," I said.

"So you coming out for the team?" Theo asked.

"I'm not sure."

"Then maybe you need to be recruited," Theo said. "We got the chance to knock off Mater Dei this year."

"Knock them off?"

"They won the last three regional tournaments," he said. "We haven't taken the trophy since eighty-nine, but we're good enough to pull it off this season. We went twenty-two and four last year."

"Regionals?" I said. "The tournament to play in the sectional, and then you play the super sectional, and then you play state. Regionals is the big thing around here?"

"I can tell he's a freshman," Luke said.

"Regionals are the thing around here," Theo said. "We've got like two-hundred kids in this school. Even Mater Dei gets their ass handed to them in the sectionals, and they've got three times our enrollment. Being the best around here is what really matters, and a banner is a banner."

"Looks like you've got a tall team," I said. "How does the point guard lead the team in scoring? Big men that bad?"

He smiled. "Hands like frying pans."

Preston laughed a little too hard at the joke. I just took a drink of my complimentary Coke. "Especially Luke, and he's going to start at center this year," Theo added. "We need a perimeter game, a three-and-d guy."

Scorers like Theo love the three-and d guy, who typically does all the hard work on the defensive end of the court and shoots just well enough to space the floor on offense—when defenders are on a shooter they can't leave open, Theo only has to beat one guy to the basket.

"You know someone like that?" he asked.

"More pressure isn't helping matters," I said.

"What's pressure? Ball don't lie," Theo said. "Come out for the team. Seriously. I think it would be awesome for you, all things considered."

That was at least a polite way to draw my scars into the conversation, so I let it slide.

Jenna joined the cafeteria line, laughing with her friends as they shuffled to the sloppy joe trough.

Theo followed my line of sight and saw an opening. "You know Jenna?" he asked.

I shook my head.

"She's a cheerleader. Loves defense."

He nudged my shoulder and got up to join his friends.

"You guys can sit with us if you want," Theo said. Preston couldn't grab his tray fast enough.

"I'm done eating," I said and let Preston join the rest of the legitimized basketball players.

I headed for the gym, walking against the grain of the cafeteria line with my good side showing, slowing down as I passed Jenna. What did I want? A glance? A wave? Should I stop and thank her for putting Jackson on blast during first hour?

She never even glanced at me, and I never stopped.

I snuck into the gym, grabbed a ball, and started to shoot.

MOM

When I got off the bus and keyed into the house, I smelled meatloaf and knew that Mom was home.

My mother was a waitress at a truck-stop diner called the Red Hen over in Sesser and a bartender at the Elks Lodge past the railroad tracks in Herrick. I never could keep track of her schedule because she was the kind of woman who never said no to a shift. When I got home from school, I'd either hear the *Mamas and the Papas* wailing on her favorite oldies station and catch a whiff of taco beef, or the house would be dark and silent and I'd find a note on how to reheat the meal she'd prepared before she left for work. Her instructions were oddly detailed. Last night was lasagna: *Leave foil on tight! Preheat oven to 400, bake for 47 minutes. Then take out, turn on broiler, and put on top rack for four minutes until cheese turns brown.*

Some kids complain about their parents. "You were never there for me," they say. I'd tell them that proximity doesn't equal love. I barely saw her since she took on extra shifts at the Elks, but I know the bills from my burns ate through a lot of the money Dad had left us.

When I was hospitalized, my grandparents rarely left my room in the burn unit while my mother kept working to keep up good graces at the Red Hen. Some nights, she'd get to my hospital room about eleven p.m. after a double, visit with me, watch me sleep, then be up at four a.m. to get back to work, leaving me to do puzzles and read books with my grandparents all day.

I sat down at the dinner table, but she only had one plate ready.

"You're not eating?"

"I have to work, hon," she said.

"You didn't have to cook. I could have heated it up myself."

"It's your first day of high school," she said, sitting down. "I wanted to make your favorite."

"Thanks," I said, busting off a huge forkful.

"Well? How's life as a Fighting Griffin?"

"Fine," I said. An accurate answer. Fine meant that no one stared too hard or made fun of me within earshot.

"You decide on basketball yet?" she asked. My mother was only thirty-six, but veins of silver ran through the bun of her hair, making it look like a mound of coal that had just begun to crack. She wore a lot of makeup, the kind that filled in the crevices that are etched in overworked faces.

"No," I said.

"Why wouldn't you play? You love basketball."

"Maybe that's why I don't want to play," I said. "I'm a freshman now. I may never see the court. I may just sit the bench. Why do that when I'd rather just go to the rec center and play all I want?"

"I understand if you're a little scared," she said. "But you'll be fine. You always are once the game starts. At least go to tryouts, okay?"

"Maybe," I said.

"So, meet any new friends?"

"I talked to Preston a little," I said.

She checked her makeup in the dark reflection of the microwave glass. "Any cute girls at school?"

That one I didn't expect. She never asked about girls in junior high, which was a relief. I never talked to girls—it felt like test-driving a car you could never afford.

"There's this girl named Jenna," I said, stopping myself before I finished a complete thought. What was I saying? I stuffed a piece of meatloaf in my mouth.

"Really?" Mom said. "Well go on, buster, tell me about her."

"It's nothing," I said. "She's cool."

"That's it?" she said.

"That's it," I repeated.

She smiled. My mom would like Jenna. Of course, she'd like any girl who was kind enough to come home with me and meet her. Mom could tell me I was handsome and the burns meant nothing, but it would always feel like mom-talk. I needed someone to corroborate her story, someone to hold my hand and tell me how none of the scar tissue mattered, and somehow make me believe it.

PARTY

Miss Harrington didn't assign seats, but most of us sat in the desks we'd grabbed on the first day of school. For two weeks, we ingrained ourselves into the same seats, the same routes to the lockers, the same tables at lunch, etching a routine so deep it was only noticeable when it was disrupted. So when Jenna traded desks with Avery Jensen to sit by me, everyone noticed.

I tried to ignore the anxious thoughts insisting this would lead to dating, marriage, children, and matching plots in East Fork Cemetery. I scribbled notes and kept my eyes on Miss Harrington, who held court at her whiteboard. Jenna kept glancing at me. I didn't dare turn my head. My scars were pointed at the bank of windows, and changing the angle would flash a reminder that I was disfigured.

I held firm, and when class was over, I gathered my books, dropping them into my backpack one at a time as the class scurried into the hallway.

Jenna didn't follow them.

"Did you even notice I sat by you?" she said, standing at my desk, an English textbook tucked under her arm.

"Yeah," I said, braving eye contact. What color were her eyes? No idea. Green, hazel, blue—is enchantment a color? I couldn't hold the gaze long enough to figure out the puzzle, but I was an expert at breaking eye contact—I could scratch my scars, obscuring them while I tended to a fake itch. I could check the clock, or make sure my pen was clicked shut, or look out the window.

"You don't have to be so shy, Wilder."

Was her hair a true red? Highlights swirled in her ponytail, golden vapor trails swept up and bound with an elastic tie.

"Earth to Wilder," she said.

"Sorry," I said. "Shyness is like breathing; I can only turn it off for a few seconds at a time."

"I'm having a party at my house tonight," she said. "You know, back to school and all that. You should come."

"I should come," I said, botching the delivery. I meant for it to sound like a question, just to make sure I didn't misunderstand her, but instead it came out monotone, like she'd just Jedi mind-tricked me.

"Great!" she said. I stammered to revoke my accidental RSVP, but I was too late. She was gone.

I followed her into the hallway, where she was already chatting with a group of friends.

Preston came up behind me, putting his arm around my shoulders.

"You've got the sickness, boy," he said.

"What are you doing tonight?" I asked.

"Oh shit—you got a personal, engraved invite from the lovely hostess herself?"

"I don't even know where she lives. I don't have a car. I don't—"

"Chill," Preston said. "I got you. But I don't even know where you live. Part with that classified information, and I'll pick you up around seven-thirty."

Just like that, I was headed to the ball. Too bad I was one fairy godmother short.

———

Mom was at work, but she'd left a pasta bake to heat up. After spending a dinner with SportsCenter, I took a shower, which didn't help me relax. The heat of the water tended to brighten my scar tissue, so I didn't bother wiping the steam off of the mirror.

With a couple hours to kill, I wandered into Mom's bathroom and took out her makeup case.

I didn't know blush from rouge or foundation. I picked the most flesh-colored powder and gently dabbed it onto my facial scars. At first, I thought I had a winning formula. The makeup was subtle, and it took the edge off of the redness. Seconds later, droplets of sweat carved gunky trenches in the makeup.

Since the whole thing was doomed to failure, I doubled down on the makeup, slathering it on to try and completely cover the scar tissue. The colors and hues didn't match the rest of my flesh, and the terrain of the scars refused to be hidden.

The sweat caught up to the makeup again, turning my cheek into a mud hole. Preston wouldn't be there for a while yet, so I took another shower, this one cold so I wouldn't redden the scars again.

He knocked on the door five minutes early, which was surprising. He seemed like a five-minutes-late kind of guy.

"Wild man!" he exclaimed then tried to walk inside. I awkwardly blocked him off.

"We can just go," I said.

"Not unless you want me pissing my pants. Your house off limits or something?"

"No."

"Your mom home?"

"No."

"Then what's the big deal?" he asked.

"I just don't want to be late."

"Fine, I'll skip washing my hands."

I had no choice but to let him inside. Our house was a shining example of the classic redneck cottage style, with wood siding diseased with paint blisters, some boards as black and brittle as rotten teeth.

Inside, the floor creaked with every other step. We barely ran the thermostat, so it was cold in the winter and hot in the summer. The ceiling in the living room had a brown patch where the roof was leaking. Mom kept a bucket by the television for when it rained.

She tried to keep the place together, but her handyman talents were limited to cleaning tricks like making blood disappear from a cotton shirt.

I trailed Preston into the kitchen.

"The bathroom's around the corner," I said.

"Dude, this is like the cleanest house I've ever seen," he said.

He had a point. The house was a turd, but it was a polished turd thanks to Mom's obsessive cleaning habits.

He disappeared into the hallway. I waited in the kitchen, running my finger along the porcelain apron of the sink, the surface as clean and slick as new teeth.

"Holy shit, is this a PlayStation 2?"

I almost ran into my bedroom. Preston was holding a copy of *Madden 2001*, purchased for three bucks at a pawn shop.

"This is retro as hell. Is that the old *Metal Gear*?"

"Yeah."

"I don't see any shooters. You good at shooters?"

"I've played them."

"*Call of Duty*?"

I shook my head.

"My man, you are missing out. What's your gamertag?"

"It's not online," I said. "I mean, we have the internet, it's just not fast."

He walked over to me and put his hand on my shoulder. "You look like a Doberman69 to me. Come over to my house sometime and we'll hook you up, play some *COD*. I'll show you how to beast out against those little shits that play the game 24/7 and sound like Micky Mouse. But then we have to grind through *Metal Gear* on your PS2 together, okay?"

I didn't know what to say.

"Okay?" he repeated.

"You just didn't seem like the gamer type," I said.

"I'm the ass-kicking type," he said. "And in *Call of Duty*, you gotta get in there and kick some ass."

I followed him out of the house, shutting off lights along the way. Before I locked the front door behind us, I said, "Didn't you have to go to the bathroom?"

"I can hold it," he said, grinning as he got in the truck.

———

Jenna lived in an enormous house with a detached, four-car garage and an oak sapling in the front yard no taller than me, the trunk tethered to a pole to help it endure the wind that tore across the cornfields behind the subdivision.

The party was in a shed behind her house. The camper, bass boat, speed boat, and four-wheelers were all parked outside to make room.

Preston also picked up Theo and Luke Conant, whose charisma matched the clunkiness of his "frying pan" hands. As we entered the party, I followed them through the door, unnoticed.

No one danced even though the songs had the bass-drenched spine of electronic music. Sodas were crammed into plastic kiddie pools and covered with ice. Jenna's mother dished out finger foods at a table near the back of the shed. Teenagers broke off into circles of conversation, not much different from the bleacher talk just after lunch. Maybe when the adults went to bed and everyone snuck nips of contraband they'd brought from their parents' liquor cabinets, the dancing would blast off, but for now, I found the awkwardness comforting.

Theo and Luke got sucked into the tractor beam of their basketball teammates, and Preston stuck to the rules he'd explained in the car.

Rule one: "Find a girl you know and hug her." He theorized that this move incited the curiosity of every girl at the party. Is he taken? Are they together? Why is she hugging him?

Rule two: "Disappear for a while at least once." Builds more curiosity, ensures against looking desperate or oversaturating the party with your presence.

Rule three: "Smile." Always look like you're having the most fun, even if you're faking it, and girls will want to talk to you because they want to have a good time, too.

I grabbed a Coke and hovered around Preston. He said hi to Talisha Slater, and I'll be damned if he didn't get a genuine hug out of her, grinning at me over her shoulder. He started chatting up Talisha, who was there with Lane McKenzie.

Talisha was hot, but in that try-hard way that tarnishes it, wearing a T-shirt that showed off her shoulders and belly-button. She was going for sexy, but to me, she just looked cold.

Lane was buried in a jean jacket and a mismatched turtleneck, her hair so unmade I couldn't tell if it was a hip thing she had done on purpose. Lane and I didn't talk with Preston and Talisha; we were observers, orbiting their conversation.

I decided to disengage hover mode and headed for the open garage door, holding my Coke with the swagger of James Bond gripping his signature martini.

As I neared the door, Jenna came in, chatting with a friend. I made eye contact with her, and just as she was giving me a friendly wave, Preston yanked me away.

"This is my boy, Wilder," he said. "This is the lovely Talisha Slater." Now I could see she was holding a Sprite. Ugh. "This is Lane," he said, drained of enthusiasm when introducing her.

"Is your name really Wilder?" Talisha asked.

"Yeah," I said.

Talisha laughed. "Is that like when you call a fat guy 'Tiny' or a tall guy 'Shorty'?"

"Oh, so your real name is Chastity?" I said. No one laughed but Lane. She put her hand over her mouth to stifle it.

"So, is it weird to ask what happened to you?" Talisha asked.

Of course this was the whole damn point of Preston calling me over. He was friends with the freakshow and could unveil me for their own personal showing, a high school version of show-and-tell. Maybe later when they were making out, they'd feel so much better about themselves because they had complete faces.

"Not weird," I said. "Natural curiosity."

They waited.

"So do you remember on the news a few years ago, when they said a meteorite was coming close to hitting the Earth, but it didn't?"

Talisha nodded. I could have made up any news story, and she would have nodded.

"Well, it didn't miss. It was going to hit us unless we sent a team to drill a hole in the center of the rock, drop a bomb inside, and split it in half. My dad is an oil driller, and I went with him on the mission, and got hit by some shrapnel."

"Oh my God," Talisha said, believing it, and the next words out of her mouth would be those of fake sympathy, but Lane spared her the embarrassment by interrupting.

"You're joking," she said. "It's that old Bruce Willis movie, right?" she hinted, but she knew.

"*Armageddon!*" Preston said.

"So I guess you don't want to talk about it, then," Talisha said.

"I was ten years old and a thirteen-year-old kid broke into my garage," I said. "His name was Randy Meadows. When I caught him siphoning gas, he shoved me down, right into a bowl he was using to collect the gasoline. Then, he lit me on fire."

I sprinted through the story as I usually did, not pausing for dramatic effect.

"That sucks," Talisha said.

"What happened to him?" Lane asked. I noticed the half-moons under her eyes, her rounded shoulders, and how her shirt sleeves extended over her wrists, limp and oversized.

"I don't know," I said. "I was busy recovering. I don't think about him much at all."

"I'd find him and kill the shit out of him," Preston said. "Not just if he did it to me, either. I'd draw blood in your name, dude. He's got it coming."

"We all got it coming for something," Lane said.

With the story over, Preston asked Talisha if she liked watching the Herrick Fighting Griffins battle on the basketball court. They squared their shoulders away from me, an official announcement that they'd paired off and this was no longer a group conversation.

I tapped him on the shoulder and told him I was going to get another Coke.

"Not too many now," he said. "You may have to drive later." The joke was mostly procedural, lacking the tenor of humor. My story had done its job, as usual. People wanted to know, but once they did, they didn't expect to feel so damn bad about it.

I wasn't the only one left adrift. Lane had her arms crossed, and our eyes caught.

"It was nice to meet you," I said.

"Do you really drink that much soda?" she asked.

"I'm a fan," I said. What the hell was I going to say? That I enjoyed holding a soda because it gave me something to do with my hands and made me feel less awkward?

"Be careful or you'll be a diabetic fan," she said, smiling. When she smiled that heaviness left her, if only for a moment.

"Hey, before you go," she said, leaning closer. "You were lying before, right?"

"No," I said, hurrying back into the details of my story. "Randy kicked a bowl full of gas onto me. My vision got fuzzy from the fumes, but I heard him light a book of matches." I would have kept going if she didn't put her hand on my shoulder.

"Not about that," she said. "About not knowing what happened to him since that happened. About never thinking about him."

"Why would I lie?"

"You tell me."

I wanted to make a sleep joke just then, even though I didn't know the context. I wanted her to stop smiling, to stop looking me in the eyes.

Instead, I tossed my Coke in the trash can, faking a cough as it landed in the garbage so that Lane couldn't hear that the can was still half-full.

I plucked a fresh can from the kiddie pool, finding myself alone on a stage of finished concrete. I sensed dozens of curious eyes, all of them scattering like cockroaches whenever I turned to face them.

I had nowhere to go. Theo was talking to the basketball guys. Preston and Talisha were tucked away in a corner, their body language set to "do not disturb."

Lane was the only one still looking at me, now sitting by herself. She raised her eyebrows at me. I had no freaking idea what that meant, but it made me feel found out.

I wasn't equipped to stand alone in the middle of a party. I felt evaluated, as if each angle of body language were being measured. I switched poses, each of them feeling more stiff and rehearsed than the next. I couldn't even decide what to look at, everyone wondering just how friendless and lame I truly was, my coolness on public trial.

My choices were to slip outside and kill time or to find a conversation. Lane was the closest thing I had to an invitation, so I looked at my cellphone and pretended as if I'd just seen an important text, then headed for the door.

Jenna caught my arm. She'd been social-butterflying around the garage, making sure to talk to everyone. Now it was my turn.

"I'm so glad you're here," she said. "Thanks for coming." She sounded sweet enough to rot your teeth.

"Wouldn't dare miss it," I said.

"Are you okay?" she asked.

Only Wilder Tate could mess up a casual greeting from the party's hostess, but Lane had jabbed me in a tender spot, and I suppose the reeling was visible.

"Maybe I just can't handle my Coke." I held up the can. "The soda, I mean. Not the hardcore street drug. Although I don't think I can handle that, either. But I wouldn't know."

"Wilder," she said, "don't be nervous. It's just a party."

"It's not the party that's making me nervous," I said, incredulous that I could say it without punching myself in the face. Telling a girl she makes you nervous is the exact same thing as telling her that you like her, only disguised enough to slip by your internal defenses, and trust me, I had vast arrays of tracking missiles ready to explosively pre-empt anything that could expose me to rejection.

"You're sweet," she said. More importantly, she didn't immediately leave.

Guys like me didn't talk to girls like Jenna Weaver. When I first saw her, I could see myself secretly loving her for a couple of years in a state of distant terror, but here we were. Talking.

"Are you having fun?" she asked.

"I am now," I said—and my God, was this an out-of-body experience?

"And I thought you were shy," she said.

"I am," I said. "I don't get it, either."

"If you need anything, let me know," she said.

"Funny you should ask," I said, thinking that maybe she was setting me up. Maybe she'd sensed the pattern of my last two responses and was fishing for me to say that I needed her, or needed to talk to her, or needed to take her out on a date sometime, or marry her, or become an astronomer and search the universe for a new constellation if only to name it after her.

Or maybe she was just being an excellent hostess and was praying for the burned kid to quit hinting that he liked her with all the subtlety of an excited puppy.

"I need to go outside and get some air," I finished, finally.

"It's a beautiful night," she said. "Give me a few minutes and maybe I'll join you."

I couldn't get out the door fast enough. The walls of the garage sealed out the party, except for the dull and steady beat from the dance music pounding away. The bricks soaked up moonlight. The breeze swept away the last of the humidity, rustling the tassels of the corn.

In a few minutes, the view would be mine to share with Jenna Weaver, of all people. Jenna. Weaver.

So I waited.

Half a Coke later, I was still alone. I paced behind the garage, my sneakers turning squeaky with dew.

She'll forget about you.

No, she's too sweet to forget and leave me out here.

If she thinks of you waiting outside, she'll remind herself to forget.

Can't you give one person the benefit of the doubt?

I made that mistake once, with you, and swore I wouldn't do that anymore.

She'll remember.

If she does, you really going to stand on this side of the garage, where the moonlight hits your bad side?

I walked to the other side of the garage. The Coke was almost empty. No Jenna. I was probably ten miles or so from my house. Walking at approximately four miles per hour, I could be home just after midnight if I bailed right away.

Voices echoed around the corner, none of them female. Theo, Luke, and Tyson Venhaus huddled together. Each of them had silver flasks. Theo tipped back a drink.

"You weren't lying. This tequila is rotgut."

"Tequila so shitty the worm committed suicide," Luke said.

Ty handed over his flask.

"I said rum, not this shit," Luke said.

"It's rum," Ty insisted.

"Yeah, but it's that Bacardi shit that moms drink."

"Tastes like I should be rubbing this on the back of some hot chick at the beach," Theo added. "What did you bring?"

"Best for last, gentlemen," Luke said, unveiling his flask. "I couldn't fill this all the way up or my dad would notice. I present to you, Johnny Walker Black."

"I take back everything I said about your clumsy ass," Theo said.

I made no effort to conceal my eavesdropping, just standing at the corner, watching them drink.

You can go back inside and talk to her, tell her about how pretty the moon looks tonight, like the asshole poet bookworm you are.

I'd have to interrupt a conversation. No way she's just sitting there alone, waiting for someone to talk to her.

Then go talk to Lane. Make Jenna jealous.

You're disqualified for the rest of the night. That's just plain stupid.

Go have a drink with the basketball guys, then.

I've never had a drink in my life. Being drunk is more terrifying than sex, only you don't puke after sex. Most of the time. I think.

Maybe she'll come out and see you being all cool and social and then one day you'll get to have sex thanks to your enhanced social status.

That logic won't get you reinstated.

Luke saw me. "Whoever is over there better get to stepping before I get to swinging." He might have had hands like frying pans, but he had a voice that seemed destined to convince perpetrators to get down on the ground and put their hands behind their backs.

"Hold up," Theo said, peering around Luke's thick shoulder. "Wilder, that you?"

"Dumbass freshman," Ty said.

"Not freshman—Doberman," Theo said. "Get over here, dude."

I stepped out of the shadows.

"Doberman, you drink?" Luke said.

"No."

"No as in not often, or no as in never-ever?" Theo asked.

"Never," I said.

"If I were you, I'd be drinking every day," Ty said.

"Shut up," Theo said. "Don't mind Ty, he's just pissed you're going to take his starting spot."

"Hell no he's not," Ty said. "He's a Doberman, but I'm motherfuckin' Cerberus."

"The three-headed dog?" Luke asked.

"Damn straight. Drop those threes all day. All money, no bank."

"And no defense," Theo said.

"Oh man, check it out, dude's got a Coke," Luke said. "Match made in heaven. We bring the booze, and the freshman brings the mixers. Let me top you off there, son. Ty, give me that Bacardi."

"No, no, no," Theo said. "That chick stuff won't do. He needs to go one-on-one with Johnny Walker."

"Veto," Luke said.

"We're trying to recruit him, and it's his first drink ever," Theo said. "Let's make it a memory."

"You're the only one trying to recruit him," Ty said.

"If I have a vote," I said, "I think I'll just take a rain check."

"Hundred percent not raining," Luke said. "I vote Bacardi."

"Johnny Walker," Theo said and glared at Ty.

"Oh captain, my captain," Ty said. "Johnny Walker it is."

"Settled," Theo said. "Democracy says drink the Johnny Walker."

"Aren't I kind of the dictator of myself?" I asked.

"You could say no," Theo said, "and then a little piece of freedom dies. Do it for your country."

We toasted. Theo and Luke drank, and when I had my flask up to my lips, Ty smacked the bottom, tilting it, sending a gush of Johnny Walker into my mouth, lighting up my throat like Listerine. He put his finger against my Adam's apple.

"Swallow that shit down, freshman!" he yelped. "Don't waste the good shit!"

I did not waste the good shit.

We rotated flasks, but Theo forfeited his turn with the Johnny Walker so I could hit it again.

"He's a baller!" Theo said.

The next round was the reprieve of the Bacardi, which is how I imagined rotten coconut might taste. At least it didn't burn.

I glanced over my shoulder. No Jenna. No rescuer of any kind.

"You meeting a hot date back here?" Luke said.

"Freshman! I'm impressed," Ty said.

"I bet it's Lane McKenzie," Theo said. "I saw you talking to her earlier."

"Ouch. Not impressed anymore," Ty said, dropping my empty Coke can and stomping it flat.

"What is the deal with Lane?" I asked.

"Besides the cringey weirdness, her demonic stares, and her nerdcore dress code? Just a few loose screws," Ty added.

"What about her and sleep?" I asked. "Jackson made a joke about her sleeping, and Miss Harrington shredded him for it."

"A while back, she ate a fistful of sleeping pills," Theo said.

"That was after she tried to kill her mom. They don't live together anymore," Luke said.

"The mom thing, who knows," Theo said. "The pills? That's verified intel. Teachers talked to us about her and everything."

Luke drank. Then Theo. We all stayed quiet for a while, contemplating a change of subject.

"She seems okay now," I said. "I met her. She was here with a friend. Talisha."

They all laughed. "Talisha don't have friends," Luke said.

"Yeah, she's got handmaidens, and when she's done with you, off with your head," Ty said.

"Smoking hot body, though." Luke tried to whistle, but he was so drunk even his whistling was slurred.

"I'll drink to that," Ty said. The flasks tipped again. Theo would drink and then hand it to me, and everyone would watch me take the last pull of the round. The bite of the alcohol reminded me of the hospital.

"Anyway, don't fuck with Lane," Theo said. "Rumors aside, Lane's got a short fuse. She snapped on Shelly Gamble last year. That cheerleader with the scar on her chin? Lane did that. The suspension along with her pill incident carved off enough of the school year to have her repeating freshman year."

"Whatever puts her in the rearview mirror is fine by me," Luke said.

"All right boys," Theo said. "Booze armor engaged, am I right? Let's go do some damage."

"Honeys galore in there," Ty said, smacking my shoulder in a frat boy sort of way.

Luke nudged Theo. "You gonna finally hook up with Jenna tonight or what?" he said.

Theo's eyes widened, and I couldn't hide feeling the sting.

"You nuts?" Theo said, stammering, buying time. "I'd love to, but I hear she's got the hots for the Doberman over there."

The sting turned to a blushing heat that overcame the sizzle of the booze in my belly.

"She would," Ty said. "She's bookwormy, and freshman over there looks like a dude who reads a lot."

They started to wander back to the party.

"You coming, or you gotta bury a bone or something?" Ty said.

They all laughed. "Yeah bro, bury that bone!" Luke called out.

"I'll be in soon," I said. The guys turned the corner, and I was alone again.

Did Jenna Weaver really like me?

Fuck no. She's got no reason to like you. You're a freshman. Social standing, zero. Looks? Two out of ten, and those are sympathy points. You don't have a car, and she's got this house. I mean look at this fucking place. Don't be stupid.

Why did Theo say that then, huh? Riddle me that.

He's got the hots for her, but he knows you've got the hots for her, and doesn't want to piss you off because he wants you to join the team. So he backtracks and decides to deliver you some good news instead of being love's executioner.

I read that book.

Don't change the subject.

I think I'm just going to keep waiting.

She's not coming.

I know. But I don't want to puke on her garage floor.

I leaned over, my mouth watering in revolt. I gave up to the will of my stomach, and a dry heave rippled through me. The next wave would carry a tsunami of dinner and Johnny Walker. I waited.

"Wilder, my God, I'm so sorry," Jenna said, finally outside. "You've been out here all this time?"

I clenched the brakes on the vomit.

"You okay?"

"Yeah," I said.

I was most definitely not okay.

———————

Priority one—don't vomit on Jenna Weaver.

Priority two—be charming.

Priority three—be brief.

"I'm not feeling the best right now, that's all," I said. "I was nursing a stomachache, but didn't want to miss the party, so I rocked some Pepto, and now I guess it's wearing off."

"By Pepto do you mean whiskey?"

Busted.

"Yeah, that's what I meant," I said, stifling a laugh and a massive thunderclap of puke. "Theo and the guys were out here, and the peer pressure was too much."

"I left you out here. Sorry." She brushed stray hair away from her forehead.

"No worries, you're the hostess, you've gotta work the room." I meant to say more, but I had to stop breathing and focus on stemming the glorious release of the chum swirling through my innards.

"At least you're not an asshole when you're drunk," she said.

"I'm a green drunk. Not like new-green either; like, I feel actually green. Seasick green. That would be an awesome Crayon color. Do I look seasick green?"

"It's dark," she said. "Can't tell."

"Do you like me?" I asked. "Don't answer. Don't say why or why not. I didn't mean to say that. I'm drunk."

"Wasted."

"Hammered."

"Seaweed green," she said.

"Seasick green," I countered.

"You need me to get Preston?"

"No," I said, even though I needed her gone so I could unleash the epic barf dammed back by nothing but willpower.

"For the record, I do like you," she said. "You're sweet and cute, but there are different kinds of like."

"Give me something you like on a somewhat equivalent level to me."

"What?"

"You said different kinds of like, so you like me as much as a good meal? Finding ten bucks in your jeans? Stubbing your toe? You can't leave me hanging."

"I like you as much as I like basketball," she said. "And I like basketball quite a bit. Just don't get so excited you drink or so depressed that you drink, okay?"

"No more drinking," I said. "None. On the wagon."

I think she smiled as she left, but I couldn't tell because thick lenses of water pooled in my eyes, and when she was gone I blinked away the tears of struggle and lurched into a ten-heave puke session so intense it sprayed from my nostrils.

I was hovering over a steaming puddle of vomit when Preston saw me.

"Jesus," he said. "You need me to call the coroner?"

"Just unlock the truck," I said. "I'll sleep in there until he gets here to bag my ass up."

He put his arm around me and helped me to the driveway. The haze of my first experience with alcohol was tilting the horizon, so I leaned on him to keep my balance.

"She likes me," I said, letting Preston take on the brunt of my weight. "Jenna Weaver said she likes me. Jenna Weaver."

"Kick back a few shots and charm the boobies off of Jenna Weaver—I have to say, that's some hall of fame shit right there."

"She's so hot," I said. Was I truly drunk, or just letting the placebo effect amplify my thoughts? "And sweet. And she likes me. This can't be real."

"I hope it's real and not some drunken fantasy." He leaned me against the hood of the truck, a weathered F150 that he'd dubbed "Old Rusty," and went to open the door.

"That's it," I said. "A fantasy. No way. Not a girl like her. Not a guy like me."

"You get that shit out of your head," he said.

"What shit? The truth?"

"Luke's clumsy. Theo is short. I've got one nut that hangs way lower than the other. You've got a fucked-up face. If you can't deal with it by now, Jenna or no one else is gonna ever be able to deal with it. You're not the first guy to take an at-bat way outta his league. So no excuses. Deal?"

He held out his fist. I bumped it. Then, he hoisted me into the back seat.

"I'll say goodbye to everyone," he said. "Won't be long. Pass out if you want, but don't vomit on the upholstery or you're cleaning that shit up."

I nodded. "Thanks," I said.

"Yo," Preston said. "Jenna Weaver likes you." He smiled and shut the door. I fell asleep wondering just how much Jenna really liked basketball.

TRYOUT

On Monday afternoon, I meditated over a two-bag lunch of Ruffles, stealing glances at the lunch line, hoping to get Jenna's attention.

In English class that morning, she sat in her normal seat, three rows over. Not a great sign.

There are different kinds of *like*, and so far she appeared to like me about as much as the bottom pancake of a short stack, the one that gets drowned in syrup and gouged with a butter knife and left for the busboy to dump in the trash.

But it wasn't her job to follow up. It was mine. No excuses.

Jenna stood in line, talked to her friends, and never looked over as I grazed on my chips. Preston was near the back of the line, late to lunch as usual. Lane waited for her lunch tray, wearing the same jean jacket from the party even though it was too hot for any jacket at all. She looked down at her feet as if they contained the secrets to the universe. The girls in front of her and behind her left a force field of airspace between them.

Preston sat down next to me and asked about my non-party weekend events. I told him I finished a book and cut the grass, and he was less than impressed.

"I set up a clan in *Call of Duty*," he said.

"An online team of players?"

"Exactly."

"How many guys on your team?" I asked.

"So far? One." He forked some shredded chicken into his mouth. "What can I say? I'm an online Rambo."

Theo sat down with us, and Luke wasn't far behind.

"You hear about your boy?" Theo said, nudging Preston. "Blew up that Johnny Walker Black and zeroed in on Jenna Weaver."

"I'm sitting right here," I said.

"The Doberman!" Preston said, playfully punching me in the shoulder.

"Speaking of which," Theo said, "you decide on basketball yet?"

"Tryouts start after school," Preston said.

"Not tryouts," Theo added. "Conditioning. Coach Ballard is going to kill us for a week. Makes his job easier when a few guys quit before he has to cut them."

He knocked on the table to get my attention. "You in or what?"

I shrugged.

"Should I go nuclear on him?" Theo asked Luke. Luke, whose mouth was full of mashed potatoes from his lunch tray, nodded emphatically.

"So when lunch is over," Theo said, "all these tables get folded up, and after school is out, this is where the cheerleaders practice. Usually, that first week, when they're done, they'll peek inside the gym, see us running our suicides and sweating our guts out, but I have to tell you, seeing those faces, the smiles, the giggles—man, I run harder. Luke, you run harder?"

Luke nodded again.

"You going to run harder?" he asked Preston.

"Hell yeah," he said.

"What about you?" Theo asked me.

I ignored him, pretending to be interested in something else, checking out the exciting action in the lunch line. Lane was setting a roll of silverware into her tray. I wondered where she would sit, expecting her to take a solo seat in one of the empty tables near the back of the cafeteria. Instead, she left the cafeteria entirely.

Where did she eat her lunch? I imagined someone sweet like Miss Harrington offered up her classroom as a safe haven and told Lane encouraging platitudes over a feast of rubbery chicken.

"What am I talking about—you're the Doberman," Theo said, convinced I wasn't going to answer. "You run hard regardless, right? But you know who's going to see you in there? Jenna. She's a hoop fiend. She cheers just to get courtside seats. You want in with Jenna, you gotta play hoops, my friend. Am I right?"

Preston nudged me out of my trance.

"You're right," I said.

I was the burned freshman, the recluse who was destined to be shunned and ridiculed, at least according to my asshole inner voice, yet here I was, fresh off of a starring role at an awesome party, getting courted by the captain of the basketball team, and the prettiest girl I'd ever seen not only knew my name but flirted with me.

So I tried out for basketball.

———

By Friday, the final day of hell week, we were down to twenty-five players. All week long, we couldn't quit for the day until at least one of us finished a full-court suicide in under thirty seconds, with everyone having run it in at least forty seconds.

This after we spent two hours tracing every line of the gym with defensive slides, sprinting outside in the cold with ten-pound plates held over our heads, and pushing weight sleds in the muddy grass.

But Coach had a surprise in store for that last day: "We're not done until someone hits twenty-eight seconds."

"Fuck my life," Luke muttered. Coach Ballard heard him, even though Luke was gassed and the swearing was more of a wheeze than actual speech. Coach heard every swear word, as if there were some secret military technology in his brain, and the fine for every swear word was ten pushups. No more, no less, but they had to be perfect, and they had to be performed immediately. Luke rattled off a set of ten pushups and rejoined us just in time for the final push.

All week, Theo and I were logging times in the twenty-nine-second range. Right then, I knew I made the team. We all had, because twenty-eight seconds was unlikely, if not impossible. Coach Ballard knew that— he meant to run us into submission to root out any remaining quitters.

The seniors called me a "try-hard" all week, but now, I was their savior. Theo and I were the only two guys with a shot to crack thirty seconds, and even then, we had to dig hard to do it all week long—and didn't always make it.

We had our strategy worked out—Theo would dog the first attempt, and if I didn't make it under twenty-eight, then he'd push hard for the next attempt while I took a breather. Coach Ballard had to sense what we were doing, but that was probably the result he was looking for—teamwork and rooting for each other.

Coach lined us up for our final suicide runs.

Preston was on my left, doubled over from our defensive shuffles. "I am literally going to die," he said.

"You don't have permission until someone hits twenty-eight," Coach Ballard said, with a little extra glee than usual.

The cafeteria door opened, and the cheerleaders peeked in.

Theo nudged me. I looked up, and Jenna saw me. Then, she waved.

"I'll go first," I said.

"I bet," Theo answered.

Coach Ballard lined us up.

"You do know that nice guys finish last?" Theo said. "You a nice guy, freshman?"

"I'm a fucking Doberman," I said.

The whistle blew, and I didn't feel the lactic acid. Not once. I glided from line to line and touched off the final baseline with everyone else shambling in behind me.

Everyone stood around, our hands on top of our heads, allowing our aching lungs to expand and recover, looking at Coach Ballard, who was smiling at the stopwatch in his palm.

"Twenty-seven-nine," he cried out, and everyone let out a massive cheer. The team mobbed me, cheering as if I just nailed a last-second shot.

Through it all, I saw Jenna, and she was clapping.

The guys hit the showers, but I stayed behind in the gym. This wasn't unusual. I liked to get a few shots in while everyone else showered, and Coach Ballard usually shot on the opposite hoop, waiting for the players to file out of the gym before locking it up.

Preston was my ride home. He showered with the first wave of guys and emerged from the locker room with slick hair, as if he didn't have the energy to dry off completely. His cheeks were still red from the sprinting.

"This isn't a damn chauffeur service," he said. "Shower up and roll out, son!" The threat was playful, and Coach Ballard answered with an equally playful, "If it weren't for him, you'd still be running."

He waited dutifully in Old Rusty while I was the last guy to take a shower, which also made me the last guy in the gym. When I left the locker room, Coach Ballard had racked the basketballs and was just waiting to lock up the gym behind us.

"I didn't make that suicide in twenty-eight seconds," I said.

He tested the push bar, satisfied the door was locked. "Twenty-eight-one," he said, matter-of-factly. "If anyone deserved a couple courtesy tenths this week, it's you."

"Don't give me anything else," I said. "I've overdosed on pity over the years. I want to earn it."

"You did," he said.

Preston usually waited behind the wheel, jamming the radio, but when I walked outside, he was sitting on the tailgate. When he saw me, he started dancing in the bed of the truck.

"What got into you?" I said, tossing my duffel bag into the truck. He hopped down, a halo of steam around his head. He was still overheated from conditioning.

"Jenna wants you to call her," he said, handing me a piece of a paper with her digits rendered in immaculate, feminine handwriting. "You could have talked to her yourself, but you insist on showering like a slug. Your mistake."

I saved the number in my cell phone. "This is good news, right?"

"Chicks don't give out their phone numbers to dudes they despise," he said.

"What if it's just indifference to a dude?"

"You got a number, and that means she not only wants to talk to you, but wants to talk to you in the future. It don't get any better than that."

He fired up the truck, chewing up parking lot gravel as he pulled onto the highway.

"Now I have to call her," I said.

"Are you fucking insane? Text, man. Just text. But wait a day or so," Preston said. "If you text right away, you seem desperate."

"Feels rude to wait," I said. "And everyone texts. Calling is terrifying, but wouldn't that stand out more?"

"Feel isn't real," he said. "And calls are terrifying—for her, too. She won't answer. She'll just text you back. So skip right to the place this is going to end up anyway. Don't die on this hill, bro."

"That makes no sense," I said.

"You do you," he said. "The wild man, a digit collector. Awesome. Awesome."

"What do I say?"

"Exchange recipes. Recite Bible verses. How should I know?"

"Because you've probably texted a girl before?"

"Aww shit," he said. "Sorry. Look—just be yourself. That's always good advice."

"Mom-approved advice."

"Honestly though, how often are moms wrong? Like in the long run?"

"Studies have proven moms are legit."

"So there you have it. Be yourself. But if you panic, make sure you have a funny story to fall back on. Not a joke—I mean don't be going all 'knock knock' in the middle of a text string. Just something funny that happened to you recently."

"Good advice," I said.

"Mom-caliber shit right there," he said. "Just remember, no matter what, do not call her right when you get home."

NICE

I called her when I got home.

I just dialed the number, trying not to think about what I was doing until I was two rings deep—far too late to obey my fears and hang up.

She picked up the phone, totally not surprised that I had called her so quickly.

"So, Wilder Tate's a caller, not a texter?"

"Calling means more," I said. "I also write handwritten letters instead of emails."

"With a fountain pen?"

"Of course. And I use the pony express to mail them."

She laughed. I pumped my fist.

"What a treat to be talking to the fastest guy on the team," she joked.

"Some of those drills aren't about who's fast," I said.

She finished the thought for me: "It's about who wants it more," she said, and navigated right into, "Wilder, you're such a nice guy."

You should have waited to call her. Nice guys do finish last.

Courteous guys call promptly.

Courteous guys are for single mom dating sites, not high school.

"I kept thinking about how I told you I liked you," she said. "And I do like you, but just wanted to let you know that I like you in a friendly way—a wave-in-the-hall, chat-in-class kind of way."

Figures.

Yup.

Told you so.

You did. Now shut up.

"I guess it's pretty obvious I like you in a totally more intense, unrequited sort of way," I said.

"It's sweet," she said.

Neither of us talked for an uncomfortably long time.

"I had this funny story rehearsed for when things got awkward," I said, finally. "You want to hear it?"

"You're not mad?"

"No," I said. "You don't even know me. I stand out in your mind for all the wrong reasons."

"It's not like that," she said.

"It's the truth," I said. "It's a burden, to have the burned kid crush on you."

"It's complicated."

"With girls, it's always complicated," I said.

I paced the living room, doing laps around the coffee table.

"I'm flattered, you know," she said. "So many girls are prettier than me, nicer than me, smarter than me."

"You stood up for me on the first day of school, which makes you the sweetest girl I know. Being intelligent and beautiful is just a bonus."

"I'm not beautiful," she said. "I'm tall and out of proportion, a bundle of sticks about to fall over, only with crappy skin. God, the freckles and constant sunburn."

"Maybe all that's true," I said, "but I don't think it disqualifies you from being beautiful. I think maybe what you dislike about yourself is exactly what sets you apart."

I waited for the compliment to melt her, to turn the tide, to win her over. I paced two full rotations around the coffee table before she answered.

"Oh, Wilder," she said. "I hope you see yourself that way, too."

Not what I was expecting.

"What makes you think I don't?" I fumbled the answer. It wasn't as "gotcha" as I thought.

"Tell me your funny story," she said.

"I'm not sure if it's even funny," I started.

"I want to hear it."

I told her how I liked to mess with people who asked about my burns by using the plots of old movies. My favorites were shark attack (*Jaws*), acid burns (*The Dark Knight*), and the elaborate setup to drill into a meteorite (*Armageddon*). When I told her that Talisha fell for the *Armageddon* story, she laughed.

"So I guess I'll let you go," I said, figuring that if I was the one who ended the conversation, it wouldn't feel nearly as bad. Jenna could have made the most polite attempt to get off the phone and my heart would have shattered.

"I have a feeling you won't," she said. "You're the guy who wants it more, after all."

I smiled.

"I'll be pulling for you at the games, Wilder. You're gonna do great."

When we finally got off the phone, I plugged my phone into the charger, grabbed my basketball, and went outside to shoot.

STARTER

I began the season as the sixth man for varsity and got plenty of minutes, but I wanted to be a starter. I wasn't crazy about getting my name announced in the pregame, but I wanted my mother to hear it. Whether they were cheering for me or just the Fighting Griffin logo on my jersey, Mom wouldn't know the difference. She'd love it and worry a lot less about me.

The rest of the team wasn't all that interested in playing defense, so Coach Ballard couldn't keep me off the floor for long. I was logging more minutes than a couple of the starters already. The situation was perfect, allowing me to perform without the pressure of being a starter, without getting dirty looks from the senior whose status I was stealing away, while still getting plenty of minutes, even in the game's critical moments.

But I wanted my mother to hear that name on the PA before the game, and yes, I admit it, I thought that being an official varsity starter would help turn up the heat between myself and Jenna.

In class, when we talked, it was basic with a dash of flirty. I gave her every opportunity to make eye contact with me in first hour, and sometimes, she reciprocated. She smiled at me in the hallways. She cheered hard for me during games.

Yet I was firmly imprisoned in the friend zone. Being a starter gave me a shot at breaking out.

Our fourth game of the season was against Cohen High School. Before running out for warmups, everyone was just relaxing in the locker room, waiting for Coach Ballard to get done talking to the jayvee guys.

Theo lost himself in some Beats headphones. Preston had one Apple earbud in, the music so loud I could hear the bass from across the room, bobbing his chin so that everyone knew just how much he was enjoying his pregame music. Luke was putting the finishing touches on his ankle tape.

Coach Ballard walked in and started writing on the whiteboard. In the upper left-hand corner, he started listing the starters, as he normally did. Then he'd go over the plays we'd be emphasizing that night, go over some defensive strategies, and review the scouting report on the other team. He wasn't an inspiring coach as much as he was a prepared one, and most nights when we were done with practice, he would drive across the county to scout out the teams we'd be up against in conference play.

I didn't even realize he wrote my name on the white board until I heard a few players clapping and Theo crying out, "Letting that Doberman off the chain tonight!"

Ty Venhaus wasn't cheering. He was the player I squeezed out of the lineup.

"Ty's done a great job for us so far this season," Coach said. "Expect plenty of minutes, Ty. But tonight's about defense. Cohen has a big shooting guard. Number twelve. He's in three-point range the moment he walks into a gym, and he'll let it go from half court if you don't pick him up. I'm dead serious. Wilder's gonna shadow him. Old-school box-and-one."

He started scrawling on the whiteboard, and I zoned out. The nervousness of starting wasn't a pleasant tingle—it was a nauseating freight train smashing into my stomach full-steam.

I held it together until we were lining up, then I ran into the locker-room bathroom stall to puke. Nothing came up. I never ate much before games, so I just heaved until my eyes watered. Coach sent the guys out to warm up and stayed behind until I came out of the stall.

"It's either nerves or you ate too much Mexican, so which is it?"

"Nerves," I said. I turned on the faucet to wash up, and Coach shook his head.

"No, cold water. Pure cold. More for your face than your hands."

He waited on me. The water was pleasantly numbing, and I felt a little better.

"I haven't started you yet because all you do is shoot threes," he said. "You need to round out your game. Drive to the hoop more often. Get better around the goal. But more than anything, you have to make your free throws. You know all this. You've worked on it."

I nodded.

"So that's me telling you that you earned your job as a starting shooting guard. Your next mission is to keep it."

I nodded then ran out of the locker room to join my teammates.

———

Theo got the biggest ovation when names were announced, being the handsome scoring star. The cheerleaders went bananas for everyone. They had a job to do, and making us feel more important than we really were was part of it.

But when I was announced, the ovation was insane. Part of it was touching; part of it made me want to puke again since everyone was hoping I'd do well and I was the only one in the building who could control my quality of play. And part of it was infuriating—some of the same kids yelling their lungs out would walk by me in the hallway with their heads down, afraid to so much as look at me during school.

The worst part of it was that my first start was a surprise, and Mom wasn't there to share it with me. Because of her work schedule, she couldn't make all the games.

Somehow, she made the first three, even one on the road at Beecher City, but she missed this one. So I had no choice but to do what Coach said and keep my job so that she could get to see the next one.

Early in the game, I was fouled going to the rim and went to the free throw line. The past few practices, Coach Ballard implored me to practice them more, and I did. I knew he was right, but honestly, the most boring play in basketball? Free throws. No one in the history of basketball ever hit a free throw at the buzzer.

I geared up for my first in-game free throw attempt. As I spun the ball in my palms, I heard Jenna through the murmur of the crowd. "You can do it, Wilder!"

I never heard much of anything while I was playing. Jenna pierced the veil I had created to keep the noise and gaze of the crowd at bay. Suddenly, I heard everything—the rattle of people sucking the last of their sodas through their straws, the random clap of hands, fans imploring me to "swish it!"

I most certainly did not swish it, nor the next one, clanging both free throw shots.

That set the tone for a tough night shooting the trey. I only nailed two of them out of about eight open shots for the entire game, which is horrendous for a supposed shooting guard. I mean, it's right there in the job description.

Theo could tell I was having a tough go of it, and between plays he came up and put his arm around me.

"It's shooting guard, not making guard," he said. "So just keep shooting. It's supposed to be hard or anyone could do it."

The frustration of not making shots fueled my defensive efforts. I took it all out on big number twelve, D.J. Renfro, a popular all-conference pick. Coach Ballard had to keep reminding me to pick him up at half court, not full court. He didn't want me to tire myself out, but there was no such thing as tired that night, and their star player didn't even sniff double digits.

Late in the game, having locked up a big lead, Coach took us out. As I was walking to the bench, I looked over at the cheerleaders, and Jenna gave me a little wave.

I waved back.

"Sit," Coach said. He knelt next to me.

"I get it," he said. "Girls and all, am I right? But you weren't all there tonight. You weren't attacking on offense the way you do off the bench. But you know what I saw you do? Wave to that girl. Let me tell you something—she does not exist between those lines. You got me?"

"Yes, sir," I said. My wave had been subtle, but if Coach noticed, I bet dozens of other kids did as well.

Coach went back to coaching, pacing the court, urging the bench players into the correct offense. I heard Luke laughing, and when I looked down the bench, a few other guys joined in.

"What's so funny?" I said.

Luke leaned over and put his lanky arm around me.

"You just got chewed for waving to a cheerleader in the middle of a game," Luke said. "You're earning your nickname, is all."

The guys laughed again, but not Theo. He was at the end of the bench, drinking water from a paper cone, barely glancing at the cheerleaders while he followed the last few moments of our blowout win.

BALLOONS

I finally got to tell Mom all about the game at dinner the next night.

She made another meatloaf to celebrate my ascension to starter and demanded to hear every play of the game, stopping me repeatedly so I could explain some of the finer points of basketball.

"Box-and-one?" she said. "I don't understand."

"It's like everyone on the team is guarding a piece of space on the floor, and I'm the only one guarding another player directly."

"Well, that's silly," she said. "A space on the floor can't score on anyone."

Bottom line? I scored six points, but the bigger feat was pinning down the other team's best player. Of course she was blown away and proud of me because moms are contractually obligated to be impressed by even the most minor athletic feats.

"Your father . . . " She trailed off, poking at her dinner. "I wish I could have been there," she said. "Your father would have killed to be there."

"I'll have plenty of games," I said. "It's not like you ditched me to get your nails done. I'll make you a deal—I won't be sad if you promise not to feel guilty. Okay?"

"Sure," she said, smiling. Of course that was impossible, people just felt what they felt sometimes, but we would pretend, and that would be enough.

I polished off the meatloaf and worked on clearing the dishes. She had just come in from a Red Hen shift and was picking up a few hours at the Elks later that night, so I tried my best to give her a break by cleaning up the kitchen.

"I'm glad high school is going well for you," she said.

"Things are cool," I said. "For a guy with half his face scorched off, I don't think I can complain."

She looked away from me when I said that, shaking her head in that subtle way she can pull off when she wants to feel like she's masking her disappointment while making that same disappointment crystal clear to anyone paying attention.

"You're just so hard on yourself," she said.

"How would you know?"

"I'm your mother."

A trump card even I couldn't deny. Jenna zeroed right in on the way I thought of myself, Lane knew I was lying about not knowing Randy's fate, but my mother was Jedi-caliber when it came to clearly seeing things about me that I never considered.

"You don't have to be all sorry for me," I said. "You know I hate that."

"I used to think it was all so unfair, but now maybe you're the one being unfair. Do you get bullied at school? Does anyone say mean things?"

"No one says much of anything to me."

"Except for Preston, and the basketball players, and your coaches and teachers, and this Jenna girl?"

"Kids in the hallway. Kids on the bus. They can barely stand to look at me. They don't talk to me."

"That highway runs both ways, Wilder!" she said.

"I don't need this," I said, stomping out of the kitchen. I was about to vanish into the hallway when she said, "I'm quitting my job at the Elks."

I stopped. "Good," I said. "I miss you."

"Do you even know why I killed myself these last few years with all those shifts?"

"The burns were expensive?"

"That's all paid for," she said. "This isn't." She pulled a brochure out of her purse and slid it across the table.

Tissue Expansion and You. I opened it. The pictures were mostly middle-aged women, their breasts ravaged by cancer, but convincingly reconstructed by tissue expansion.

"You want me to get a boob job?"

"Be serious."

The photos deserved every syllable of the word serious. These weren't even the cartoon graphics you get in some medical brochures. These were real pictures, taken from the neck down, the breasts gone, the remnants looking like two giant, closed eyes without eyelashes.

She waited. I read the entire brochure. Two of the before-and-after photos were burn victims. The results were astonishing. Swaths of scar tissue buried by skin that the body is tricked into growing over surgically implanted balloons.

When the surgeons first brought up tissue expansion to us years ago, they never showed me pictures. They only described the procedure, which, to be fair, sounded grueling as hell.

First, the surgeon implants silicone balloons underneath strategic regions of healthy skin. Then, he'd slowly inflate those balloons over the course of a couple of months to get the body to grow new skin. When the balloons are removed, the expanded flesh is available to patch up old scars, covering them for the rest of the patient's life.

The surgeon in the brochure, Doctor Eli Iacabucci, had the white teeth and tanned skin of a man who had many country club memberships and knew a lot about wine by smelling it.

"But your insurance policy is about as useful as one-ply toilet paper," I said.

"I have enough cash saved up for the operation," she said. "Over seventy-five percent of it, anyway. The clinic has agreed to finance the rest."

With fully inflated expanders, the patients looked even worse than they did with just the burn scars. Yet, it would be worth it. To be normal again? To have the scars gone? Since the first day they described the possible results of going through the tissue expansion, I wanted to do it. I would roll around in broken glass and swim through lemon juice to get my face fixed.

"I want you to know I did this not because I care about what you look like, but because you do," she said. "You can wait if you want. Or don't do it at all. No matter what your decision is, I love you."

I focused on the after photos, the patients smiling, their burns waved away with the wand of innovation.

I deeply cared about what I looked like, although I never admitted it to Mom, or anyone else. The fantasy of change is unstoppable—I couldn't shake visions of a Wilder without scars, walking down the hallway, head up, with a new hairstyle and clothes that weren't secondhand. Girls smiled, looking away—they are the shy ones now. The guys greeted me with high fives, fist bumps, nods. I am as popular as a member of a trendy boy band, only I'd be the one who breaks out of the group as a star and avoids a shitty solo career.

At the end of the hall, Jenna pushs through the crowd to get to me. She takes my hand. We walk to class together and kiss on the lips before going inside.

At my desk, the sun blasts through the bank of windows, and I sit on the opposite side of the room now, proud to show off the right side of my face, daring everyone to see the thin, pink repair scar that runs below the collar of my shirt, all but invisible.

Jenna sits beside me, and before the bell rings, she leans over to whisper something: "I can't wait for tonight."

Tonight! What's tonight? Before I could hit the fast forward button on my daydream, Mom interrupted.

"Are you okay?"

I smiled at her.

"Let's meet with the doctor," I said.

MONSTER

We drove to the hospital for a consultation at St. Louis Children's Hospital, where my life as a burn victim began on the eighth floor over six years ago. Perhaps it could end on the first floor in Doctor Iacabucci's office.

Doctor Iacabucci was flanked by two residents who took furious notes as he examined the extent of my scar tissue. Most of his attention was focused on my healthy tissue, and where he'd insert the balloons.

I couldn't understand all the technical jargon they were using among themselves, but he eventually gave it to me straight—to do it right, the procedure would require six balloons. One would be in the cheek of my good side, and two would be directly in the flesh of my neck, directly under my jaw. One on my chest, one on my arm, and one on the flesh of my burned side that remained untouched, right under my ear on the side of my neck.

He showed me pictures of what I could expect—the bubbles turned the healthy parts of the patients into gross, blue-hued mounds of distended flesh.

"How long would I have to look like that?" I asked.

"All factors considered," he said, "including the distance and frequency at which you could come to the hospital for saline injections, we're looking at six to eight months."

"We could wait," Mom said. "Time it to where the worst of it, near the end, happens over the summer. That way, you can be recovered in time for your sophomore basketball season."

"January would be optimal, but it's almost over," the doctor said, flipping through his paperwork. "I'm afraid February isn't possible. We're looking at sometime in late March, possibly early April."

"That might work," I said. "I could finish this season, and I may be back in time for regionals next season. The tournament is what really counts."

"Shall we get you scheduled, then?" Doctor Iacabucci asked.

I looked at the before-and-after pictures again, this time rendered on the computer. My face made whole, a reflection that was foreign to me, a fantasy made real. The right side of my face was restored, no scars left but the skinny, white suture lines he rendered to show how the flaps would be sewn together, leaving tiny scars of their own.

From a distance, no one would be able to tell I was even burned, but those were just pixels. Some surgical brand of Photoshop. A sales pitch.

"Would I look just like that?" I asked. "That's the best-case scenario, right? There's no way I'd improve that much."

"I'm the Michael Jordan of this particular surgery," Doctor Iacabucci said. "I don't deal in anything other than the best-case scenario, and I'm ninety percent certain your after photos would match that rendering you're marveling over right now."

The scars were on the ropes, and I could land a knockout blow if I just had the balls to say yes.

Yet the cost would be looking even worse than a burn victim for the better part of a year, and sacrificing the early part of the upcoming sophomore basketball season. I had a shot with Jenna, but if that was going to work out, I needed to stay on the court and stay in school enough to see her every day. Closing the deal would be tough enough with burn scars. Adding the expanders would knock me out of the game in more ways than one.

"Can I sleep on it, at least?" I said, finally.

"You can do more than that," he said. "It's your body. Take a couple days. If you do this, there are no half measures—you have to go all in. It's not fun, it's not pretty, it's not easy. You understand?"

"I'm definitely not used to easy," I said.

Just like that, he clapped his file shut, shook my hand, and left the room with one of the residents scurrying behind him. The other one stayed behind to show us to the window where my mother picked up her paperwork, which would presumably turn into a significant bill if I said yes, paid off by a double-shift-fueled nest egg, the rest financed at terms that would make a car salesman blush.

On the way home, Mom suggested stopping by the mall for frozen yogurt. We ate our treats in relative silence—she knew better than to press me on the issue while I was thinking it over, and I wasn't ready to talk about it.

"Maybe you'd like to browse the bookstore for a while?" she asked and gave me a weathered ten-dollar bill out of her purse.

"Get yourself something for once," I said, refusing to take it.

She placed it on the table. "I'd rather you get a book than me get a cheap pair of shoes."

There hadn't been a bookstore in that mall for a long time, not since I was little, but there was a massive Barnes and Noble across the plaza parking lot.

Browsing books was one of my favorite things to do. I sometimes liked it better than actually reading them, because when you read the back of the book, your imagination builds up the entire story—sometimes actually reading the whole book is a disappointment. Possibility is always better than the reality, and maybe that was true for the tissue expansion surgery. I had this fantasy of going through the operation without a hitch and walking out of the hospital with nothing but a thread of scar tissue. The reality was that eight months was a long time, and the scars weren't as ugly or terrifying as the inflated expanders themselves.

Don't talk yourself out of it.

I'm not. Just putting all the cards on the table.

It's hard and painful because it's worth it. You want this.

Maybe it's just you that wants this.

Jenna's never going to let your disfigured ass out of the friend zone. A big makeover, a huge sophomore basketball season, star of the school? She'd be nuts not to wise up by then. Play the long game.

I'm going to read now. You always shut up when I'm reading.

I'm courteous that way.

The bookstore was busy, with plenty of teenagers milling the aisles. Veteran's Day fell on a Wednesday, so everyone was off school. I didn't mind wasting a holiday at the hospital, either—it meant I wouldn't have a mound of makeup work to worry about when I got back.

After leafing through a few sports magazines, I browsed the fitness ones with good-looking, muscular guys on the cover. I liked reading those—each of them made you think you could look like that in eight weeks or less.

The current *Men's Health* had a vertical leap workout, which was perfect for stoking the impossible fantasy of dunking a basketball.

"Mommy?" A little girl's voice, scared and timid. I glanced at her with my peripheral vision, and she was gawking at me. I could almost feel her thudding pulse from ten feet away. She backpedaled into her mother's leg, who was scrambling to shove an issue of *Cosmo* back into the rack.

"Is that a monster?" the little girl whispered. I made eye contact with the mother, the embarrassment lighting up her face with red swirls. I felt sorry for her.

"I apologize," she said to me, kneeling down to hug her daughter, who said, "It's a monster, Mommy, a real-life one."

"No, honey," she said. "Shhh."

She picked her up and said, "I'm so sorry," then carried her daughter away.

I took the *Men's Health* to the coffee shop area, then sat down by myself in the corner, pointing my scars at the wall. I stared into the vertical leap workout.

Kids don't know any better, but it was just a reminder that the only reason adults didn't say things like that was because of tact and judgment. The unvarnished truth was that I did look like a monster.

"So dunking is on the agenda next, huh?" I looked up, and Jenna was pulling up the seat across from me.

Of course she'd show up during your lowest possible moment. That's so Wilder.

You're actually me, so when you say stuff like that, it's kind of hypocritical.

I'm not the one who believes the silly dream of dating Jenna. You just going to stare at her? You're even creeping me out.

I was staring at her. Once I realized it, I shrugged at her question. Talking felt impossible.

"Did you just totally expect to see me in the bookstore?" she said. "Am I that nerdy?"

I just stared at the fitness model coiling his legs to do a plyometric tuck jump.

She reached across the table and put her hand on my forearm. "Wilder, what's wrong?"

I smudged away a single, runaway tear before looking up.

"Not a good time," I said, my voice wavering.

"What happened?"

I considered not telling her. It would sound like I was cruising for sympathy, but I was so embarrassed I didn't have a choice.

"A little girl asked her mom if I was a monster," I said.

"Kids can be awful," she said.

"They can also be right," I replied.

"She's wrong."

"That's just your opinion," I said.

"What, my opinion doesn't count?" she said. "Well, maybe it's a fact that you're not a monster."

"How do you figure?"

She thought about it for a moment then smiled, the curve of her lips fueling a devious brightness in her eyes.

"Monsters don't get dates, do they?"

"Jenna . . . "

"Don't you dare tell me no," she said. "I'm asking you out, and I do not take rejection well."

"You came over to say hi," I said. "Not ask me out."

"Is that a no, then?"

Yeah, she felt sorry for me. She liked me the way you like getting a drink refill at a restaurant without having to ask the waiter or finding a front-row parking spot on accident, but monsters didn't get dates with Jenna Weaver, so I said yes.

PUMPKIN

The weekend after our serendipitous meeting at the bookstore, Jenna Weaver knocked at my door for our date. Having her pick me up was embarrassing enough, but Jenna didn't have her license yet and her father had to drive us. His Audi looked more expensive than my house.

"I didn't know your dad was driving us," I said, translated from *What the hell is your dad doing here? Aren't you old enough to drive?*

"Don't worry," she said. "He's a lot more puppy dog than grizzly bear."

I opened the Audi door for Jenna. She got in the back seat, a move worthy of a mental fist pump—that meant she planned on sitting by me during the drive.

Shit's getting real. You gotta hold her hand.

Not on the way there. You nuts?

Go for the hand on the thigh, then.

That's even more sexual than hand-holding. Jesus. Her dad's in the front seat.

How do you think he became her father? By not putting his hand on a good woman's thigh?

You are all the worst things about being a man.

"I'm Wilder Tate, sir," I said, poking my open hand into the front seat. I expected a chisel of a handshake that could crack stone, but I did all the squeezing. He was afraid he'd break me or intimidate me. Sympathy ran in the family, I guess.

"I know who you are, young man," he said. "I watch the basketball games just as closely as I watch Jenna's phenomenal cheerleading squad, if you can believe it."

"You know you love cheer," Jenna said.

"I'd love a regional championship even more," he said, his expectant eyes finding me in the rearview mirror. He was bald with a thick crease in the middle of his forehead. He looked like one of those guys that shaves his head to be bald on purpose.

Speaking to the Father of the Girl You Like is always terrifying, but basketball felt like a safe place to score some points.

"Did you go to Herrick, sir?" I asked.

"I'm a North Central man, myself," he said. "Hell, it was Herrick that beat us back in eighty-nine. Hell of a team. Those farm boys played some defense, now. It was like five Dobermans."

That was why basketball, and regionals, meant so much in that little slice of Southern Illinois—the enrollments and budgets were too small for most sports, and the graduates stuck around, working family farms or settling down with sweethearts they met in eighth grade. Rivalries could ripen over generations, families could take over towns, and the basketball court is where it mattered most.

Herrick had a half-dozen baseball banners that no one seemed to care about, but rivalries weren't best settled at four in the afternoon when the daylight hours were long and farms needed to be worked and the weather was too nice to scream at the umpire. Baseball never made the front page. But in early February, parents and fans would turn on the four-wheel-drive to get through the roads that were just too rural for the state to salt them, all so they could sit shoulder to shoulder on the bleachers, turning the gym humid with body heat, ready to scream and smile and have something to talk about during their predawn coffee at the diners the following morning.

He dropped us off at the theater, where we shared a bucket of popcorn as big as a trash can. The container served as a blockade between us, keeping me from doing something silly like trying to kiss her.

The movie featured conflicted superheroes and an alien invasion and so many explosions and fights it was like watching someone else play a video game for two hours, but I didn't have time to pay close attention—I was sharing popcorn with a girl. I had to focus on timing my reaches into the bucket so that I wouldn't stain the back of Jenna's hand with my buttered fingers.

Late in the movie, her hand bumped into mine as I foraged for the last few kernels, and for a minute I thought she was going to interlock her fingers into mine, and we would kiss and get married and buy a house and have kids. Instead, she just waited for me to finish digging for popcorn, her eyes glued to the screen.

The movie ended. Even after waiting through the credits for a bonus scene to tease the next movie, her dad still wasn't picking us up for another half hour, so we chilled in the lobby.

I busted a dollar in the change machine, and she absolutely took it to me at the air hockey table. I wish I could say that I let her win. I probably would have if she weren't the Sidney Crosby of air hockey.

When it was over, she shrugged. "We have it in my basement."

So on top of cute and smart, she was the kind of girl that had an air hockey table in the basement of her Tony Stark-ian house. I could try my ass off to be sweet and funny and win her heart, but I didn't see myself delivering an arcade-quality game experience right in the comfort of her home.

"I bet your bathroom has heated tile," I said.

"I wouldn't know; the butler carries me all the way to the toilet."

We looked at movie posters and passed judgment on upcoming films based on pictures and taglines. I counted three "oversized star's head" posters, and she found four "orange-and-blue contrast" posters, explaining how the color combo catches the eye. So she won that game, too.

When her dad picked us up, we gave him our lukewarm reviews of the movie, and then the back seat turned into a monastery all the way home.

We arrived at my house, and even though it was Jenna walking me to my door, in a weird gender reversal of all of the romantic movies I'd seen over the years, I could still reclaim the moment. All I had to do was show some mettle. Just go in for a kiss.

Lean in, grab her face, and make this motherfucker a Notebook-*caliber kiss.* It's not even raining.

Don't stall. She's going to leave.

Wait, we saw *The Notebook*?

Stalling again.

Our fingers didn't even graze during the movie. Too soon.

There's soon and never and no in-between.

Sounds fancy, but kind of makes no sense.

Jenna grabbed my hand and gave it a hard squeeze. "Bye, Wilder," she said, lingering, and the porch light highlighted the shine of her eyes and the curve of her hair.

"I'll call you," I said, meaning, *Don't leave.*

She didn't leave. She glanced over her shoulder, just slightly.

"He's not watching," she said.

I leaned in probably two inches before I froze.

She smiled. "You're freaking adorable," she said then kissed me on my cheek. The non-destroyed one.

I tried to say something. My mouth opened up with the express intention to tell her goodbye or thank you or I love you but instead I just remained silent and rooted to the porch.

"Practice your air hockey," she said, and then she was gone.

WALK

I called her on most nights after school, or after practice, or after games. We talked about things, but not important things like "Are you my girl-friend now?"

She talked about cheerleading and how much she loved Harry Potter, and how she wanted to go to college to be a veterinarian because she loved animals. I talked about basketball, about going to college wherever they gave me a scholarship, about how bad I wanted a driver's license, not bothering to tell her I didn't have a chance in hell of affording an actual car.

The night we beat Fulton Grove to tie for first in the conference, I got home, showered, and gave her a call.

I was feeling rambunctious after that game—it was the first time all year I had more points than Theo, and I held Fulton's all-conference guard to six points, mostly free throws. He even picked up a technical foul for throwing a fit after I picked his pocket in the third quarter.

Jenna told me I had a good game and that she was proud of me, and I went right into it, just as I had rehearsed it on the bus ride home: "I like you the way a starting shooting guard likes basketball, and I'd like to take you out again."

"Okay," she said, after a long pause. "But let's do something like a picnic. Something where we can be alone and talk."

I had just the place—the railroad tracks behind my house were torn out a long time ago, leaving a rock path into the woods. The trestle that spanned the creek was gone, but you could sit by the edge and look down into the muddy water, a redneck ocean where I used to camp out with my grade-school friends. We built fires against our mothers' wishes, roasting packaged hotdogs and acting like we were survivalist badasses.

That's what I planned to do with Jenna. Build a fire, impress her with my Boy Scout skills. Roast s'mores and drink Cokes. Now, that was a damn picnic meal that beat the pants off of cold-cut sandwiches.

The thought of sandwiches made my stomach quiver with anticipation. I headed to the kitchen and peered into the fridge for a snack. Mom sat at the kitchen table, jotting down one of her many lists—shopping lists, checklists, reminders. The spot near the kitchen phone was always wallpapered with little, yellow blocks.

"Sounds like you two get along quite well," Mom said.

"Yup," I said, grabbing a baggie of ham.

"I've seen Jenna at the games. She's adorable."

"I have to agree," I said.

"A first girlfriend can be scary," she said, putting her pen down. "I'm here if you want to talk about it."

"We have yet to file girlfriend/boyfriend paperwork at the local courthouse," I answered.

"I'm just saying you can talk to me."

"We're most definitely talking, right?" I said, placing the entire wedge of ham between two slices of Wonderbread.

She picked up her pen and continued writing. I ate half my sandwich standing in the kitchen, waiting for her to press me. She didn't.

"I think I want to do the tissue expansion," I said.

She dropped her pen. "Are you sure?"

"Yeah," I said, leaning against the counter, already wanting to make a second sandwich before the first one was even finished.

"If that's what you want," she said. "But I think it will be good for you, sweetie. You especially."

"I agree," I said.

"I'll call Doctor Iacabucci sometime tomorrow and let him know," she said.

"You better write down a reminder."

She shot me a sarcastic look then broke into a smile.

"I'm off on Saturday morning," she said. "Do you want to do something? Maybe go out to lunch?"

"I have a date with Jenna on Saturday," I said. "Do you work tomorrow night?"

"I'm working nine to twelve at the Elks, but I've got a few hours between shifts. Why?"

"I thought you said you were quitting."

"I am," she said. "Eventually."

"I'm taking Jenna on a picnic," I said. The ham was gone, so now I was just buttering the Wonderbread, folding it in half, and eating it as a standalone snack. "I'd like to get some supplies."

"That sounds sweet," she said. "I'd love to help."

"Can we go to the mall?" I asked.

"Honey, we can fill a picnic basket at the local SuperValu."

"I know," I said. "But there's something special I hope you'll help me buy."

———

Two days later, during first hour, Jenna invited me to take a walk through the biology class's nature trail just after final bell. As if things couldn't get any better, now we were stealing away some private moments before we needed to be at practice.

I had bought her a bracelet with two charms—a basketball and a ruby, which was her birthstone. A sterling silver story of us, and the story was just getting started. The whole works was three-hundred bucks, which my mother agreed to pay out of my surgery savings.

I dressed out for basketball practice and threw on my coat. We'd been well into those Midwestern days where you had to run the heater in the morning and the air conditioner at noon for weeks, but now, the colder days had come to stay. The bracelet's felt box was inside my coat's breast pocket, its contact with my chest feeding my elevated heartbeat. I'd been carrying the bracelet with me everywhere ever since the clerk wrapped it up and handed it to me at the Fond Memories store in the mall.

Jenna had changed into track pants and a T-shirt for cheerleading practice. She tossed on a hoodie and met me in the parking lot.

We headed to the nature trail that cut through the forest behind the school. One day, we'd have to walk through the trails during biology classes, capturing leaves and insects, an all-business trip. But now it was just a romantic walk in the woods.

"I just have to say, I'm totally moonwalking on clouds right now," I said.

"How can you walk on the moon and clouds at the same time?" Jenna joked.

"Mixed metaphors aside, I'm just really happy." We walked next to each other, lapsing in and out of sync. Her hand bumped into mine, and I grabbed it, squeezing it. She didn't yank it away. My heartbeat rose even higher.

"I'm looking forward to Saturday," I said.

"Wilder," she said, trailing off.

She stopped walking, unplugging her hand from mine. She looked at me. In my fantasies, this is how it went at our picnic. She looked me in the eyes, and then I'd reach into my pocket for the bracelet. I intended to wait, but the weariness of her smile and the way her eyes wandered off into the woods had me reaching for the bracelet prematurely.

I offered her the jewelry box.

Jenna took a step back. A literal step back, as if I'd drawn a gun.

"It's just a bracelet," I said. I opened the box, the silver and ruby glimmering, even in the shade.

Jenna wouldn't even look at it.

"What's wrong?"

"Last night," she said. "I went to the movies with Theo."

She reached out and closed the box, never taking it from my hand.

"We kissed," she said. "I like him, Wilder. I have since the start of the school year. Heck, since I was a freshman."

"But you invited me to your party," I said, sifting through my memories, looking for evidence that she was wrong about liking Theo. "You gave me your number. You said all those nice things to me. You kissed me on the cheek after our date."

"And I meant all of that," she said.

"Don't say that," I said. "Please."

I rubbed my eyes before any tears could fatten their way into existence.

"I got all our picnic stuff," I said. "You pretended all this time. You could have pretended a few days longer."

"I couldn't let you fall any harder for me," she said. "Now was the time."

"The worst time."

"There is no right moment for a thing like this," she said.

"I already fell for you," I said.

"Wilder," she said, delaying before she decided to go ahead with her confession. "It's better you hear it from me—the full truth—instead of someone at school. Word may not get around, but there's always a chance, and I feel it's the right thing to tell you."

Again, she hesitated.

"What is it?"

"Theo wanted me to invite you to the party and flirt with you so that it would be easier to convince you to join the basketball team."

The cold air scorched my throat as I took a short breath, gearing up to tell her off, but all I could say was, "How could you do that to me?"

"I'm stupid, and I liked Theo," she said. "But I wasn't going to do it. You have to believe me. That's what got me talking to you, but I do like you, Wilder. If it weren't for Theo, who knows—"

I turned around and launched the bracelet, box and all, into the woods, then started walking away.

"Wilder! Let me finish!"

She grabbed me by the shoulder, and I jerked away from her.

"I hate this. You're a nice guy."

"I'm sick of being called nice," I said. "It's like being called beige, or that you taste like oatmeal."

"I didn't lie to you, I swear."

"You knew how much I liked you for weeks and kept me dangling on the hook, L-O-L."

"You're not just any guy," she said.

"Looks bad to break the freak's heart," I said. "The monster from the bookstore."

She walked to me slowly, reaching out for me. I flinched at first, but then let her palm settle on the scarred side of my face. She leaned in, looking at me with her glistening eyes, and my anger fell away.

"I'm having an operation," I said. "It's going to fix my face. I'm going to be normal. I'm going to look normal, it'll just take a few months. Maybe then—"

"Walk me back," she said, not letting me finish. "We're late."

She took her hand off of my face. My scars were numb, the nerves fried away long ago. Still, her touch lingered. I followed her back to the school.

"Have a good practice," she said. I didn't respond, just standing there like a schmuck in the hallway as she disappeared into the cafeteria.

I looked through the tempered glass of the gym doors and saw the basketball guys—Theo stretching out with the team, laughing, as Coach blew the whistle to start the first round of drills.

I couldn't share the floor with him. I couldn't stand to even look at him, the way he put his arm around me, feeding me booze and pushing me at Jenna.

"Why aren't you practicing?" The voice managed to scold and sound concerned at the same time. Lane McKenzie stood behind me, her backpack slung over one shoulder, her hip jutting out to balance the load.

"Why are you still at school?" I said. "The buses ran already."

"I hope they run far, far away," she said. "My dad's picking me up. What's with you?"

"Nothing," I said, ducking away from the gym door.

"Bullshit. What's wrong?"

"Why should I tell you?"

"I was in a psychiatric hospital for four months. I'm practically a doctor," she said. She wore a frizzy sweater even though the heater was cranked up to match the climate of the equator. Dots of sweat gathered on her forehead. She sleeved them away, leaving behind little bits of wool. "Here's my prescription—the library is a good spot if you need a cry," she said.

"I don't need to cry."

"Try it. You'll feel better."

"Jesus. Isn't your dad here yet?"

"Yeah," she said, glancing out the front door windows. "You just had this look on your face like someone slapped your puppy."

"I don't have a puppy."

"You don't have Jenna Weaver, either," she said. "She finally stiff-arm you?"

"Your dad is polluting the environment as we speak. Best get going, for the rain forests and all."

She adjusted her backpack and wiped her forehead again. "There's a box of tissues on the A shelf, behind the Jane Austen books."

"The ozone layer is screaming at us. Somewhere, an elephant is choking to death."

Mercifully, she started migrating to the main door. She put her hands on the push bar, then stopped.

"Wilder," she said. "Jenna acts like a McGoodGirl, straight off the rack, but I bet she masturbates with cucumbers and has a pile of dead clowns buried in the crawlspace of her house. Fuck her."

I couldn't even react before she bolted out the door.

I looked into the gym one more time then snuck out of the side door of the school. I walked nine miles to get home, and when I was about to cry, I thought of clowns and cucumbers and couldn't help but smile.

QUITTER

With Mom working until midnight, the house was my own personal palace of sulk. I baked a sleeve of cinnamon rolls for dinner and ate half the icing before the oven timer beeped, an act I immediately regretted—rolls with sub-par levels of icing are among life's most bitter disappointments.

Not as disappointing as your dream girl liking you about as much as Hannibal Lecter likes veganism.

I'm not even in the mood.

About as much as the modeling industry likes your face.

Now that's just mean. That's your face, too.

Nope. I'm just a voice. I'm sexy as hell.

Okay, then.

I tried rationing out the icing onto the rolls when someone knocked on the door.

A knock was cause for alarm in my world. Mom watched a lot of *Dateline NBC*, so she always thought that killers, kidnappers, and all sorts of evil lurked behind every knock.

I was in just the right mood to open the door and embrace the gleaming butcher knife of a supernatural murderer.

Of course, it was just Preston.

"Why'd you ditch practice?" he asked, letting himself in.

"I walked home," I said.

"Was this over Jenna and Theo? Come on—you knew that was growing into a thing, right?"

"Did everyone know about them but me? She told me she liked me."

"I like applesauce. Big whoop."

I felt myself wanting to cry, but I couldn't. Not in front of Preston. Maybe I should have taken a break in the library after all.

"You have to leave," I said.

"Oh man," Preston said. "You actually didn't know. Dude."

That's when Preston hugged me, and I started to cry, brushing my tears onto my shoulders before he could get a close look at me.

"There's this surgery that can fix my face," I said. "I'm going give it a shot."

"If that's what you want, that's awesome," Preston said. "But you don't need to fix your face, man."

"I know Jenna liked me, somewhere in there," I said. "It's not what she thinks of my scars or even what I think of them, but what it's got to be like walking down the street holding the burned kid's hand, the stuff haters are going to stay behind our backs. I'm not worth the trouble."

"That's the stupidest thing I've ever heard."

"It sounds stupid, but it's not," I said. "We'd love to think we live in this amazing world where every precious soul is worth the trouble, but when you're Jenna or any of the other billion girls on the planet and you can have a non-scarred dude with zero emotional baggage and no history of mental and physical trauma, I'm at the very least handicapped against the field."

"I don't know what imaginary field you're up against," Preston said. "But in a field of vanilla pricks, your face is the one that people will remember."

"I can't knock being a vanilla prick until I've tried it," I said.

"Then your decision is made. Fix your face, be a vanilla prick. I've got your back if that's what you really want," Preston said. "See you at practice tomorrow?"

"That's the thing about the surgery," I said. "It takes a long time to make it work. It takes months. So, I'm quitting the team."

"I take all of my noble support for your plight back. You can't quit," Preston said.

"I sort of just did," I said.

"You haven't even thought it through. You're just upset," Preston said. "Have you even considered what life would be like without basketball for you? I know you like to play it off like you don't care, but you're the kid that shoots around before the bus comes. Then, you shoot around in the gym before class starts. You shoot after lunch. You shoot after school, before practice. When practice is over, you go home, you eat, and if there's enough light, you shoot."

"I don't need to be on the team to shoot. Or love basketball."

"Shots mean nothing without a game," Preston said. "Games mean nothing unless you play them for a trophy, and we can win it. Everyone says so. Do you know what that trophy means around here?"

"I can't play with Theo," I said. "I can't play with Jenna on the sidelines."

I had a pre-op appointment with Doctor Iacabucci but no firm time-frame, other than his promise to try and schedule it in March. Regardless of scheduling, I had no intention of sharing a court with Theo ever again, let alone trying to make a free throw with Jenna cheering me on.

"Don't quit," Preston answered. "Don't let Theo or Jenna or anyone else make you sacrifice this."

"I wouldn't call it a sacrifice."

"Bullshit," he said. "You're our most important player. We can't win without your defense."

"I don't care."

"See now, that just pisses me off," he said. "I'm lucky I made the team. I just want to be a basketball player. I only wish I was as good as you."

"Why? That's stupid."

"You know what it feels like, just wanting to fit in," he said. "Right? I'm not the smartest, not the best looking. I'm a basic bitch. I need that uniform, but that uniform needs you."

"Why the hell do you care so much about what I do?"

"Because you're the only real friend I've got on the whole damn team."

I didn't want to hurt him or desert him, but I couldn't let anyone else talk me into thinking I didn't need to fix my face. I could tolerate the scars if I lived in a fairy tale, but the world was superficial and harsh, and it didn't get easier once you graduated high school. I'd have job interviews. I'd have a first day of freshman orientation at a college full of kids I didn't know. I'd share eye contact with hundreds of girls who might have been the love of my life if they could only tolerate holding that eye contact for just a little longer without glancing at my scars.

I couldn't let Preston push me away from what I had to do just because he needed a friend on the team. I couldn't be dumb enough to think a Jenna Weaver could somehow fix me. I sure as hell couldn't lie to myself, thinking that if I could just accept the way I looked that it wouldn't matter to anyone else.

Accepting yourself sounds like it's always the right choice, but it takes even more bravery to reject yourself and make a change. I was getting the surgery, and Preston would come around to support that decision, or he wasn't actually my friend.

"You could have told me about Theo and Jenna," I said, changing the subject. "If it was so obvious I should have figured out, a friend would have given me the heads up."

Preston let out a sigh, then opened my fridge. He grabbed two Cokes.

"I didn't want it to be true, either," he said. "But if I put that seed in your head on a hunch and ruined the whole thing, it would be my fault. Theo was careful enough. Don't feel like a douche because you didn't figure it out."

I cracked the tab on my soda and took a pull. Acid and sugar bloomed in my mouth.

"Let's go to my place, get wired up on sugar and caffeine, and shoot people online."

"As long as we don't talk about basketball," I said.

He raised his can, and we toasted, sealing the agreement.

———

Preston dropped me off back home around midnight, my ears still buzzing from the grenades and gunfire in my headset. Our new clan, *W1ldBunch*, won plenty of pickup games. Some games *Doberman69* unleashed hell, in other games *FullCourtPreston* carried the team.

I woke up the next morning bone-tired after crappy sleep haunted by the instant-replay moment when Jenna told me she kissed Theo.

I wanted to squirm out of going to school and could easily get a day off if I just confessed the depths of my heartbreak to Mom, but I didn't feel like seeing the sympathy on her face after I had tossed a bracelet worth a week of Red Hen tips into the woods.

I showered and ate breakfast, and she gave me her customary kiss goodbye. When I was a little boy, it was on the lips, moving up to my cheek as I approached junior high. The kiss had now migrated to the top of my head, an annoyance I knew I'd miss when those days were gone.

When I got to the front door that morning, I turned around and peered into the kitchen. She thought I had left. I never looked at my mother that closely before—what kid does that? She looked tired but beautiful, her coffee steaming in her right hand while she wrote out a shopping list with her left. The radio mumbled in the background. She was immersed in the rare moments she had in her life that weren't dedicated to me or working her ass off to make sure I had a chance to grow up right.

The house was shit, we didn't catch many breaks, her car was junk, but I felt like the luckiest guy in the world for just that moment. The feeling didn't last long. I had trained myself out of feeling good, more scar tissue I could attribute to the burns, only no surgery in the world could treat it. Maybe fixing my face was the first step.

"Mom," I said, startling her. "I love you."

"Love you too, honey," she said, her black hair cross-hatched by the early sunlight that was carved into bars by the kitchen blinds.

I took the bus to school and stared out the window, wishing the ride would never end because I knew I had to walk the first hour and Jenna would be sitting there. She'd look at me or try to talk to me or ask if I was okay, and I wasn't ready for that. I wasn't okay, not with her, not with anything.

The goal was to just make it a bank robbery–type day at school—get in, get out, try not to let anyone see you.

Except for Coach Ballard. I would have to see him, since I'd decided he was the only other person I'd tell about my decision to quit the team.

Then again, it wasn't a decision now, was it? It was a medical necessity. At least, I could make it look that way.

I made it a point to get to class before everyone else, that way I could bury myself in my textbook until everyone was seated and Miss Harrington took over the attention of the class.

I couldn't tell when Jenna came in, not until someone thin and pretty in a cashmere sweater was standing by my desk, demanding my attention. I looked up from my book, and of course, it was her.

Without saying a word, she placed the blue jewelry box on the corner of my desk. I looked at it, the corner muddy from where it landed in the woods behind the school.

Then I looked at up at her. The eye contact didn't last long before she walked away, forfeiting her usual seat to sit in the back row on the other side of the room.

My scars were pointed out the window so that no one could see them, but that was just a trick, wasn't it? She saw them clearly. Perhaps more clearly than me.

During seventh-hour study hall, Coach Ballard peeked in and asked Mr. Gilliam if he could have a word with me in the hallway.

"We missed you at practice," he said. "Everything okay?"

I told him about the tissue expansion, how it would knock me out for the season and most of the following year if it all went according to plan.

He put his hands on his hips, a pose he frequently used while watching practice.

"Coach, please," I said, "Don't make me feel bad for quitting the team."

"You know what? I can't promise I won't make you feel bad," he said. "I promise you this, though—one day, when you're older and married, you'll laugh at yourself for ever wanting to go through all that just to be rid of that scar tissue. Sure, it may look smaller in the mirror after those expander things, but whatever is left is just going to feel bigger. Trust me on that."

This wasn't the supportive coach act I imagined I would get, but that's Coach Kevin Ballard for you, the kind of guy who went from a genuine smile to spitting fire as you blasted out suicide after suicide for messing up an out of bounds play.

"I just know it will be worth it," I said. "I thought it through."

"You know what I see when I look in the mirror?" he said. "I don't see this receding hairline, the turkey neck, the wrinkles, the gray hairs. I see the guy that swaggered up and down the hallways of this very school, decked out in my letter jacket, smiling at the ladies and high-fiving my friends. He didn't need knee braces or Aleve or Rogaine. And even after this surgery, you're going to look in the mirror and remember what those scars used to look like before you fixed them up. The surgery won't erase your memories, so it won't change the way you feel."

The bell rang, unleashing students eager to start their weekends.

"And you'll never forget the price you paid to try and fix them."

I walked to the bus, trying to choke down the anger.

Coach didn't know shit. He had bad knees, not a bad face. My mother saved for this operation knowing it was the best thing for me. She didn't care about the regional championship or a basketball scholarship.

She wanted me to be happy. He wanted a trophy for himself. End of story.

When I got to the bus, I pulled the tissue expansion brochure out of my backpack. I browsed the before-and-after photos, skipping over to the burn repair pictures and staring at them until I got home.

RECOVERY

Once I quit the team, rumors about the severity of my upcoming surgery began to surge through the school. Some kids told me they heard half my jawbone was removed and replaced with a prosthetic, others heard that an experimental gas would be pumped under my skin via a six-inch needle.

Before the start of first hour, Lane didn't even pause to drop her book bag. She blazed a direct route to my desk.

"What's this I hear about you getting inflated with a bicycle pump?" she asked.

"Just your run of-the-mill, intensely surgical saline fluid balloons," I said.

"That's supposed to fix your face?"

"Yes," I said, stopping myself before adding, *it has to.*

"Didn't anyone ever tell you that chicks dig scars?"

"Too much of a good thing, I suppose," I said. "Kind of like that jean jacket."

Her shoulders melted, and she turned away from me—just another asshole making fun of her.

"I didn't mean it like that," I said. "I was only joking."

"You suck at comedy."

"Where do you go at lunchtime?" I asked.

She couldn't tell if I was scraping up intel to use as insult-fuel against her like the mean kids, or if I honestly gave a damn about her lunchtime routine, so she just stood there, arms crossed, processing the question.

"You don't have to tell me," I said, finally.

"I don't like to eat alone in front of everyone, okay?"

"I don't like to be a burnt freak in front of everyone," I said.

"You might be weird, but you're not a freak," she said and headed to her desk.

———

I caught up with Preston at lunch. The latest annoyance in his life was his dad's obsession with his new metal detector. On Sunday nights, he pulled Preston away from *Call of Duty*, and they drove to the public beaches at Carson Lake and scanned for treasure.

"So far, our greatest find was a necklace with a diamond stud," Preston said. "My dad turned it in at the visitor center. I asked him what the point of all this was if we weren't keeping the junk we found, and you know what he said? 'I like the beach, but I can't swim.' I volunteered to teach him, but he's content scanning the sand."

"I think it's cool," I said.

"You would."

"The lost relics of other people," I said. "Very Indiana Jones."

"Yeah, without the beautiful love interest and adventure."

"And Nazis," I added.

"Nah, I think there's a few of them. You ever been to Carson Lake on a Sunday? Yikes."

He spooned some cafeteria corn into his mouth while I opened by bag of Ruffles.

"You still dead set on quitting the team?"

"I told Coach Ballard not to expect me back, so yeah, pretty much."

"You can't pretty much quit. You do or you don't."

"I quit, then," I said.

"Maybe, but it sounds like you want someone to change your mind."

"I don't," I said.

"We would have won last night with you. No doubt."

Sumner High beat us the night before, and if the chatter around the lockers was to be believed, it wasn't all that close. Sure, it was a road game against a conference opponent, and I heard it was a loud gym, a tough place to play—but Sumner was under five-hundred.

"How the hell did Sumner beat us?" I asked.

"Their point guard went off. He got to the hoop at will."

"Who guarded him?"

"Theo," Preston said. "A wet towel would have double digits against his sorry-ass defense."

A tray clapped down beside me—Theo. Luke was with him, as usual.

"I hope the towel at least has a solid crossover," Theo said.

Preston started to apologize.

"Chill," Theo said. "You're not telling me anything I don't already know. When it comes to defense, I'm no Doberman."

I dumped the remainder of the chips into the palm of my hand, looked at him, and then crammed them all into my mouth, crunching furiously, trying to get the meal over with.

"I understand if you're pissed," Theo said to me. "Jenna said it all wrong, though. She was just supposed to flirt a little. We just wanted you on the team, man!"

Crunch. Crunch.

"She likes you," he said. "The whole team likes you. I like you. I'm sorry it went down the way it did."

I swallowed the chips. Theo pawed at his French fries. After a few gulps of soda, I placed the can down, took a deep breath and said, "If I play, it will be because I want to play," I said. "If I don't, it will be because I've got more important things to handle, and also because you're a manipulative asshole."

I couldn't believe I actually said it and didn't wait around for it to sink in.

I went to the gym and shot around, never once glancing at the bleachers to see if anyone was looking. I don't think I was ever more locked in. I could see the rings where the net looped into the orange metal, focusing on the center eyelet every time I shot. I made twelve three-pointers in a row that day, hitting the last one just as the bell rang, leaving my hand up as if I were some NBA all-star who had just beaten the buzzer.

CEREMONY

That night, I was microwaving leftovers in my kitchen when Preston made a surprise visit.

"Your mom at work?" he said, hanging his coat over the back of a kitchen chair. "When she back?"

"Late," I said.

"Good. We need to talk."

"We really don't."

"I heard you got Jenna a bracelet," he said. I had no idea anyone beyond her knew that I had gotten her an expensive piece of jewelry. If Preston knew, most of the school knew. Theo probably knew. My face flushed, so I turned to the microwave, watching my lasagna rotate from hemisphere to sizzling hemisphere.

"She gave it back, right?" he said. "You still got it?"

I ignored him. He sat down at the kitchen table.

"How long I got?" he leaned back, getting a look at the microwave. The lasagna was frozen—four minutes. "You remember Cassie Inman?" he asked.

Cassie was the alpha queen of our middle school, morphing into the prettiest girl in our class around sixth grade. By eighth grade, she was a green-eyed unicorn worthy of adolescent worship.

"God, I loved her, man," he said. "Loved with a capital L. Why? Hell if I know. She was all I thought about before I even talked to her. Sounds so freaking stupid. But I did. I think I'll be fifty years old and know that I really did love her, dumb as it was."

What the hell was he talking about? Cassie Inman adored Preston, and everyone knew it, but for some reason, he wouldn't date her. All through eighth grade, she wanted him. She wasn't even a cheerleader, but joined the cheer squad just to travel with the basketball team that year.

"I wrote her a poem back in sixth grade. Can you believe that shit? Me? A poem? I worked on it for weeks. The first time she ever heard from me, it would be via the first and last original composition I ever created. The title of the poem was 'Your Name,' and it was all about Cassie."

"You let her read it?" I asked. The best poems are vulnerabilities, and I couldn't fathom handing one over to a girl I had a crush on.

"I gave it to her and watched her read it, right there in class," he said. "She laughed, then showed it to one of her girlfriends. I didn't get to know what she thought of it, but the laughter wasn't exactly a good sign, you know? When class was over, she walked to the door, turned around and looked at me, then she threw it in the garbage can. She wanted me to see that."

"No way," I said. "Cassie was obsessed with you."

"I was obsessed with her first," he said. "Then she did that to me. She broke my heart. I cried for three days. I'm not even lying. Every day for three days. Why? What was I missing? I tried to write down three reasons I loved her. She was pretty. That's as far as I got. When the crying was over . . . I was mad. The right kind. The kind that makes you want to work out a little more and practice hoops twice a day."

"This is a big pep talk to get me mad?"

"Get pissed. Finish the basketball season. Be a champion. Outshine Theo. Take the expander surgery right after, beat the shit out of your rehab, and come back by midseason next year."

"I wish it were easy to just fast forward through the hard stuff."

"You said they'd have to inflate those things two or three times a week? Make them do it three or four. Do anything you have to do to get past that phase in your life. Fix your face up if that's what you want; I won't be some disingenuous dick who wants to deny you that. You can have it all, man—you just need to decide to take it, and sometimes motivation like that takes some anger."

"I hope no one licenses you in therapy," I said.

"Cassie regretted throwing away that poem. When she apologized, you know what I told her?"

I shrugged.

"I just thanked her and walked away. Stone-cold left her standing there. She was hot for me ever since, and I wouldn't give her the time of day. I started working out. I studied harder. Tried to expand the range on my jump shot. All because I got pissed. And Cassie? One day she'll be forty years old with a couple of kids and a husband, and she will think about what life would have been like if she didn't throw away that poem. For reasons the human race has never figured out, even if she has a perfect life, that thought will cross her mind."

He put on his coat. "What's Jenna gonna think about when she thinks about you twenty years from now?" He patted me on the shoulder. "Probably the first time she kissed her husband? If she marries Theo, I'll eat my Cubs hat with a side of shit on toast," he said.

"Well, she's not marrying me," I said.

"Probably not," Preston said. "All the more reason not to scrap two seasons of basketball over a girl and an asshole teammate. The only way anyone can take anything else from you is if you give them permission."

"That's right," I said. "And I'm not letting anyone take this surgery away from me. It's all I'm focused on. I need it, the same way you need to be on the basketball team even though you know you'll never be great."

"If you say you need it, you need it," Preston said. "But two seasons? If you say you can't delay it to fit in this year's regionals, I'll take your word for it."

He held out his fist for me to bump it, his typical punctuation at the end of a supportive comment. Instead of returning the bump, I took a long breath, then said, "I won't get the operation until late March," I said. "It's looking like April is a lot more likely. As it turns out, surgeons are busy people."

Preston lowered his fist, nodding. He wasn't exactly playing a precise version of verbal chess, but he finally got the truth out of me.

"Then why the hell did you quit the team?"

He was asking the question, but he knew the answer. He was just giving me a chance to say something other than the obvious.

"Maybe I just needed someone to change my mind," I said.

I walked into my bedroom and got the blue jewelry box from my sock drawer. I placed it on the kitchen table. He smiled. I opened it.

"That is one damn fine piece of jewelry," he said. "I wonder what Jenna will think when she hears about what happened to it."

"And what's that?" I asked.

"You asked me to drive you out to Carson Bridge, then you threw the son of a bitch into the Kaskaskia River. I'm sure she'll enjoy hearing that story."

"Not a story," I said, grabbing the jewelry box. The microwave went off.

"Taking it to go?" Preston asked.

"It can wait," I said, and we headed for the truck.

Operation "Give Jenna Some Regrets" was a green light. We boarded Old Rusty and headed for Carson Bridge, energized by the thought of chucking that bracelet into the muddy water.

I'd banish that bracelet and all thoughts of Jenna and start fresh. I'd return to the team, get the tissue expanders right after regionals, and attack the shit out of my recovery. I'd grind each day until I could dribble better with my left hand and expand my scoring prowess in the lane. I'd try like hell to return in the middle of my sophomore basketball season, looking and playing like a new Wilder.

The quickest way to Carson Bridge was to take the side roads toward the lake, but Preston took the main blacktop that cut through the center of Herrick. Don't confuse Herrick's main street with anything resembling a busy highway or an interstate. The road had two narrow lanes, faded center lines, and plenty of cracks. Still, it was the finest paved surface Herrick had to offer. We passed shuttered businesses, along with the one cafe that stayed open only because it served coffee and breakfast and closed at noon. Two churches were on either side of town—one Lutheran, one Methodist. The Catholic church was on a nicer plot of land a few blocks over, with three acres to itself. We passed the First United Methodist Church of Herrick and then the First Bank of Herrick. Was there ever a second bank? Or a Fifth United?

We passed plenty of residences that lined the blacktop. As we neared the edge of town, where the speed limit finally bumped up to fifty-five miles per hour and the landscape turned into nothing but farm fields, I saw Talisha Slater carrying shopping bags into her house, a ranch-style home with blue shutters and an oversized porch.

I knew then why we were taking the long way to Carson Bridge. Preston was hoping to catch a glimpse of a girl he had probably crushed on since we went to Jenna's party. And why not? Talisha was hot.

He tapped the horn. Talisha recognized Old Rusty and waved.

I turned my attention back to the road and saw a weathered Grand Am lingering at a stop sign. Only a bushel of brown hair was behind the wheel. No face. No eyes. Was this some weird hair creature?

No. It was a girl with her head turned to the left like most drivers do when they're easing into a right-hand turn.

The wheels started creeping forward, but they weren't angled—she wasn't turning. She meant to cross the blacktop and didn't see us coming.

I tried to warn Preston, screaming his name, but by then, avoiding the collision was impossible. Maybe if he didn't slow down when Talisha waved, we would have gone fast enough to prevent the accident. Maybe if he didn't wave back, giving Talisha his full attention, he would have seen Lane McKenzie crossing the intersection in her dented Grand Am.

As Lane crossed the road, Preston cut the wheel to avoid T-boning her car. Instead, we cleared her nose, and she t-boned us instead, slamming into the driver's side door of Old Rusty.

As we bore the impact, Preston's right arm barred across my chest. Neither one of us were buckled up—finding the ancient seat belts on Old Rusty was a geological dig into the upholstery we never bothered with—and Preston thought that holding me back with a straight arm would somehow protect me.

Instead, it exposed his sternum to the steering column, which crunched into his chest and ribs as the tires left the pavement and we started to roll down the hill.

Just outside of town, the blacktop was elevated, flanked by bottom-ground farmland that sprouted corn in the summers. We went airborne, the truck twisting in the air, cartwheeling into the muddy field below.

Without seatbelts, we rattled around the cabin. My skull crunched against the roof as the truck landed upside down before flipping again, the metal groaning like a living thing, the windshield busted into kaleidoscope shapes. Old Rusty continued to roll, and I saw the dark sod of the side of the hill through the broken windows. For a moment, I felt weightless, no part of me touching any part of the truck's interior. Gravity was pulling me back into the blender of the truck, and the ground was moving across the passenger window. My destiny was clear—I was going to face-plant into the turf before the truck crushed me.

Then, the truck flipped again, the blur of the sod transforming into the drollness of the gray sky with the instantaneousness switching of a TV channel. I was outside of the cabin, thrown through the smashed-out passenger window, weightless again, then falling.

I struck the field with a thump, my shoulder driven at least four inches into the mud by the impact. The tips of my fingers buzzed with heat, and my feet felt like they weighed a thousand pounds as I willed myself onto my back.

The pale sky felt close enough to suffocate me, and I couldn't turn my head to escape it. The buzzing throbbed in the base of my skull, my nervous system gonged by the impact. I took the tingling to mean I wasn't paralyzed.

I was alive. Another brush with death, another escape. I scanned my body, trying to feel the rest of my injuries. A fresh wound was opened up on my left arm, pocked with broken glass, bleeding into the dirt. I tried to raise my right arm, knowing my hand was chewed up without being able to see or feel it. My elbow rose three inches, and I tried to look down. I saw my mangled fingers, a blood-soaked claw at the end of a swelling forearm.

Steam rose around my broken limb. I tried to move my hand, and my thumb responded, but I couldn't make out if it the rest of my fingers were broken or sliced away completely. I turned my hand, palm-up, my muscles twitching in revolt, but there was something in that palm, a memory I couldn't make out.

I heard Talisha screaming, I heard sirens, and I heard people calling out for me, thinking I was trapped in the truck. I didn't hear Preston. He was either dead or horribly injured, but as long as I could lie in that field and not get up, I wouldn't know it. I cherished not knowing, so I didn't call back to them.

Instead, I stared at my palm and saw a long-forgotten memory. I saw snow.

The year I was burned, I was stuck in the hospital until just before Christmas. Infection is the biggest threat to a burn victim, so I was in a room without windows, and even though I could tell what nurse was walking in by the squeak of her shoes, their faces were masked, their bodies gowned up. Ghosts tended me in the burn ward, and sometimes I wouldn't even recognize my mother in her scrubs and mask. The haze of the drugs dulled me too much to make out her blue eyes, or the strands of black hair long before stress turned her roots as gray as stone.

When her sterilized hand would hold mine, I always knew her touch, and she would say through the mask that it was raining outside, or the sun was out, or it was overcast, or it was morning.

She told me about the passage of time because when you're in the burn ward, time doesn't unfold through sunsets and clocks and boxes on a calendar; instead, time is measured in debris scrubs, Demerol shots, whirlpool baths, and grueling reps with the physical therapist.

When I was long past the worst of my infection risk, I woke up one morning feeling a refreshing numbness in my palm. She'd brought in a mug of snow from outside, scraped some out, and placed it in my hand.

We didn't say anything. I smiled at her and watched the snow dissolve into water, and watched the water find the seams between my fingers and drip down my wrist, and then droplets would collect and fall onto the tile where they'd evaporate and rise and become snow once again someday.

The calming memory didn't last long.

My mangled hand fell back to the ground, the last of my strength wrought out of my traumatized muscles.

The bystander who found me in the field was a pastor who stopped to help. "I have another one over here!" he screamed, and I opened my eyes. For a moment, my eyes didn't work—I felt my lids spread wide but no images were registering with my brain. Was I blind? Finally, I started to take in the information and saw a frail man who had taken off his coat to shield me from the shear of the wind, he himself trembling as he introduced himself as Pastor Dan.

I felt sleepy and let my eyelids drop.

"Don't you sleep," he said. "You're concussed. I'm no doctor but seeing that truck, there's no way around a brain bruise, so you stay up and talk to me, okay?"

I tried to talk, but couldn't. The act of speech just felt too hard, and I wanted to sleep.

"I'll talk then," he said. "Just keep those eyes wide and listen to me until help gets here."

His coat flapped in the wind, and his parchment cheeks had already been whipped red by the cold. "God was looking out for you today," he said.

If I had the strength to talk, I would have asked him if that was the absolute best God could have done for me that day. If that was His idea of looking out for me, I was switching my allegiance to Zeus or Thor, someone who was cooler to have on a T-shirt and might let me go a few years without a traumatic injury.

A helicopter churned overhead as the paramedics arrived. They strapped me onto a backboard and loaded me into an ambulance. By then, I could finally muster up the word "Preston," only it came out as one jumbled syllable and woke up an icepick headache.

They didn't understand what I was asking, but they put me into an ambulance while the chopper touched down in the field. I wasn't the one getting airlifted, and you don't airlift corpses, so Preston had to be alive— but there was no guarantee he'd be alive for long.

TRAUMA

My view in the trauma room was of the freckled tiles of the drop ceiling. I couldn't turn my head. The pressure of the straps was torture, the back of my head burning from the prolonged squeeze, hurting worse than the lacerations and fractures. A fleet of doctors and nurses positioned exam lights, their intensity blurring the edges of my vision.

I didn't need to turn my head to know what surrounded me. Stainless steel carts and matching trays laid out with instruments and stacks of gauze, ceiling-mounted booms and columns that held monitors and instruments, a wall of pre-fab cabinets with additional supplies ready at the doctor's command.

"Talk to me, Wilder," the doctor said. He was just a voice behind a white mask, his hair color obscured by scrubs, a blue droid with white gloves like the rest of them.

"I've been here before," I croaked.

They were checking me for signs of paralysis, squeezing my toes and fingers, commanding me to attempt movements. For some reason, they jammed a finger up my ass and asked if I could feel it, and I most definitely passed that test.

"When were you burned?"

"When I was ten," I said.

The doctor barked out rapid-fire jargon. One team was picking through my crushed right hand. My broken arm was splinted, and a pair of nurses were stitching up the gash on my left shoulder.

"Preston," I said. "Is he okay?"

I started to shift against the straps.

"You need to hold still," the doctor said. "Everything is looking satisfactory, but I don't want any excessive movement from you until we get the MRI and CAT scans completed."

"Then give me some fucking Demerol," I said, which drew a laugh from the trauma crew.

"Kid knows the good stuff," one of the nurses said.

"We treat our repeat customers well around here," the doctor said and ordered a load. They drove a needle into my IV, and minutes later, the pain and discomfort from the strap pressure was gone. I felt like I was melting into the board.

"Where did you go for your burns?" he asked.

"Children's," I said, my voice thick with the effect of the drugs.

"They're our lovely neighbors to the north," he said. "You're at Barnes-Jewish."

"A trauma room is a trauma room," I said. "Do I get a punch card or something? A free sub sandwich after my fifth trip?"

More laughter. I had a career in standup if only they'd send me home with some Demerol.

"You're a lucky boy. Today is all the Jell-O and ice chips you can eat day around here."

"So how fucked up am I this time?"

"You'll get your report card after more tests."

"Don't bullshit me," I said. "You're just confirming stuff you already know, right? Isn't that how this works?"

"In this case, no," the doctor said. "Obviously you have some cuts to fix up, and I don't need an X-ray to know your right arm is broken, but neither do you. Same goes for the sustainment of a nasty concussion. Your hand concerns me. Multiple breaks and lacerations. Your neck concerns me, but for that, I need to see the scans. Fair enough?"

Fair enough.

———

I didn't get the full verdict until the next morning, after they funneled me through every scanning device in the hospital and took me in for hand surgery. After waking up from that, I puked everywhere, ate two bites of the Salisbury steak dinner they provided me at one a.m., and tried to go to sleep.

Mom waited all night for me to get out of surgery. She pulled her chair up next to my hospital bed, and said she'd stay within arm's reach all night.

"You should sleep lying down," I said. "Use the pull-out. Please."

"You act like I'm going to sleep at all," she said, her hand gently planted on my left wrist, comforting me.

My right forearm was pinned together and casted, and my right hand was mostly a club of plaster.

They hadn't told me officially yet, but I knew that I had lost a finger due to the accident. Possibly two. On my shooting hand, no less.

As for the spinal injuries, I'd have to wait until morning to know how the scans turned out. They had me in a Philadelphia collar, the upper portion supporting my lower jaw, the base of the collar spanning across my shoulders and most of my thoracic spine. The meat of my throat was sweating and itchy, but the pain meds pushed that urge far into the hazy distance.

You only need three fingers to shoot—the thumb, index, and middle finger. The other two are a liability anyway. Fuck 'em.

Do you know who you're talking to? No way I lose the exact ones I could tolerate losing. I'm not in the business of lucky breaks.

Your left hand is fine.

You're being awfully supportive during this difficult time. What got into you?

I just want to wait to see how bad the damage is before I can really be accurate about filling you with doubt and dread. Let's sleep, okay?

Okay.

I tried to sleep but couldn't. Even the cocktail of drugs didn't help. Mom's hand didn't leave my wrist. I opened my eyes and saw that tears had carved trenches in her foundation. She still wore her white shirt from bartending at the Elks Lodge, her hair in a simple ponytail.

"Have you heard anything about Preston?" I asked.

"Still in surgery," she said.

The flipping truck spared him, coughing him onto the highway pavement, but not before his right leg got caught in the metal. His femur was fractured, and his right ankle was shattered, the only injury requiring surgery. Despite his colossal mistake of exposing his chest to the steering column, fractured ribs were his only other significant injury.

"I'm sorry about all this," I said.

"You have absolutely nothing to be sorry for," she said. "It's not your fault."

Just as Randy Meadows was the boy who burned me, Lane McKenzie would be the girl responsible for my latest scars while everyone called me lucky and brave.

And I would let them do it.

LOSS

In March, the Herrick High Griffins played in the regional championship game versus the Mater Dei Knights. Our early-round games were closer than they should have been—Theo scored a basket with two seconds left to secure a 54-52 win in the first round against the South Herrin Speedboys, and in the second round we beat the North Central Cougars by a dozen, although we were only up four with a minute to go before desperate fouling stretched the margin of victory. Neither game gave anyone confidence that we would stack up with Knights.

I watched the game from the first row of bleachers behind our bench, still wearing the Philadelphia collar two months after the accident. I should have been out of it already, but my neck wasn't strong or healed enough to go without the support of the collar just yet.

My neck ended up being broken. Even though the X-rays were clean, the CAT scan showed a fracture so small I couldn't tell anything was wrong, even when the surgeon was pointing it out to me. The impact of landing upside down, directly on the top of my head, delivered a massive concussion and cracked off some bone at the C1 region of the spinal cord. At least I convinced them to give me a chance with the Philadelphia collar instead of going the more conservative route—drilling a halo onto my skull.

The expansion surgery that could have taken place in March, preserving two shots at unseating Mater Dei as regional champions, was now pushed back to August so I could finish healing and rehabilitation.

An August surgery assured that I would go through the worst of the procedure during the school year, while offering zero hope to return to the basketball team as a sophomore.

Not that I'd ever be the same player. My right arm remained casted, as did my hand, after a second round of surgeries. I lost the top half of my right-middle finger. If you could pick one half of one finger most critical to shooting a basketball, that's the one piece you can't do without. A pure shooter's release has that finger centered on the ball, and it's the last piece of the hand to part with the grained, leather surface before it's launched at the hoop.

My stable of doctors was getting impressive. Doctor Iacabucci postponed my tissue expansion surgery until I got the cast off and my broken neck was cleared. Then I had my neck specialists, the ones who MRI'd and X-rayed me into oblivion, exposing me to so many radioactive waves and magnets I thought I'd emerge from those noisy tubes as a superhero.

I hated watching the tournament games, and not just because we were getting our asses handed to us on a piss-soaked paper plate. I hated feeling like a mascot. I hated being reminded I couldn't physically play basketball for a long time. I hated seeing Theo, because it all started with him—he pushed Jenna into my life, and if not for that nudge, there's no heartbreak, no bracelet, no spontaneous truck ride to dump that bracelet into the river.

If not for Theo, Preston would be sitting the bench, and I'd be in the game guarding Mater Dei's all-state guard Robbie Imming, who was draining shot after shot as the lead for Mater Dei kept growing and growing.

Halftime was just a stay of execution. We were down 47-24, and Robbie had more than half their points.

I couldn't handle watching the blowout continue, so I left the game early. One tried and true benefit of being heinously injured was that you could leave any event early, and no one ever asked you why.

So I dragged myself out of the gym, the deflated crowd barely noticing my exit, and tried to catch Preston at home before the painkillers knocked him out.

He had started physical therapy for his leg and ankle, and therapy days were the only times he took his hydrocodone. The femur was the riskier injury but healing fine on its own. His ankle, however, was broken into more pieces than a dropped coffee mug, with the added bonus of having every tendon shredded. He'd walk normally again "someday," according to his doctors. He took the news like he was going to be wheelchair-bound for life, but I wasn't going to spare him the dramatics. I knew the therapeutic value of pessimism.

Since the accident, I'd gotten to know Preston's parents, Mary and Dan Brenner, a lot better. Before the crash, they would just warmly greet me before we disappeared into Preston's room for our *W1ldBunch* gaming sessions. Now, I had to make small talk before Mary took me to his room.

Dan was slumped into his recliner, remote dangling from his right hand, a tumbler of iced tea in the other. I asked him about foraging the beach with his metal detector.

"I haven't gone lately," he said. "Walking through sand strengthens the foot, I've heard. When Preston's ready, I'll dust it off, and we'll get back at it."

Mary was one of those interrogative moms. She asked me about school, about my mom, about my hand, about my neck.

"That brace looks medieval," she said.

"Beats a few bolts in your skull," I said. "Although, that would help me really complete that Frankenstein's monster look."

"He had the bolts in his neck," Dan said. "Skull bolts would be more like *Hellraiser*." He smiled as Mary admonished him, but I couldn't help but laugh.

I walked into Preston's room. His foot was elevated on a stack of pillows, his mouth ajar, drool gathering at the corners. *Call of Duty* was on the TV screen, the controller limp in his hands. Too late. I turned around to leave.

"You're here early," he said, his voice stretched out by the drugs. "I take it you guys weren't busy cutting down the nets?"

"Mater Dei should be snipping them right about now."

I pulled up a chair next to him. He stirred in his bed, trying to sit up.

"Was Robbie as good as they say?"

"Yeah," I said. "Moves without the ball. He's not lazy. Earns his points."

"He ain't earned them," Preston said. "Not until he puts them up on you."

"He'll be gone by the time I play again," I said. "He's a senior next year."

"Play him next year then."

"Once this brace is off, that puts the tissue expansion into August after rehab, according to the docs. I'll work hard to get back, but I'm going to miss the season unless the laws of physics cease to exist in my body."

"You could postpone," Preston said.

"Why would I postpone now? I won't be right for a while, and I need to learn to shoot left-handed. Might as well regroup for a year, fix my face, come back strong as a junior when Theo is gone."

Preston's elevated leg was clamped into an air cast up to his hip.

"How's the leg?"

"Femur's mended up, but my ankle is trash."

Preston achieved a clean sweep, breaking all three major ankle bones and tearing most of the primary tendons. He was lucky they could salvage his foot, but was bummed out by the twelve-week healing timeline.

"I'm going to have more pins and screws than the Terminator," he said.

"There's worse things in life than being half man, half machine."

"I'll never go through an airport metal detector without creating a scene for the rest of my life," he said.

"At least you have your sights set on traveling."

"I need to fly. I'm sure not walking anywhere."

"You'll be back to normal after therapy."

"Normal," he said. "They keep telling me, normal function in a few months. That just means I can get along on my own. I'm going to need a cane for months after that. I'm going to have a limp for even more months on top of that, maybe even forever."

I remembered his pep talk to me about crushing my rehab. I was going to say something similar but thought it would come off as condescending.

"Don't worry, man, I'll get pissed eventually," he said. "Secret weapon. Hell, I should be pissed now."

"At Lane?"

"No. At the chick on the Progressive insurance commercials. Of course Lane."

Lane wasn't injured in the accident—she had her seat belt on, and the air bag bloomed on impact. They checked her out at the hospital, and she was released hours later with nothing but bruises.

Still, the only person who had missed more school than me since the accident was Lane McKenzie. After hurting us, the worst of her bullies declared open season. New voices joined in. Teachers were just a little slower to come to her aid, and students loved to come to me with the latest rumors and gossip she hit us on purpose—suicide attempt. She was high on pills—suicide attempt. She was pregnant and wanted a reasonable way to lose the baby since her mother was pro-life. I heard them all.

The worst part is, I think Lane heard them all, too. Repeatedly. To her face. On the days she came in, she always left early, clutching her books to her denim-armored chest as if they could shield her from the righteous honesty of Herrick Community High.

Preston wanted to believe most of the rumors because he needed the anger, but I thought Lane was just a young driver who made a mistake.

Lane told the police she meant to turn right, then decided to take a detour and see a friend first, which meant crossing the highway. She just forgot to check traffic to her right before crossing the road.

Preston still saw it as an unforgivable mistake from a girl who had no business behind the wheel of a car. The McKenzie lawyers were also pushing blame on Preston, saying he was too distracted to avoid the accident. So, of course, he took that as Lane lying about him.

"How does none of this freak you out?" he said.

"This?"

"Thinking about the accident, how we should be dead or paralyzed, and it's not even our fault."

Just because it wasn't my fault didn't mean I didn't deserve it.

"Don't even tell me you're just used to it," Preston said. "The burns couldn't have fucked you up that bad."

"Maybe they didn't," I said.

Mary knocked on the frame of Preston's door and delivered the official, final score of the basketball game. We lost by thirty-five.

"Robbie's lucky," Preston said. "No Doberman."

I hated the word *lucky.* Since I was burned, people would either call me the luckiest kid alive or the unluckiest kid alive.

I had no idea which one was the truth.

BLAME

A winter storm kept us out of school for almost an entire week near the end of March. When students returned from the impromptu vacation, piles of dirty snow were gathered around the pole lights in the parking lot. They became iceberg-hard when the sun was strong enough to start a thaw, and they lasted almost two weeks longer than the inches that had gathered on the ground itself.

Three months had passed since the accident. Preston was back in school full-time, although he needed a cane to get around on his own. I somehow managed to endure my fully neck-braced days at school without jumping out of a second-floor window. Thankfully, the school year was almost over. Just a couple more months of answering the question "How are you doing?" an incalculable number of times. Seriously, I came close to having a T-shirt made that said, "Fine, thanks."

In study hall, Jackson Kuhn asked if he could sit by me—he had something to tell me. I prepared myself for the latest Lane McKenzie Car Accident Theory(TM), information gleaned from a friend of a friend whose mother knew a cop who was involved with putting together the accident report.

Jackson's big revelation? Lane waited at that intersection for the better part of twelve minutes.

"The intersection had cameras in the caution light," he said. "She was there for twelve minutes, man! Twelve! Three other cars passed before you guys came along."

He waited for my outrage. Instead, I just stared at him.

"Don't you get it?" he said. "She was targeting you guys."

I eye-rolled the conversation to a close when Talisha Slater turned around to chime in.

"I wouldn't even come back to school if I were her," she said. Talisha, who once stood shoulder to shoulder with Lane at a party, was now The One Who Witnessed The Accident, and she was going to lecture us on The Right Thing to Do. "She should just go somewhere else and get a fresh start. No way I could come back here and look you in the face knowing what I had done."

She had a point. Lane was used to bullying, but going to school with the boys you almost killed had to suck.

"If she were here right now," Talisha said, "what would you say to her?"

Both she and Jackson leaned in.

"I guess I'd tell her Jackson's a fucking idiot."

While Jackson considered punching a burn victim who was wearing a neck brace, I considered a more serious answer to the question.

Everyone wanted me to hate her, but I didn't.

Everyone had a rumor, but I didn't believe them.

Everyone blamed her but me, and she needed to know it.

———

Lane's house looked like a run-down White House knockoff thanks to the pillars on her front porch. The paint lost its grip on white a long time ago and was now the shade of well-worn socks.

The inside of my neck brace was greased with sweat after the walk. After skipping the bus, I didn't have any trouble getting her address from the secretary in the office, who wasn't going to torpedo my mission of forgiveness.

Her driveway was empty, and I saw a television flickering in the bay window.

I didn't even have to knock. Lane opened the door and said, "Meet me out back."

The ground was mushy from the melted snow and cold rain, as if the body of winter refused to decompose and submit to the looming spring. Her backyard was a sea of oak leaves neglected since fall, black and soggy, clinging to the side of the house.

A wicker patio set was on a cracked slab of concrete. She sat down, and I followed suit, the wicker chewing into my hoodie.

"My dad would like to crush your balls with a spatula," she said, burying her hands in the front pockets of an oversized sweatshirt. "He blames you for the tidal wave of bullshit I have to deal with at school."

I thought she'd lead off with The Apology. Instead, I was on defense right away.

"He blames me?"

"As if you personally ordered the student body to devour me."

"That's nuts," I said.

"Nuts is a big part of the dad-code."

"I wouldn't know," I said. "My dad passed when I was little."

"I'm sorry."

"Don't be," I said. "You didn't kill him."

"Oh shit, someone killed him?"

"No," I said, stumbling over my words, already off balance by how quickly she responded to everything, the way she asked questions without taking the time to quality-check them for rudeness. I finally managed to stammer out the words "Heart attack."

She nodded, as if she knew all along.

"What about your mom?" I asked.

"What about her?"

"I don't know. I just thought I'd be polite and ask?" She unplugged her hands from her sweatshirt and crossed her arms. "What are you doing here, Wilder?"

I asked myself the same question a hundred times on the way over and still didn't have it figured out.

"I know what's going on at school with you, and I guess I just want to say that I've got nothing to do with it, and you don't deserve it."

"Please don't be a little bitch about this," she said. "I don't deserve it from them. I deserve it from you. Vent. Blame me. I can take it."

I looked down at the glass table, which hadn't seen Windex in a long time.

"I can't blame you," I said. "I've got my PhD in shit happens, and shit just happened to both of us."

"Blame me," she said. "I hurt you. I got a ticket for running the stop sign. Everyone knows it's my fault."

"Accidents happen," I said.

"You're so mushy," she said. "There's a difference between shit happens and getting used to the taste."

"I'm trying to do the right thing."

"I prefer the true thing," she said.

"Which is?"

"You can't forgive me until you blame me," she said. "You're scared. So you came here to offload all of this onto destiny's lap. I won't let you do it."

She wouldn't stop looking at me. I tried to drop my gaze to the glass table again, but she wouldn't allow it, leaning down, tapping the table.

"Up here," she said. "Look at me."

I saw her anguish, and understood it.

"It was my fault, Wilder, and I'm sorry."

"I forgive you," I said, surprising myself at how pure and genuine the words felt.

Her chin quivered as she licked her lips. She pressed her sleeve against her face, a preemptive strike against the threat of tears.

She had a hardness to her. It crackled through the tone of her speech, the way it alternated between pithy and philosophical. The hardness was earned through lonely hours in the tear-soaked library, her heart tempered by lacerating rumors, cruel jokes, and prescription drugs. Seeing her fight tears prodded me in unexpected ways.

"I do know what happened to Randy Meadows," I said. "You were right. I lied about not knowing."

"Why?"

"I just want it to seem like I don't care," I said.

"The more interesting question is why you're afraid to care about what happened to him."

"Do you want to know what happened to him, or not?" I asked.

"I already know," she said. "He's in a federal prison in Memphis. Drugs and armed robbery."

"How did you know?"

"Didn't anyone tell you why I'm so screwed up in the head? I'm psychic." She touched her temples and closed her eyes, faking meditation, waiting for me to react, but I couldn't. "I'm fucking with you," she said. "Google. Took me like three minutes."

"Don't make me laugh, the neck brace rubs my chin when I laugh."

"They should give you an even bigger one. When does a neck brace become a body brace, anyway? That thing has to be close."

I laughed, and yeah, the brace rubbed my chin, but the dirty little secret was that laughing was always worth it, no matter how much it hurt.

EXPANSION

Just as the school year ended, my physical therapy for my neck was just about to begin.

Let me tell you, wearing a Philadelphia collar in the summer, then doing physical therapy in the hottest July on record is the *Transformers 2* of summer vacation experiences, one out of five stars, a shitshow that leaves you begging for it to end.

So how did I spend the few non-miserable moments of my summer vacation?

I visited Preston, who graduated to using a cane, and the *W1ldBunch* kicked ass at the new *Call of Duty, Destiny 2,* and *Star Wars: Battlefront II.* We were hellbent on resisting Fortnite as much as possible.

I took walks as part of the exercise regimen my doctors had recommended, and those walks kept getting closer and closer to Lane's house in the center of town.

I watched movies and read books.

I exercised my hand, even though not having most of my middle finger would permanently hinder my basketball shot and make it look weird if I tried to flip someone off.

I spent time with my mother, mostly trying to downshift her out of freak-out mode. She was back to working doubles, trying to pay off the credit cards and medical payments that piled up while she took off work to care for me after the accident. A settlement would erase most of it, but lawyers and insurance companies juggled offers and counteroffers as the threat of a trial hovered over everything.

I didn't tell my mother I had gone to see Lane. Lane's dad didn't like me; my mom wouldn't exactly high-five Lane for almost killing her son, so it was best left alone.

So as summer ended, I was on another surgical table.

As they laid me down for surgery, I wished my father was alive and in the waiting room to visit with me post-op. I only remembered flashes of him. He had a deep voice and a mustache, a ghost who visited me in pieces of a perfect dream where my face was still whole. We played catch and watched movies like *Star Wars* and *Lord of the Rings* behind Mom's back since she always thought they were too violent for my age.

I remembered him once saying, "We don't do censorship in this house."

That house is gone now, just like him.

Just like my scars could be gone, if I could just push through more surgery, more recovery, more rehab.

I was ready. Roughly six years after the burns left me disfigured, Doctor Iacabucci and his fleet of residents stood over me, ready to insert bubbles into my flesh that would grow the skin I needed to put that day behind me forever.

The hissing mask went over my face, and the cold anesthesia snaked its way into my nostrils. I counted backward from ten, dreading the nausea that would accompany my waking from the surgery. As the world faded around me, I was in the garage again, where it all happened.

I saw the gasoline ignite as the little boy just stood there. I begged him to run away, but I was just mumbling into the mask, my voice lost to the hiss of the anesthetic as it snaked into my nostrils.

The stupid boy just stands there as the fire takes him, and then there is nothing but darkness.

PART TWO
SALVAGE

SOPHOMORE

When I boarded the bus for my first day of sophomore year, my tissue expanders were the size of baseballs.

Sophomores aren't supposed to have first-day jitters thanks to the advantage of familiarity. I knew the layout of the classrooms, the timing of the bells, which bathrooms had stall doors that worked. However, the thought of debuting my new face blunted the comforts of the ordinary. I was reintroducing myself to friends and teachers, with new scars and new stories.

They'd want to know how the bubbles got inflated. The inflation procedure had a pit crew feel to it, with Doctor Iacabucci pressing butterfly needles into my valves and pumping me full of saline.

They'd want to know if the bubbles hurt. Short answer? Yes. After just a few sessions, the expanders were already pushing the elastic limits of my flesh. Bruises smudged the edges of the expansion sites. Each session ended with me feeling on the verge of exploding in a starburst of blood, salt water, and tissue. The stretching flesh stoked the deep ache of getting kicked in the balls, only all over your body. I felt each heartbeat echoing off of the bubbles.

They'd want to know how long I had to endure the expanders. I took Preston's advice and convinced the doctors to try out a more frequent inflation schedule so I could get done with the procedure sooner. With one extra session per two weeks, I could compress the timeline to seven months, but after just one month of extra appointments, I didn't know if I had the constitution to pay that price.

They'd want to know how big the bubbles would get. Even I didn't know an accurate answer to that one. As big as they needed to be, based on my physical limitations, my tolerance, and my body's adaptation. The bigger they got, the more extra skin I'd have, and the better the results would look in the end. I was prepared to go all the way and see the bubbles get as big as Jupiter if it came down to it.

Thankfully, no one asked me anything on the bus. I sat near the back, the right side of my body facing the window instead of the aisle.

If not for the accident, I wouldn't have had to bother with the bus. Preston would've picked me up most mornings until I got my own license, and then we could split the duty. But now, neither of us could drive. His parents had yet to get him a truck to replace Old Rusty, not because they didn't want to or couldn't afford to, but because it was a waste—he lacked the strength and coordination in his right foot to safely drive. He had to walk with a cane, his right foot suffering from bouts of numbness that hindered his recovery. Late in the summer, he got the bad news—he needed a bone graft. Another round of surgical repairs and physical therapy.

The end result was a walking boot on his right foot and a lack of fine motor skills required to operate the pedals of a vehicle.

Despite this, he promised that he wouldn't let his parents drive him to school—he planned to board the bus with me that first day so that we could endure the stares together.

Preston got to the second step with his cane before the driver engaged the parking brake and helped him aboard. He limped back to my seat and sat next to me.

"Your arm is fucking huge," he said. "Tissue expanders work better than steroids." He rested the cane between us and settled back into his seat, sweating from the effort of boarding. "I forgot how much I hate the bus," he said.

"Think of all the cool cars in the student parking lot," I said. "You know what they don't have that we do? A private driver."

He laughed, a sound I missed. There was far too little laughter between us during the difficult summer.

"So, who you got first hour?" he asked.

"Miss Harrington again," I said. "Thank God."

"Jenna in that class?" he said. Decoded: *Do you still have a hopeless crush on her?*

Horrifically, I did. I settled on Theo as the enemy, and she was just the manipulated victim in need of love and rescue.

All that said, I had no idea if she was in my class, so I shrugged.

"I know it's a sore spot so I won't talk about it if you don't wanna," he said. "But I ran into Luke at the mall the other day. We talked, and Theo's name came up."

Had their high-school-sweetheart relationship survived the honeymoon phase? Surely, she was too smart to put up with him for more than a few months.

"You know they're still dating, right?" he said.

I didn't know—social media had become so photo-based that my barely active accounts gathered dust. Why would I add Jenna? To see selfies of her and Theo on dates?

"Luke said Theo got her a promise ring."

"Seriously?"

"Right? Lame."

"Not nearly as cool as a charm bracelet," I said.

"Wonder if he got on one knee with his fifty-cent ring," Preston said, nudging me.

"You know what we should do?" I said. "Grab that promise ring right off her finger."

"Yeah," he said, picking up on the joke I was crafting. "Borrow a big truck. One with strong seat belts. Head for the bridge."

"Take a detour around the highway intersection, for sure."

The bus hit a bump, and we both flinched in pain.

"I'm getting too old for this shit," Preston said.

———

I shuffled down the hallway with the speed of a zombie. Not even one of the fast zombies from all the modern zombie movies—I'm talking the old-school, black-and-white movie zombies that inched along at what can best be described as a casual shamble. The balloons wobbled under my skin if I moved too fast, waking up a horrendous ache.

A girl I'd never seen before, perhaps a freshman, was thumbing her smartphone and ran right into my left arm.

When she saw me, she stopped mid-sorry, as if shifting down for something more apologetic and finding nothing but shocked silence.

"It's okay," I said. "I won't explode. And if I do, they're full of confetti." She flexed a smile.

Then, I saw Jenna trying to part the crowd and get to her locker. I hadn't seen her over the summer, and—just my luck—she was even more beautiful. Highlights of gold were spun into her red hair now, and her freckles had faded, as if they belonged to her childhood and were getting left behind. She wore dark jeans with tight cuffs above her ankle, showing off a rainbow-colored sock and her Chuck Taylor sneakers. I didn't know if I wanted to marry her or just hire her to give me style lessons.

Theo came up behind her and wrapped his arms around her waist, nuzzling her playfully on the neck. No easy task, since he hadn't gotten any taller and it looked like Jenna had grown a couple of inches. Theo was thicker through the shoulders, making his graphic tee look too tight. Maybe that was by design, but I had a strong suspicion he spent the summer lifting weights for the wrong reasons. He wasn't a post player— the extra beef would only hurt him on the perimeter. Thick shoulders just make it harder to slip through screens, and a developed chest is almost totally worthless for a sport that doesn't require any kind of upper body pushing. How could someone who continued to get things so completely wrong get to be captain of the team and winner of Jenna Weaver's hottie-encased heart? Cue Wilder Tate's patented, feeble-ass locker slam.

I was ready for some of Miss Harrington's trademark perkiness. She looked completely and totally the same as she did my freshman year. She had obviously reached the age where everything got frozen, like Han Solo in carbonite. She did her makeup the same way each day. Every outfit, even her new ones, exuded the same style. Her height was frozen, her shoe size finalized. She was at the top of the bell curve of time, and every few years she'd look in the mirror and see signs of riding that slope on down—a wrinkle here, a gray hair there, until the shriveling accelerated in earnest. She was in the sweet spot, after things were scary and fast and changed without warning, pausing just before things got scary and fast and degraded without warning. I never wanted to be thirty years old more than I did in that moment.

When taking attendance, she looked me in the eyes as she always had and gave me a genuine "Welcome back," but I saw so much pity pooled inside her irises I wanted to stab my balloons with my pencil.

After first hour, I saw Jenna again. Theo flirted and nuzzled. I almost screamed. I was infected, having downloaded Jenna into my psyche a year ago, and no amount of rebooting could purge her from my system. I couldn't fix the problem by telling myself to not see her in the hallway, which was akin to saying "don't find the pink elephant."

So during third hour, I decided I'd look for Lane in the hallway when class ended instead. I didn't find her, so of course I witnessed another session of Jenna and Theo PDA.

At lunchtime, I ate my chips standing in the hallway, occasionally peering into the cafeteria. Preston sat by Theo and the basketball boys. His cane leaned on the chair next to him, saving me a spot.

I didn't want to show off my brand-spanking-new deformities in the well-lit arena of the lunchroom. Not yet, anyway—the day had been rough enough already. Dragging myself from class to class was tougher than the therapeutic walks I'd taken all summer. The trip to the lunch table felt like more of an odyssey than a stroll.

By the end of the day, I fell asleep on the bus before we were out of the parking lot. I hadn't felt exhaustion like that since the hell week of basketball conditioning.

My backpack was full of homework. The mental burst to take care of it during the school day was non-existent, buried in a humid fog that lingered just behind my eyeballs.

Someone nudged me awake.

"You can sleep all you want when you're dead," Preston said.

"Wouldn't want to miss a party like this," I said, and on cue, the driver downshifted as we slammed into a pothole. We both grimaced.

"Don't banish yourself to the hallway during lunch," Preston said.

"I don't know. I feel so on display."

"You think I have it any better?" Preston said. "The only guy who looks cool with a cane is Gandalf."

"You should learn magic," I joked.

"I'd put a spell on you," he said. "Make you forget about Jenna. Make you forget to care about what you look like."

For the rest of the trip, we talked about the Bulls, the new *Call of Duty* coming out, and how he and his father found a woman's lost engagement ring on the beach with their metal detector.

"I can barely move on the sand," Preston said.

"Sand is good exercise for your feet and ankles," I said. "So I've heard."

"Dad's like a shitty superhero," Preston said. "He can sense metal, so he swoops in and snatches up beer cans and earrings for the good of the republic."

"He learn to swim yet?"

Preston shook his head. "I'm not in the best condition to teach him."

"You can use me as a life preserver."

"Shit floats, after all," he said and nudged me, just to make absolutely certain I knew he was joking.

"Mom says you should come over for dinner this week. Back to school special. Lasagna? She says it's your favorite."

"It's okay."

"You eat like three bricks of that mess every time we have it."

"It's just to keep her from making the goulash," I said.

"Amen to that." The bus pulled up to Preston's house. He got up and steadied himself on his cane.

"Hey, Preston," I said. "Work on your magic skills. Forgetting isn't easy."

"Easy as walking," he said, winking at me. It took him two full minutes to limp off the bus.

LIBRARY

I again spent lunch lingering near the vending machines, scarfing down a bag of Ruffles.

In just the second day of school, the cafeteria territory was marked, boundaries drawn. Preston once again had my usual spot reserved with his cane as basketball players filled up the table. The band kids gathered at another table, and baseball players at yet another.

Jenna sat in the same seat at the same table with the same cheerleaders. I recognized Alexis Gyles, a perfect girl for one of those movies where the ugly duckling just takes off her glasses and is instantly gorgeous. Avery Jensen sat beside her, the LeBron of cheerleaders and current holder of the "hottest girl in school" crown. She was a lab-built Frankenhottie who could do a shitload of backflips in a row and still look groomed enough for a shampoo commercial.

My chips were gone, and the line to the vending machine was empty. I used dimes to buy another bag, putting the coins in one at a time. Then I hit the change release button, picked up the dimes, and started again.

The lunch monitor noticed me in the hallway and told me to finish up and take a seat, so I pocketed my dimes and escaped into the bathroom where I engaged in the proven time-killing strategy of pretending to take a shit.

The bathroom traffic lulled during lunch. The occasional pisser would drop by to lash the deodorant puck with a stream of urine and then pretend to wash his hands, the door swinging shut before the automatic faucet even clicked off.

I thought I would run out the clock on lunch without incident. That's when the door swung open again, and two boys were laughing as they squared up the urinals.

Scientific rule: as the number of boys in a high school bathroom rises, so does the volatility and likelihood of shenanigans.

"How hard did Ballard ride your ass about it?" The questioner hid his meekness. I could all but hear his glasses and acne, and the word "ass" sounded foreign coming out of his mouth.

"It was just dicking around in study hall," the second boy answered, his voice vaguely familiar.

"He could bench you when the season rolls around."

"He's not gonna bench me." Ty Venhaus. The preening tone was more of a giveaway than his voice. He sounded more like an asshole than he really was—we always got along on the team, especially after our little bootleg drinking session behind Jenna's garage.

"Maybe he doesn't start you," the meek kid said.

"You think he's going to start the mongoloid instead?" Ty said.

The meek kid laughed. "You're going to make me piss on my shoes."

"I should have been starting all along anyway. Tate isn't even that good; he's just a fucking try-hard. The Doberman? I hope he can lick his balls, because no girl is ever going to do it."

More laughter. "He can't lick his balls with those things on his neck."

"They're going to get bigger," Ty said. "It's going to look like a gigantic ass underneath his face."

"If you were a girl, what would you rather kiss? His burns or his bubbles?"

"Oh man, that's a brain buster," Ty replied, flushing the toilet. "Deep-fried Wilder rinds or artificial anus? I'd just shoot myself."

The faucets clicked on. They washed their hands far longer than the solo practitioners. Peer pressure at work.

The air dryers blotted out the back end of their conversation but not the giggles as they exited the bathroom. The door swung shut.

I flushed the empty toilet and pretended to wash my hands and headed for the library.

Mr. Darden, the math teacher, caught me in the hallway and asked where I was going. I wasn't crying, but he saw enough in my face to give me immediate permission to sit in the library and offered to tell the lunch monitor my whereabouts.

Calling it a library was generous. More accurate: somewhat organized, outdated book storage. Teachers donated age-appropriate hardcovers and paperbacks with spines so arthritic you could barely read the title. Lots of phased-out textbooks and outdated encyclopedias, but weren't all encyclopedias out of date? I couldn't imagine a world where you had to look something up in alphabetical volumes instead of typing it into Google. How the hell could you trust that information? It's a wonder old people knew anything at all.

So I'd spend the last twenty minutes of lunch staring at old books and waiting for the bell and trying not to cry. Awesome.

When I entered the library, I heard the unmistakable rustle of a bag of potato chips. Sun Chips, to be exact. Thanks to my shitty nutritional habits, I had a Sherlock Holmesian ability to identify anything from the snack machine by sound.

Lane was eating her lunch and staring out of the window. Her hair was stringy and unkempt, her eyes glassy with anguish.

"Sloppy joes," I said, sitting down across from her "The horror."

I got a tiny laugh from her, and for a moment my eclipse of despair lifted.

"You look different," she said.

"No shit."

"Taller. Yeah, that's it. At least two inches."

She must have been joking. They always measured me at the doctor's office, both height and weight, but as the expanders tightened and got heavier, it affected my posture. Even when I tried to stand up straight, I had lost a half inch of height over the past few weeks. Impossible, of course—no teenager had a reverse growth spurt—but no one could notice if a reverse-hunchback grew a couple inches.

"Those going to get bigger?" she asked.

I nodded as best as I could. "I'm gonna go from the human blister to shuffling around saying 'I am not an animal, I'm a human being!'"

She was less than impressed by my Elephant Man impersonation, going back to her chips.

"I thought that was funny," I said. "I can't tell you how hard it is to try to be funny right now, okay? So maybe just laugh. Snort. Something. Tell you what, if it was funny, blink twice."

She blinked once, just because that's what humans do.

"That's once!" I said. "Wait for it . . . Wait for it."

A smile started to spread across her face as she strained to not blink. She looked down, hiding both her blink and a laugh. "Stop it," she whispered.

"So, what are you in for?" I asked.

She didn't answer.

"Me? I overheard Ty in the bathroom. My neck's too thick for me to lick my own balls, I'll never get a girl, I suck at basketball, the expanders are hideous."

"Lick your own balls?"

"They call me the Doberman."

"Because you can lick your own balls?"

"Are you going to tell me what happened, or do I literally have to try to lick my own balls right now?"

She took a drink of Coke. Not Coke Zero or Diet Coke but the red can, dissolves-your-teeth-but-it's-worth-it heavenly Coke.

"Ask Preston what happened," she said. "Or more accurately, ask his girlfriend."

"Bullshit," I said. "He doesn't have a girlfriend."

"Yes, he does," she answered.

"Who?"

"Talisha, Queen Megabitch, first of her name."

"Did he change his relationship status on Facebook?" I asked.

"You don't have Preston on Facebook?"

"I don't have Facebook, period," I said. "It's the 'face' part I have problems with."

She laughed and looked me in the eyes for a long time. I let her.

"I'm sorry," she said. "I'm even sorrier now than I was last year. I don't mean to pull other people into my black hole of suffering."

"You can tell me what happened," I said. "I've got my merit badge in suffering."

"I don't even know where to start."

"There are things we can't help but think about, and they make us feel bad," I said. "So just start listing them and see what happens."

"Oh God," she said. "My mother. My father. My soon-to-be stepmom. My mother. My molester-ass uncle. My mother."

That paragraph she just put together was full of so many questions, so many landmines, so much heaviness that I didn't know how to unpack it all. When someone brings up a molester, you just assume that they were the ones that got molested, right? How the hell do you talk about that? Were you allowed to speak about that if you were within two-hundred yards of a school, even?

The bell rang. She gathered up her wrappers while I sat there like an idiot thinking of something to say, but I wanted to say something. She hurt, and I recognized it, and I didn't want her to feel that way anymore.

I stood up and saw the encyclopedias, and for some reason, those make me think of science, and science makes me think of shit I don't understand, not entirely, like black holes and suffering.

"What happens when two black holes get too close to each other?" I asked.

"Light has twice as much trouble escaping," she said, leaving me sitting in the library.

I went up to the encyclopedias and grabbed the "B" volume. Black holes were inside. Nothing about black hole collision, just a murky definition that I needed a physics class to understand.

I checked the copyright on the volume, and, naturally, it was 1993.

TALISHA

I figured I'd catch Preston on the bus ride home and prod him about Talisha. Not that I cared all that much if he dated her—he didn't have to report to me, even though I'd finally accepted that we were actually friends and dating someone was one of those things you voluntarily reported to all of your active friendships.

He never boarded the bus.

The doors shut, and we started rumbling out of the school's circle drive, a fleet of buses scattering to the far corners of the county. On the way out, I looked out the window, into the parking lot where Old Rusty used to be loyally posted, waiting for Preston and me to get out of basketball practice.

Cars were lined up at the mouth of the parking lot, waiting for the buses to clear. Some kids were gathered in little clusters, talking to each other before heading home for the day.

I saw Preston stuffing his cane into the back seat of a metallic blue Ford Escape, and even though I wasn't sure whose car it was and couldn't make out her face behind the wheel, I could tell her hair was black, and that was plenty enough evidence to figure out it was Talisha.

What did she do to force Lane to the library?

Lane had endured the names well enough, all the catcalls of psycho, crazy, busted, wack, suicidal, nutjob. I once heard Billy Kennings say she was crazier than a skunk fucking a football in a turnip truck, which got a good laugh from everyone within earshot, further proof that no one really unpacks jokes to make sure they make sense before offering up a laugh.

I didn't laugh at any of it. I knew the names they called me, the jokes they made when I wasn't around. That Wilder, he looks like Mel Gibson, but from *The Man Without a Face.* Darkman, Backdraft, French Fry, Blister Head, Crusty, Original Recipe, to name a few. But for some reason, they respected me enough to at least try to do it behind my back and have their laughs in private. Maybe because most people felt sorry for me, thinking it wasn't my fault that I looked the way I looked.

But Lane? Someone had decided that she chose the fate of outcast and this judgment permeated throughout the student body, a universal permission slip to make sure she heard exactly what people thought of her. I still didn't understand the root of it.

In high school, you simply are your worst moment. Kyle Loddeke made the mistake of saying aloud, in Miss Harrington's class, that his Jedi name was Jai-Ku Gammon, and we were going on year two of him being called DD, which stood for Darth Dipshit. Marylin Tally fell down the stairs and was now permanently called Trippy. Hell, for a while there I thought it was her last name. And Cade Jarrett—dear God, Cade Jarrett once popped a boner in the boy's shower after practice. I obviously wasn't in there with them, stalling while I waited for everyone to get out, but from then on, he was Popper. Even in practice, they'd yell out "Pass the ball, Pops" or urge him on in games, "Come on, Popper!" Coach Ballard thought we called him that because he was a good free throw shooter.

That's how they boil you down, because to remember you for something great would be an affront to the fragile egos of the typical asshole teenager personality. So many times, they were moments we couldn't control, like falling down or getting burned, but with Looney Lane McKenzie, it wasn't so simple. She'd made the horrific mistake of being responsible for her own worst moment, at least in the psyche of the various cliques around school.

When the bus dropped me off, I went right to my bicycle and zipped over to Preston's house.

Mary opened the door. The first words out of her mouth were, "You rode your bike over here?"

I wasn't supposed to be riding my bicycle. She'd offered to come and get me whenever I wanted to visit, a standing offer I never took her up on just because asking an adult for favors, especially another friend's mom, was never comfortable for an introvert like me.

"I needed the air."

"Well, I insist on driving you home."

"Okay," I said, not wanting to fight her about it.

"You want some dinner?"

"I just had a huge snack," I lied. "And my mother's bringing me something home."

"Okay then," she said, and I veered from the kitchen into the hallway. Preston's door was closed. I knocked.

I heard him rustling for his cane, the rickety floor of his old house thumping every time he put the brunt of his bodyweight on his stronger foot.

He opened the door, saw me, smiled weakly and then let it swing all the way open.

"I was hoping we'd get to whip some ass today," he said. The *Call of Duty* title screen was pulsing on his television.

I sat on the bed, and he sat on the floor, leaning against a beanbag, stretching his legs out awkwardly as the bag digested him.

"Missed you on the bus," I said.

He picked up his controller. The lobby timer on the TV screen was counting down as he selected a soldier sporting a colossal machine gun to do his online destruction.

"I caught a ride today," he said.

"With Talisha, right?"

"Yup."

Silence.

"So are you two a thing?" I asked.

"Yup," he said again.

"Why didn't you tell me?" I just figured I'd get right to it, leaving myself open for all kinds of "why should you care" or "I don't need your permission" comebacks.

"You sweet on Talisha or something?" he said, surprising me. "I figured you'd still be caught up with Jenna for God knows why."

"No," I said. "If I liked a girl, I'd probably tell you, and if I were officially dating one, I'd definitely tell you."

He took a deep breath as the game started, paused it, then decided to shut the PlayStation down. As the console's humming stopped and the TV turned dark, he just sat there looking at the blank screen, both of us reflected in the black glass.

"I really wasn't looking forward to this," he said.

"Why? She's cute. I think it's cool. She seems nice." Maybe not a lie but far from the truth. If she cut into Lane the way I figured she might have, she wasn't all that nice, but I didn't want to get things off on the wrong foot.

"First of all, she's hot, not cute," he said—a correction I somewhat agreed with. Talisha was blessed with perfect skin that belied her age and a blossoming, shall we say, womanhood that had other girls whispering, ludicrously, "implants."

"Second, it is cool, and I do think she's nice, but we're in a tight spot here, man."

"I don't understand."

"Talisha is kind of all about me," he said. "It's that new relationship smell. I've been there a time or two, and I'm digging her and all that, but she's talking just a little too much shit about you for my taste."

Now, this was surprising. She didn't seem nasty enough to say stuff about my scars.

"She was a little weird at the party about my scars," I said.

"It's not that, doofus. She knows better than to say shit about that. It's Lane."

"What?" My face turned hot.

"Oh my God. You're blushing. When did you last talk to Lane?"

"What?" I said again, so incapable of saying anything else I felt like I was a computer that needed to be power cycled.

"Simple math. Psycho hits us, shatters my ankle, and adds another injury to your impressive laundry list. I've got a resentment about it, but you don't, and it's not like everyone knows that—plenty of people think you're good and pissed about what she did—but she told me that you got defensive about Lane at the end of last year, when Jackson was trying to cheer you up."

"By cheer me up, you mean making up awful shit she didn't do?"

"We don't have to make anything up. What she did was awful enough already. She never even apologized."

"Not to you," I said.

"What?" Preston said, his eyes hardening. "She apologized to you? When did you talk to her?"

I drew out a sigh, stalling for time.

"That day with Jackson, I felt sorry for her. I went to see her, to tell her that I forgave her."

"Are you fucking serious?"

"So are you against forgiving people?" I asked.

"Did you forgive her before she apologized, or after?"

"Why does it matter?"

"Did you try to forgive her for what she did to me?"

"She didn't mean to hit us," I said. "Come on, Preston. You don't need a psych degree or a Bible to know that not forgiving someone isn't the worst for your long-term mental health."

"You blushed when I mentioned Lane," he said. "You better not have some Stockholm shit going on with her. It's one thing to forgive her, but to start liking her? No fucking way."

"I saw her in the library today," I said. "I just asked her what was wrong, and she said some girl was picking on her."

"Some girl, huh?" Preston said. "That could be a hell of a long list."

He wasn't coughing it up voluntarily, so I just went for it. "Was it Talisha?"

He didn't have the gumption to turn around and face me. We looked at each other in the turned-off television.

"What makes you think that?"

"Perhaps she didn't say some girl. Maybe Lane said, 'Talisha picked on me today' when I asked her."

"I can't believe it. She's got me using a cane, and you want to bang her."

"No," I said. "I just know what she's going through, with people saying stuff and everything."

"No, you don't," Preston said. "This 'woe is me, shit' is all in your head. I went to grade school with you. No one said jack shit about you."

"We're in high school now," I said, thinking of Ty and his little buddy giggling in the bathroom.

"I walk like a zombie now," he said. "You don't have a monopoly on suffering anymore."

"Come on, Preston. It's a broken ankle," I said. "You really think it's as bad as all . . . this?"

"You don't need a cane."

"I needed a neck brace. And skin grafts. And steroid injections. You don't have half a finger permanently missing. And now I get saline injections three times a week."

"Talisha told Lane that if only she took a few more sleeping pills, she wouldn't have been alive to ruin our lives," Preston said. "Call it mean, but Talisha's right."

I swallowed hard. "My life isn't ruined," I said. "Is yours?"

"When's the last time you shot a basketball?" Preston asked.

I held up my maimed hand. "With this? I haven't."

"There's plenty ruined, then," he said. "You're just too dumb to notice."

"Maybe I just choose to be an optimist."

"You know what man? Fuck you and your high horse," he said. "Friend to friend. Fuck you. Let me be pissed and bitter and petty, and you can sit on the mountain of morality next to the burning bush and preach the way things ought to be."

"Well," I said, groping for a response. He didn't let me off the hook, waiting on me to finish, tight-lipped and ready to burst. "It looks like I got too close to the burning bush," I finished.

The corner of his mouth started to lift, and we tried to keep the laughter in, but then we both cut loose with belly laughs and the simmering anger cooled and reduced.

He turned on the PlayStation 4 again and tossed me a controller, and we shot at online strangers until dinner time, which I couldn't resist since even Mary Brenner couldn't screw up spaghetti.

His father, Dan, came home from work early, and we sat at the table telling his parents about our day, feeling like a family.

We'd be brothers for at least a few more weeks until it all fell apart.

HOTLINE

Within a few weeks, school turned rote for everyone but me. With three hospital visits each week, that new-student feeling never wore off. Even when we switched to afternoon appointments so I could attend my morning classes, people still said "Welcome back" every time they saw me.

Basketball conditioning started. I was just happy it thinned a few guys off of my school bus, but their absence just reminded me that I wasn't at conditioning. Theo would be the one winning the suicide races. Jenna and the cheerleaders would peek in and wave. Ty Venhaus would loaf at every opportunity, knowing he would get my starting spot by default.

I missed the rim at the north end of the gym. That one got the most shot traffic before school and during lunch hour, so it was softer than the south rim. My shot had a lot of arc, and that rim always gave them a soft landing. Sometimes, I'd hit the side of the rim, then it would gently bounce up and kiss off the glass before rolling through the hoop, one of those rare moments in life where you get something special you don't even deserve.

Whenever I thought about basketball, I started squeezing my right hand. Everyone asked me if I had phantom limb syndrome, if I could feel the middle finger of that hand as if it were still there. I actually did, all the time, except for those moments when I thought about basketball, as if my body were saying, *dude, you can't. Don't beat yourself up.*

Everyone else was getting excited for our first three-day weekend of the school year, Columbus Day, and I was just happy to have a hospital appointment without worrying about makeup work. Same for Veteran's Day.

With Thanksgiving break around the corner, my expanders were now as big as softballs, and not the moderately-sized ones they use in the Olympics; I'm talking about the Chicago ones that you can catch with your bare hands.

Preston stopped riding the bus as he got closer and closer to Talisha. I never ate lunch in the cafeteria, opting to wolf down my vending machine feast and sit on the bleachers, since I couldn't shoot around. The *Call of Duty* invites dried up, and our text conversations slowed to a trickle.

My only real friendship was dying on the vine, and it was happening in the only real way friendships ever die—we were both right, but we were both wrong, and we didn't feel like arguing anymore.

Glimpsing Lane in the hallway among the other students was a rarity. She kept her head down as teenage girls side-eyed her and murmured to each other. Their smiles were knives, and I could smell the toxicity of their whispers, my burns having tuned me in to their hushed wavelength long ago.

Our first snow came early that year, a dusting just a week before Thanksgiving. Freezing temperatures and my tissue expanders didn't get along, and even though scarves were kind of douchey, I much preferred the asshole-in-an-ascot look to having ice-blue bubbles. As a bonus, it covered the bastards up, so I left it on during school.

As I was getting my books for first hour, the hallway was thinning out. The six minutes between classes kept feeling shorter and shorter as my movement got more sluggish over time. I saw Lane standing in front of her locker, alone, and though she wasn't crying, I could tell she was fighting the urge.

She turned around with the snap-footed quickness of a military sentry and headed for the library door. Then, she stopped.

"You okay?" I said, startling her.

She looked at me, her irises shiny, the rims of her eyes puffy. Still, no tears. She clenched her jaw and nodded once, then headed for class, refusing the sanctuary of the library.

We didn't have the same class that period. As she headed up the stairs, I pulled out a notebook and wrote her a note. I stuffed the notebook page into the slat of her locker, the frilly edge of the torn paper too sloppy and thick for me to punch it all the way through. I banged the locker with the side of my hand. The gong echoed, and everyone looked at me. I hurried away and ducked into my English II class, just as the bell rang.

I managed to stay awake through the numb and boring analysis of adverb use. I also managed to not create an excuse to turn around and look at Jenna, which had become as habitual as chewing fingernails. I had a whole array of moves, dropping a pencil, stretching my back out, popping my neck. Most of it had gotten more complicated with my newfound lack of flexibility, but I figured it just made me more sympathetic, and I was right—I sometimes got smiles and little waves.

When class was over, Jenna put her hand on my shoulder.

"Is everything okay?" she said.

Her touch was warm, bearing an electric hum.

"I'm all right," I said, not looking back at her, walking until her hand fell away.

I dragged myself into the hallway, which was already packed. Everyone was looking at me while trying not to look at me, and Lane was sprinting down the hallway. Students were laughing.

My note to her was unfolded, lying on the tile beneath her locker.

My cheeks felt swollen with blood, and I rushed to grab the note, having no idea what could have possibly upset her. The sea of students parted as I got to her locker and picked up the note.

I had written down my best attempt at callback humor: "Sad to report I can't lick my balls. Some Doberman. I need moral support." I also wrote down my cellphone number beneath the joke, just in case she ever needed to talk.

However, my writing had been blacked out with a sharpie. The phone number was left intact. Underneath it, two words crafted in the perfect handwriting that all girls were born with: "Suicide Hotline."

I pocketed the note and headed for the administrator's office. Lane emerged with Principal Turner beside her, his arm around her shoulders as she continued to cry, most likely taking her to visit with Ms. Ventura, the counselor.

I stepped into the office. The school secretary, Lindsay, had the phone to her ear but wasn't talking.

"Is Lane okay?" I asked.

"Principal Turner is walking her to the counselor's office," she said. "Do you know what happened?"

I placed the note on the counter. She read it and started shaking her head. "Do you know who did this?"

I couldn't accuse Talisha without proof. Even with proof, getting her in trouble would pop the powder keg of tension between Preston and myself.

"Yes, hello? Mr. McKenzie?" she held up her hand to me, giving the phone call her full attention. I backed into the hallway, which was now empty.

My biology teacher, Mr. Dinan, didn't even bother giving me a tardy—one of the few perks of looking like an exhibit from a Martian zoo was getting a long leash between classes.

I only had to last a couple more hours at school before Mom picked me up for my inflation appointment. The highlight of my day was turning out to be the ride to the hospital.

————

I spent a painful ride home with my body adjusting to a few more milliliters of saline inflation. The stretched skin turned a storm cloud hue of purple, and I couldn't sleep when I got home. The tissue expanders were swollen enough that sleeping on my side was painful. I laid blankets on top of my mattress, which was nothing but a sandwich of old springs and dust mites. It took a dozen blankets to turn my bed comfortable, and from then on, twelve was my redneck sleep number.

I started a text conversation with Preston. We carried on for twenty minutes or so, and he was asking, with as much concern as could possibly come through on text message font, how my injections had gone that day.

Finally, I warmed up to the real reason for contacting him.

"Someone left a nasty note for Lane today. Know anything about it?"

"Why u care?"

"It's my fault. I tried to leave her a note and someone messed with it. I feel bad."

"I don't."

"Do you know anything about it?"

After a long delay, my phone buzzed in my hand, jolting me from the cusp of sleep.

"Can't say that I do."

"Okay man. See you tomorrow."

"K," he texted back, ending the conversation.

I dragged myself out of bed—it wasn't even ten, and Mom was just asleep, a rare night off. She never did quit the Elks Lodge. Taking me to inflation appointments throughout the week meant that she had to drop the Red Hen job instead and keep her night shifts.

After Googling around for Lane's home phone number, I couldn't come up with anything useful. As a last resort, I dug out the phone book from the kitchen junk drawer as quietly as possible. I looked through the M's, and there was only one McKenzie. Caleb McKenzie, Lane's father.

I dialed the number. On the sixth ring, when I was just about to hang up, almost relieved, a gravel-voiced man picked up the phone.

"Sir," I said. "Mr. McKenzie—it's Wilder Tate. May I talk to Lane, please?"

A long pause. "No," he said.

"Is she okay?" I asked.

"No," he said again. "Thanks in large part to little shits like you."

"I didn't do anything to her," I said. "I'm just worried."

"I bet."

"Please tell her I called and that I'm worried about her."

"I hate to burst your bubble," he said, probably not knowing that he had just conjured up a pretty decent pun, "but I'm the one who knows what's best for her, and it ain't you. Stay the fuck away from her."

The phone clicked as he hung up on me.

"Everything okay, honey?" my mother said, standing in the doorway of my room.

I tossed my phone on the dresser. She came over and kissed me on the head, my cheek inaccessible thanks to the expanders.

"You're a good boy," she said, smoothing my hair.

She was wrong, but I wasn't in the mood to correct her.

SABOTAGE

The next morning, I barely responded to the alarm clock, but couldn't afford to hit the snooze button. I needed every possible minute to complete my morning routine. Obviously, showering was a bitch, but I couldn't consider skipping a day, needing to wash the bubbles as much as possible. The skin in the creases of the bubbles was always swampy. I needed to shower twice a day unless I wanted to smell like sour cream left on a hot sidewalk to curdle.

I dragged myself to school. Lane was absent. I asked around, trying to find out the repercussions for the note incident. No detentions handed out, no suspensions, no suspects. That's the problem with school justice—teachers and administrators aren't in the business of fair punishment. Every decision they make is to minimize disruption, so they were content to let the issue fade.

I was not content to let it fade, so I went to the office to check up on the investigation.

There was no investigation, according to Lindsay. I asked to talk with Principal Turner and offer up some evidence to kickstart the cold case, insisting that the handwriting was female and could be easily matched by taking samples from the student body. He wasn't having it.

"This isn't an episode of CSI," Principal Turner said. "We can barely afford teachers with our budget, so we can't provide handwriting analysts. Besides, what if a male student has nice handwriting? You're being a bit gender-biased, don't you think?"

I have heard rumors of principals long ago who were feared disciplinarians imposing order and justice upon their schools, and we were stuck with Jay Turner, who was such a bitch he probably didn't wipe his ass for fear of offending the toilet paper.

I almost made it through the day without incident. Mom was picking me up at one p.m., near the end of biology class. I was happy to skip Mrs. Thoman's sixth-hour sociology class. We were on politics lately, so I could finally match up a little bit of knowledge with all the crap I'd seen on TV. I had no idea that GOP stood for "Grand Old Party," and that was enough for me right there to not vote for them—when I was old enough, anyway.

Fifth hour was biology, and Mr. Darden gave us the last half of class for free study and open questions. His tests were notoriously hard, even though they were open-book, but I knew I'd be able to take it at home without any time limitations. I decided to stare at my book and space out, half-napping until I could cash in my permission slip and leave class.

"Wilder, don't you have to leave early today?" I zoned out so completely, I lost track of time. It was already one, and my mother was likely waiting. I shook off the cobwebs and closed my textbook.

"You're not gonna stick around and vote for yourself?" Twyla Roider said. She sat in front of me in biology, which I was cool with for a couple of reasons—she was cute, and she was Talisha's sworn enemy, allowing me the satisfaction of occasionally hearing her talk shit about Talisha in those social moments before the start of class.

"Vote for what?" I asked.

"They're electing prom court today," she said. "You know, because politics."

"It's November. Prom isn't until—"

I didn't know anything about prom. I just knew we had an incredibly small school, so prom was a wide-open affair, freshman through senior.

"Early April," Twyla said. "But Talisha's on the prom committee this year. All bets are off."

"Wilder?" Mr. Darden said. "Are you going to be late?"

By now, it was a little after one. "Just one second," I said, leaning closer to Twyla. "What's this got to do with me voting for myself?"

Twyla's voice lowered to a whisper. "I heard she's angling to get you on the court with her as the sophomore couple. She's definitely going to nominate you. That's her best bet to compete for prom queen."

She didn't have to spell out the reasons. I was a lock for sympathy votes, and Talisha getting me onto the court, and campaigning us as a couple, would boost her own vote.

Appearing in front of the entire school was bad enough, but by then, my expanders would be close to maximum capacity. To have a smiling Talisha looped around my arm during prom court presentations? Hell no.

"Thanks," I said. I left my desk, handing Mr. Darden my permission slip.

I headed for the office. Lindsay handed me the sign-out book. She knew the drill. "I'm going to talk to my Mom for a second," I said, pushing away the book.

"Don't you have to leave?" Lindsay asked.

"I think she mixed up the appointment," I said, offering a shrug.

Mom was idling in the pickup area. I shambled down the steps, leaning hard on the guardrail. She got out of the car to help me, but I waved her off.

"We're running late, honey," she said, jumping back into the car. I stood by her window, signaling her to roll it down.

"I said we're running late."

"I need you to reschedule my appointment," I said.

"Why?" she said, more suspicious than concerned.

"Just please do it?" I turned around, hellbent on scrubbing my name from prom court.

"Just let them vote," she said.

I turned around. "You knew?"

"Mrs. Thoman called me. She thinks you'll be nominated and wanted to check with me about it."

"What about me?"

"We both know you'd never allow it."

"Getting me away from the vote isn't going to win me over," I said. The bell rang, the sound muted by the closed doors. Fifth hour was over.

"I just thought if they voted you onto the court, you'd warm up to the idea by the time prom rolled around," she said.

"It's in April," I said. "Unless the theme this year is beauty and the beast, I'm going to freak everyone out."

She shook her head. "You're wrong, but I can't stop you."

"Thank you," I said, relieved.

"I'd just like to see my baby boy in a tux," she said. "They'll cheer for you, Wilder. I think that's what you're really scared of, and I don't know why."

She didn't know why. She'd never know, because I couldn't bring myself to ever tell her, so I didn't answer her. I just headed back up the steps.

She waited for me to get safely to the front door, and only then did she finally pull away.

The hallways were empty by the time I got back inside. I checked back in at the office, rushed through a bathroom break I couldn't bear to skip, and switched out my books. I was ten minutes late, but Mrs. Thoman didn't even ask me for a pass.

The class had doubled in size—the other sophomores that usually had study hall were crammed into the room, some of them standing to leave a desk open for me.

I glanced at the whiteboard where Talisha was standing at the head of the class. At the top was a big, bold heading in Mrs. Thoman's block handwriting.

PROM COURT NOMINEES.

I digested the contents of the board. The seniors voted during first hour, and their court nominees were underlined. The only two names I recognized were Theo and Derrick Reynolds, two basketball players. So right there, the king was elected. Theo fucking Lang was going to be the prom king. Bang me with a screwdriver.

I didn't know many senior girls, as if that wasn't obvious. I'm sure every one of them thought in their heart of hearts that they were going to be crowned queen. It's always a senior—unless, of course, Theo could orchestrate an upset, and that was already in the works, because below it, the junior class had already voted in their court—Mitch McGill and Jenna Weaver.

So now, in alignment with the politics we'd been discussing, it was only natural to have our class nominate a few sophomores and vote on them. I'll be damned if my name wasn't on the board in Talisha's handwriting, and in the column next to my name was a list of three girls, with Talisha's topping the list.

They were about to vote on the girls, but the nominees below my name were erased—the sophomore class voted me onto prom court, which was either the sweetest or cruelest thing I could have ever imagined. I figured some votes were of the sweet variety, and others were of the cruel variety, which probably made it damn near unanimous when they put it to the class.

I didn't even sit down.

"I can't," I said. "Not prom. Not in front of everyone like that."

Pleas of "You have to!" and "We really want you to do it" and "You deserve it" flowed from the class.

"These will be even bigger," I said, gesturing to my bubbles. "I don't even think they can cut a tux to fit me like this."

"My mom's a seamstress," Lori Vanover said. "We'll make you a tux from scratch if we have to, but you gotta do it!"

I looked at the whiteboard again, and Talisha was smiling at me. Fucking smiling at me, twisting the red marker in her hand, and on the board, her name was written just a little bit bigger than the others, a perfect cursive that she probably practiced every day for when she'd sign the pep posters for the boys' basketball team. Even in the cursive, she couldn't truly hide what I was now seeing in the bend of those letters, the way the S and the I had leaked out of her wrist and the pressure with which she held the marker, as unique as a fingerprint.

Unique, but I had seen her handwriting before.

"Where's Lane?" I asked. Total silence.

Mrs. Thoman spoke up. "She's home today, but I'm sending her work along. She's doing okay."

Preston glared at me. The hardness of that look wrung the pity I had for him straight out of the marrow of my bones. Talisha kept smiling, the finishing touches on her prom queen coup attempt falling into place—I'd get a mountain of sympathy votes; now all she had to do was lock down her nomination.

"I'll do it," I said, and the class cheered, but I wasn't finished.

"But I want Lane on prom court with me."

Crickets. Talisha's smile vanished.

Mrs. Thoman took over. "We have another nominee, Talisha," she said. Talisha wrote Lane's name in tiny letters at the bottom of the list.

"Now, we need someone to second the nomination," Mrs. Thoman said.

"No, you don't," I said. "Just vote. If you want me to do it, a vote for Lane is a vote for me."

My first political speech, and my first ultimatum. From what I knew from the news, maybe the GOP was my kind of politics after all.

Talisha got one vote. It was Preston's. Lane collected the rest. As our names got underlined as the winners, Talisha wiped out her own name, the body language of her eraser strokes slow and disbelieving. I found them calming, and her disappointment salved me for approximately two minutes before regret started bubbling to the surface.

After the voting was over and normal class resumed, I had the entire period to sit there and let my regret marinate until it morphed into full-blown panic.

By the time prom rolls around, they'll be able to see your freaky ass from outer space.

And what if Theo pulled that thing where he's all noble and convinces people to vote for me so they can crown the persevering burned kid? That would make a little news item, probably, and Theo—that fucker Theo—he'd be able to take all the credit.

Imagine Jenna talking to him alone after it happens. "It's so beautiful what you did for Wilder." Then they'd start kissing.

Stop.

They'd get all horny because you're the prom king.

Ratchet it down.

She'd probably make out with his dick.

Christ. Now is not the time, okay?

Preston wasn't even trying to hide his seething, and when I looked over at him, he didn't look away. It was like he had that *Firestarter* power and was trying to will me into exploding, and I'll be damned if I didn't heat up while he stared through me.

What about Lane?

Shit. You're awfully chatty today.

Talisha's going to try to crumble her ass to ground zero to take her spot at the dance. Everything that happens to Lane now is on you.

The dance gives Lane something to think about other than her own problems. Maybe some girls rally to her side. Maybe she embraces the court and convinces her dad to get her a beautiful dress. Maybe she rehearses until she could do the slow dance thing perfectly, and on prom night everyone sees that homely girl emerge from her cocoon as a makeup-encrusted, dress-twirling Cinderella. Then, I'll be the one who gets to dance with her, and there we would stand, the new and better versions of ourselves on display for the entire school, crushing our worries and blame and hurt forever.

Yeah, but do you kiss her?

Why not? I somehow afford a new car in this fantasy, and we drive off into a farm bypass road and strip away every cell of our former selves together, scrubbing off our old skins with shaking hands and clumsy kisses.

You like her?

It's just a fantasy. I like any girl I can imagine kissing me back.

Pick a girl to kiss. Lane or Jenna?

Jenna, obviously.

Then why do you think about her less and less?

I don't.

I'm your mind, fuckface. I know better.

The bell rang, and I jumped so hard the pencil flicked out of my hand. As students scurried by me, Tammy Stanford, whom I barely knew, picked up my pencil and handed it to me.

"I'm voting you for king," she said. "And Lane for queen. I think it's cool what you did, that you can forgive her like that."

"Thanks," I said, and as I turned to the doorway, I knew that Preston overheard it. He was limping out of the room, leaning on his cane.

Usually, I'd wait for him, but his eyes seemed buried under a meat-visor of his scrunched-up forehead. When Preston looked pissed, you knew it, and with that billboard of destruction advertising what was sure to be a confrontation I wasn't ready to have, I just bolted for the door.

The reprieve wouldn't last long—Preston was in my math class with Mrs. King, and we usually sat together.

I had a five-minute stay of execution.

PUSH

When I entered Mrs. King's room, Preston was standing next to her desk, waiting for me. He didn't even bother to visit his locker to switch books.

We were alone. Mrs. King was usually posted by her door, monitoring the hallway, but she was gone to visit the teacher's lounge or take a dump or God knows what, right when I needed her around the most.

Preston took a hobbled step toward me.

"What the hell did you do that for?" he said, his voice full of pain, not anger.

"Talisha didn't deserve to be nominated," I said. "Not after what she did."

Now he was pissed. "Are you talking shit about my girlfriend?"

"No," I said. "You know what she did."

"Clarify it for me."

"Why does anything I say matter? Her opinion means more to you than mine anymore."

"You want to act like I'm choosing a girl over you? Look at me," he said, gesturing to his cane. "Lane McKenzie did this to me. It's one thing to forgive her, but to get a crush on her?"

I blushed so hard it damn near knocked me out.

"Makes me sick," he added.

I took the note out of my pocket, my hands trembling as I unfolded it.

"Talisha did this," I said, flicking the paper at him. "But you knew that, didn't you? And if you're cool with what she did, you're not cool with me."

By now, more kids were walking in, but they kept a wide berth, going around us to get to their seats. After a long silence, I tried to walk to my seat, but Preston's hand shot out, palming my shoulder, stopping me. He came inches away from slamming palm-first into the expander in my arm.

"You're turned inside out, man. It always feels like being my friend is an inconvenience to you. Look what it got me, fucking around with you."

I swiped his hand away. He cocked his arm and shoved me. He needed one arm to steady himself on his cane, but even with half a push, I fought to keep my balance. He hobbled closer.

"Preston, don't," I said, but he came up and pushed me again with his free arm. He couldn't muster enough to budge me since I was prepared for it.

"You like the girl who hurt me," he said.

"You like a bully," I said.

"Talk shit about her again," he said, trailing off.

"Talisha's a fucking bully," I said.

He threw his cane aside and lurched into me, shoving me with both hands, putting his body weight into my sternum.

I flailed, losing my footing. I let myself fall backward, hoping to protect my expanders from rupturing during an awkward landing. I crashed against the whiteboard, bounced off, and hit the ground, bracing the impact with my knees and hands, trying to protect my expanders.

They sloshed hard as I hit the floor, sending a nauseating pain throughout my upper body. My hands were poor shock absorbers, giving way as I crashed forward, turning at the last second to try to minimize the impact to the expanders bulging from my neck.

I mostly succeeded, but still smacked the side of one of the bubbles in my neck. The impact sizzled dots into my vision, the kind of pain that buzzes in your eardrums.

I tried to get to my feet when a hand rested on my shoulder, and a familiar voice said, "Stay down. You might be hurt."

Theo.

"This doesn't involve you," Preston said, kneeling down to pick up his cane.

"It does now," Theo said. He was on one knee, protecting me.

"He doesn't want help from you," Preston said. For a moment, I thought he was going to jab Theo with his cane.

"I don't care," Theo said.

He helped me to my feet. The expanders in my neck were burning, and I was afraid one of them was torn or leaking.

"I need to see the nurse," I said. Theo tried to help me, taking my arm to put it around his neck. I pulled it back.

"I can walk just fine," I said. Preston was an asshole for pushing me, but he was right—I didn't want or need Theo's help.

NURSE

Our school nurse, Mrs. Boatright, had no idea how to tell if an expander was damaged. I sat in her office, waiting for my mother to come and get me for yet another hospital visit.

"How's Preston doing?" I said, thinking that falling down when he pushed me might have hurt him.

"He's in the office with Principal Turner."

"It was an accident," I said.

"I don't care what it was," she said. "You're in here, he's over there. If Principal Turner wants to talk to you about it, he will."

When she was done with me, I sat outside her office, tucked away in an alcove of the hallway by the entrance to the cafeteria.

The double doors opened, and Theo came around the corner. He kept his distance, crossing his arms a few yards from me, waiting for me to talk. I didn't.

"You okay?" he said.

I nodded.

"Are you really so pissed you'd rather have your ass kicked than have me help you?"

"Don't make this about you," I said.

"Jenna and I have dated a year now," he said. "It's not a fake thing. I love her."

"I don't care," I said.

"Don't let your feelings about me keep you from the games. We all want you there," he said.

"Why would I go when I can't even play?"

"Gee, I don't know, support your teammates maybe? Your school? We'd be pumped to have you on the bench. You're part of the team."

"A mascot," I said.

"You ever consider that maybe I'm sorry for what happened and I'm just trying to help you?"

"Robbie Imming had forty-six points for Mater Dei last night," I said. "They played North Central, so I bet you and some of the other players were at the game, maybe even Coach Ballard. You saw your chances at a regional championship get a little smaller each time Robbie hit a shot, and you're hoping I'll come back to help get your name engraved on a plaque."

"I know you can't come back, but it sure doesn't stop me from hoping," he said. "A real Doberman would be hoping to come back, too."

"If I couldn't play defense, you wouldn't give a fuck about me," I said.

"That's a lie," he said. "You can also hit the three."

I held up my right hand, still pink and scarred, reminding him about my lack of a middle finger.

"So what?" he said. "You can probably still outshoot Luke."

"And catch the ball better," I added.

"Hands like fuckin' frying pans."

We laughed.

"That's my dude, right there," he said. "I've only met that dude once, when he was knocking back liquor at Jenna's party. Going toe to toe with us, freshman status be damned."

A fun night, for sure. A long talk with Jenna, my first drink, lots of free Cokes. Preston driving me home in Old Rusty, laughing his ass off the whole way.

"You don't get to do this," I said.

"Do what?"

"Stand here and cue up the after-school music and dig me out of a tough hole, like you understand what it's like to look like me. You don't have a single scar, not on your heart or your pretty-boy face, no failures that haunt you, no staying up at night wondering which tragedies are the worst—the ones that are your fault, or the ones that happen for no particular reason."

"This is what I get for trying to talk to you?" he said. "I've had plenty of failures, I just don't wallow in them."

"Your biggest failure is on deck," I said. "We host regionals this year, so Robbie Imming is going to cut down the nets on your home court in a few months. That one's gonna sting, especially for a senior like you. Lots of seniors cry after their last game. You're a safe bet to bawl, so maybe I'll show up for at least one game this season."

He just looked down at the tile and waited for me to keep unloading, but I was done. He took a deep breath and tried to look me in the eyes, but I wouldn't let him.

"All that you're going through with those bubbles—and they're not going to fix a goddam thing," he said.

Mom and I were experts at killing time in hospital waiting rooms. The magazine selection was slim and outdated. I read through a *Sports Illustrated* NFL preview issue from three months ago, making fun of how much they'd gotten wrong now that the season was halfway over.

"Are you going to tell me why Preston pushed you yet?" she asked, leafing through a *Good Housekeeping*.

"I egged him on. It's over."

"You're a good kid," pausing, adding, "sometimes you're too good."

Again with the good kid shit. I kept my nose in my magazine. I wasn't in the mood for gooey stuff. Good kid? If only you knew me better. No one sees your scars? You're under maternal contract to not see them.

Most others in the waiting room were browsing their phones, but I didn't have that luxury. Our cell phones were prepaid, low on data allotments, and non-smart. What else would you call phones that weren't smartphones? Classical phones. Vintage phones. Dumbphones.

So when my phone buzzed, it wasn't a sports score or a social media alert or an app reminding me to update. I slid my handset out of my pocket and saw it was a number I didn't recognize.

"OMG WHY DID YOU NOMINATE ME FOR PROM COURT"

All caps, the font of choice for panic. So Lane got my number after all. "Better you than Talisha," I responded. "Screw her."

I sent it, then quickly sent another message: "I can't do prom alone."

Lane didn't respond until much later, when I was sitting on the Children's Hospital ER bed, waiting for someone familiar with expanders to check me out.

I drew a nurse whose perfume matched the floral pattern on her scrubs. I walked her through my awkward fall, and as she examined my expanders, I had to breathe through my mouth.

"The burning subsided?"

"Yes," I said.

She stepped over to the wastebasket to dump her examination gloves, and her sneaker squeaked.

"You're new," I said.

"How did you know?" she said.

"Your shoes are squeakier than everyone else's, like you just got them."

"Maybe I just got new shoes, detective."

"Just a hunch," I said. "The scrubs look super new, and you're way too chipper to have worked in the ER for long."

Silence. I sensed that the nurse gave my mother a look, and I imagined Mom shrugging at her.

"Lucky for you, I'm plenty experienced with patients such as yourself, and you've got nothing to worry about. Everything looks fine. Close call. You're a lucky boy."

"So I've heard," I said.

As we left the exam room, my phone vibrated.

Lane's response was two words: "I can't."

While my mother was talking to the nurses at the discharge station, going over that "we're too poor to actually pay for this visit anytime soon" paperwork, I stepped out onto the sidewalk and dialed Lane's number.

It rang once and went to voicemail—not a personalized message but the robotic default message that just repeats the phone number you just dialed.

I hung up before it started recording.

CONFESSION

After a quiet dinner, I told mom I needed some air.

"You're just walking, right?" she asked. "No bike rides. Doctor's orders."

So I took a walk around the block to get her off my scent, then stole my own bike.

Usually, I'd breeze through a trip of just a couple miles, but I felt more unbalanced than usual with the weight of the expanders gathered on one side of my body. I shifted my center of gravity and struggled to pedal.

Fall, and the expanders burst. Fall, and never look normal. Fall, and Mom's money is wasted, a thousand shifts at the Red Hen flushed away and for what? To watch Lane slam a door in my face?

I didn't fall, but the ride gassed me. I dropped the bike next to Lane's driveway, wondering where I'd draw the energy to ride home. Sweat blazed through my shirt. The sun wasn't down yet, but it squatted behind the trees, turning the dusk windy and cold.

I stepped onto the porch and knocked on the door.

Caleb McKenzie answered. He was shorter than me, five-eight at the most, but he had the stature of a man that built houses from storm-felled trees with his bare hands.

He stood there, his foot jammed in the screen door, holding it open so that both arms were free to cross over his thick chest.

"What the hell you want?"

"I need to talk to Lane," I said.

"Need's a strong word," he said. "Sounds to me like you want to talk to Lane, and I think I recall telling you to stay away from her."

"'Stay the fuck away from her,' to be exact," I said, not budging.

"You need to go," he said.

I noticed movement beyond his shoulder. Lane sat at the top of the stairs listening, but all I could see were her sneakers.

"I need to ask Lane something," I said. "Please."

His hands curled around the edge of the door as he spoke, the rims of his fingernails clogged with black grease.

"Ask me what?" Lane said, giving her father pause. His jaw tightened, but he waited for me to answer.

"I'm here to ask you to prom," I said.

Her sneakers didn't move, and neither did Caleb.

"Let him in," she said.

Caleb held fast. Beads of sweat quivered on the furrows of his brow. A coppery stench radiated from him, the smell of work and anger.

"Please, Dad," she said. "I can handle this."

He let a glare linger, then stepped aside.

"Thank you, sir," I said.

I stood at the bottom of the stairs. Lane sat at the top wearing an oversized sweatshirt, her dark hair bound in a ponytail. She waved me up, and I followed her to her bedroom.

The only female, teenage bedrooms I'd seen were on television. I expected a big-ass bulletin board full of photos of her and her friends, every square inch of her wall plastered with trendy posters of popular movies, boy bands, and hot dudes.

The room had an attic feel to it, both in the draft coming from the single window and the way the angles of the roof shaped the ceiling of her bedroom. You couldn't get close to one of the walls without ducking.

"So, you want to go to prom with me? Why? Because you're too chickenshit to do it alone?"

"Yes," I said. No hesitation, which stunned her a little.

"You big baby. You'll get the biggest ovation. They'll go crazy for you."

"Maybe, but half of them will clap just to feel better about themselves."

"Don't throw a pity party."

"Isn't that kind of what I do?" I said. "Throw pity parties with just one person attending? Just me, sitting in a room with a party hat on, blowing a sad-sounding party horn while I look in the mirror at the ravaged topography of what was formerly a perfectly acceptable human body?"

Laughter escaped. Cracks in the armor. "So is this your first pity party where someone else is invited?" she asked.

"Yep. Lasts until question mark, BYOB."

Her father knocked on the door. The hinges somehow tolerated the force. "Door stays open," he bellowed.

Lane rolled her eyes and flung the door open. "Can't have the door closed with a boy in the room," she said, collapsing back into her chair. "I might report for breakfast pregnant."

She winked at me. My throat was so dry, it crunched when I swallowed.

"You always this nervous around girls?"

I shrugged.

"I can't go," she said. "But you have to find a way to be brave enough to go."

"What are you afraid of?"

"I'm the crazy bitch who almost killed you," she said. "I'll just make it so hard for you. It's your moment. You deserve it."

"Don't say that," I said.

"They don't give you pity, can't you see that?" she said. "Whatever it is you've got, they wish they had it."

"They wish they had burns over thirty percent of their body?"

"They want whatever it is that makes you the Doberman," she said.

"If I didn't play hard, I'd never play."

"You don't stop. Not ever. All these things happen to you, and they're not your fault, and you just keep pushing."

She fiddled with the sleeves of her sweatshirt.

"If you can keep going, anyone can keep going," she said. "I can keep going."

She looked me in the eyes, and I couldn't hold the gaze for long, staring at the tongues of my sneakers, my chin pressing against the tops of my expanders.

"The burns," I said. "What if they were all my fault?"

"I don't understand," she said.

"The way I tell the story, I get off the bus and hear a noise in my garage out back." I took a breath to reset myself. "Randy's in the garage, siphoning gas out of our old John Deere mower into a bowl. Everyone knew he was a huffer—so I confront him and tell him to get out. He refuses, then we start screaming at each other. We scuffle, I run away, he shoves me down, right into the bowl of gas. He lights a match and sets me on fire."

"You already told me at the party," Lane said.

"I didn't tell you the truth," I said. "I've never told anyone."

She said nothing, just waiting for the rest of it, her body taking on the concerned, engaged look of the counselors we've both talked to so many times over the years.

"He broke into my garage, that much is true," I said. "He was siphoning the gasoline into an oversized bowl. The bowl was sitting on a red plastic milk crate. Looked like a dog bowl, the stainless silver murky from age and wear, something he probably found on the curb during trash day. The raw gas was in there, so when I looked at him, the thickness of the fumes made him appear blurry, as if he were at the end of a hot road."

She nodded in all the right spots, urging me along.

"We fought the week before at the rock pile. I slugged him, and he ran off, but I think it was because my friends were around. Now, we were alone, and the fear he flashed at the rock pile was gone. He told me to just leave the garage, let him finish up and not tell anyone. He said he was just borrowing the gas and he'd bring by a half-gallon within the next week or two. As he talked, he was coming closer to me, one slow step at a time.

"Now, around this time, my buddies and I were in a weird outdoorsman survivalist phase, camping out all the time. My buddy Glenn used to carry around a survival knife he bought at a pawn shop, like the one from the Rambo movies. Blade was dull as shit, but there was a compass in the hilt and a spot where he kept matches, a little waterproof hollow in the base of the knife. We'd start campfires, and he would always say you needed to have matches on you if you wanted to survive a bad situation; then he would open up his knife. I was younger than Glenn by a couple years, so

I started carrying matches around. I didn't know any better. I kept a book tucked in my sock. It was annoying, scratching against my ankle all day, but if the world ended and we needed to cook over an open fire, I had us covered.

"Randy walks past the fumes and I see him, good and clear, and I just know he's going to get his revenge for the rock pile. He's going to hit me. So I go for the book of matches. He doesn't know what I'm doing. He doesn't speed up. In fact, he stops, and I don't just show him the book of matches. I light them, a tiny hiss that gets louder as the whole book lights up."

I couldn't backtrack now. I had to tell her the real story. Even worse, I had to hear myself tell it, giving voice to the whispers I've heard raging in the back of my skull since the day I lied to the police.

"He's scared now. He even says, 'Are you fucking nuts?' and takes a step back. So by now, I feel like he's Frankenstein, and I'm holding a torch and he's scared of it. I take a step forward, he takes another matching step backward. So I decide I'm going to chase him out of my garage before the book of matches fizzles out. I run at him. He turns; he's a thin kid, so it takes a while, all the elbows and knees switching gears. I almost catch him, but one long stride and he pulls away from me. I see the milk crate at the last second, and only then does it register in my dumbass, ten-year-old mind that he's not scared of me or the matches; he's scared because of the gas. I try to jump it at the last second, but my foot catches the lip of the crate, and then everything is airborne—me, the crate, the dying book of matches."

I almost can't finish, but I've come this far. She waits, making no move to prod me along, allowing me to get to the moment all on my own.

"I remember seeing the gasoline suspended in mid-air. The whoosh in my ears is like a jet plane engine, and my world is fire, all at once. I get to my feet, and I can hear myself crackling as my clothes burn, so I start running around, leaving a vapor trail of fire. I slam my fists on the wall, like I can break through it and get outside, but there's nothing outside to save me. Then, I hear a voice saying 'stop, drop, and roll motherfucker!' and I don't know if it's an angel in my head or just my first-grade self who saw the stupid video in class one day. So I stop, drop, and roll, and when I finally put myself out, Randy is gone."

Lane is suddenly closer to me, attentive and patient.

"No one liked him," I continued. "He was the 'bad kid.' He tortured animals—he shot out the eyes of my old friend's dog with a BB gun. He stole. He fought. The first person to ask me what happened was one of the doctors. So I told them Randy Meadows set me on fire and left me to die, because the burns needed to be because of someone else. My face like that, forever, because of an idiot kid who tripped? As long as it was someone's fault and not mine, I could get past it. I could handle being a victim of violence. So I told the doctors and my parents and the police that it was Randy Meadows, and told myself that he was getting what he deserved."

"Wilder," she said, her voice achieving tones of softness I thought only my mother could produce, "Your scars are not your fault."

"Sometimes I think about when Randy and I were friends," I said. "We were little. He would come over, and we'd pretend to camp out in broad daylight. One day my mom brought us out a bag of Doritos while we were playing, and he begged me to let him eat the whole thing. He wasn't dirty or hungry because he wanted to be. He was broken, and I just made it easier for the world to flush him down the toilet."

"He's in jail because of himself, not because of you," she said.

"You asked if I knew what happened to him," I said. "I know. I've always known, because I could never risk running into him. I could never look him in the eyes, knowing what I did to him, knowing that he could tell me that every awful thing that's happened in his life is because of me, and I couldn't tell him any different."

"Yet he never refuted your story," she said.

"He didn't," I said. "I told the cops what happened. They asked Randy. He asked them, 'What did Wilder say happened?' and they repeated my story. 'Then that's what happened,' is what he told them."

I tilted my head up, hoping that gravity could keep the tears from falling. "I'm sorry," I said. "I haven't even told my mother this. I'm putting too much on you."

"Sometimes it's nice to put things on other people," she said. "The things we can't carry all alone." She came even closer. "Your neck didn't get it the worst?"

I shook my head. "My torso and my arm are third-degree," I said. "A real mess."

"Show me," she said.

The thought of stripping off my shirt to show her the decimated landscape my stomach and chest drove every strand of muscle tissue into a tense state of cramped alert.

"Settle down," she said. "Wilder, unclench your jaws. Take a breath." She touched my arm.

"Have you ever shown anyone? Other than your mom and doctors?" I shook my head.

"You think it's the worst thing in the world," she said. "And you're always going to think that unless you show someone who understands, someone who can tell you it's not as bad as you think it is."

"It's bad," I said.

"We're both hurt in places most people can't see," she said, "and we're too afraid to show other people. So show me."

"I can't," I said. "I'm sorry."

Lane wedged her hands into the bottom of her sweatshirt and pulled it over the top of her head. I looked at the open doorway. I don't know if fathers have a spidey-sense that tingles when their daughters are disrobing, but I was prepared for a tsunami of Caleb McKenzie to burst into the room. The hallway remained empty. Underneath the sweatshirt, Lane wore a *Breaking Bad* T-shirt with Heisenberg's hatted silhouette.

I'd never seen her with anything less than two layers of sleeved clothing, and as she turned her arms up in front of me, I knew why.

"I can't go to prom," she said. "The prettiest dresses don't have sleeves."

Her arms were streaked with white scars mixed in with freshly rendered cuts that had just scabbed over.

"I can't afford a decent dress, anyway," she said.

"You do this to yourself?"

"Are you so dense you've never heard of cutting?"

I'd heard of it, but I always filed cutting under "no way that's a widespread problem; who would actually do something so stupid?" right next to people dying while taking selfies and people who drink sparkling water and think it tastes good.

She picked up a paperclip from her desk and bent the outside wire until it poked out. She held it like a tiny pocketknife, dug the tip into the pale flesh near her wrist, and drew it along her forearm. Droplets of blood bubbled along the surface of the cut.

"It's not that deep," she said. "Just enough to feel it."

She blotted the cut with a tissue.

"I'll make you a deal," she said. "I'll go to prom with you, but then you have to go somewhere with me."

"Now?"

"No, sometime before prom. Maybe even after. Depends, you just have to promise to go with me."

Her ponytail brushed her shoulder. On her T-shirt, Heisenberg's chin was smudged with an old blood stain.

"One condition," I said. "I want your jean jacket."

She looked at her ravaged arms.

"I've got hoodies and turtlenecks, you know."

"I know. But I want your jean jacket. I'm not even taking it home. I'm going to burn it and bury the ashes and pour a concrete pad over the remains."

The jacket was sprawled on her bed, the sleeves laid out as if the person inside of it had just melted away.

"Fine," she said. "Then you help find me a dress with sleeves. Preferably one costing less than twenty bucks, which is my life savings up to this point."

What did I know about dresses? Nothing. I nodded anyway.

She tossed me the jacket, and we had ourselves a deal.

CHRISTMAS BREAK

The best part of Thanksgiving break is that you come back to school and it's almost time for an even longer Christmas break.

I spent most of the gap between breaks at home or at the doctor. I got pumped with saline. I also came down with a nasty cold. The doctor told me to expect a difficult cold and flu season, since my body was too busy with the expanders to give the proper resources to fending off germs.

I used to not mind a cold; that's an easy day at home playing video games with a box of tissue at your side. The expanders weren't about to let me have an easy time of things— imagine feeling like your whole body got kicked in the balls every time you unleashed a sneeze.

Lane was in school on all of the days I didn't have an inflation appointment. We didn't have many classes together, so we didn't get to talk much, but I started taking my lunches in the library so we could catch up. We typically complained about the school's food, compared our favorite TV shows, and joked about the latest rumors floating in the hallways. Our last lunch before Christmas break was the only one that turned serious.

"Why have you been eating lunch in the library?" she asked.

"I'm not eating lunch in the library," I said. "I'm eating lunch with you."

"Funny you should say that. You don't call or text me," she said. "You have my number, right?"

I nodded.

"Anyway. Fuck the library. I don't like being in here," she said. "Makes me think of all the wrong things."

"Then why do you keep eating lunch in the library?"

"I'm not eating lunch in the library," she said. "I'm eating lunch with you."

"I'm confused," I said.

"When you're at your appointments, I've been eating in the main lunchroom."

"With who?"

"Jealous much?" She punched my good shoulder, one of her favorite bits of punctuation. "Beth and Twyla, mostly. Sometimes Daityn comes over."

"I bet they were just allergic to denim," I said. Lane laughed. "You want me to eat lunch with you in the main lunchroom? In front of everyone? Is that what you're asking?"

"I don't know what I'm asking," she said. "Never mind, okay? It's fine in here. Less noisy. More private."

She attacked her pudding with a singular focus, wanting to drop the conversation. Her phone buzzed. I was holding my own cellphone, not even trying to hide the fact that I had just texted her a message: "Yes, I have your number."

"Use it over Christmas break," she said, and I intended to do just that.

Over Christmas break, without juggling makeup work with the physical toll of the expanders, things finally settled down. Mom worked a lot. I slept in a lot.

The best and worst part of the holiday break? Mom got me a new basketball for Christmas.

"I've never seen what our yard looks like with grass around your basketball hoop," she said.

Since I stopped playing, the grass that I had beaten out of existence by shooting around had come roaring back. The muddy pathways were etched with the gentle consistency of a trickle of water carving out a canyon. The grass had swallowed up thousands of shots, crossover dribbles, jumps, shuffles, and lateral cuts.

"I hate it," Mom added. "Too much mowing."

I sat there like a baby crying over the gift, and she handed me a tissue. "I know you too well to think you'll quit for good," she said. "You'll play again. You'll shoot just fine. You'll find a way."

The ball stayed in the cardboard box long after Christmas, sitting on my bedroom dresser.

On New Year's Eve, I fell asleep on the couch trying to stay up and watch the ball drop.

I woke up at 11:40 p.m. and sent Lane a text: "I almost missed it. Crashed at like nine p.m. on the couch, old man style."

"Lame."

"Yup."

She didn't text back. After breakfast, I tried her again: "So who did you make out with at midnight?"

Almost immediate: "Since I was by myself, I masturbated aggressively."

Her jabs had a way of stunning me, and she knew it. My thumbs hovered over my keypad.

"I hope your dad let you close the door," I typed.

"Obviously joking. Girls don't masturbate. Or take dumps. We're a perfect species."

She'd counterpunch me all day if I kept going, so I let the thread fade out.

I tried Preston: "What's up?"

Yes, even after the push, I still texted Preston. He would always respond, but it would take hours or days between responses, and each conversation died young—if you could even call it a conversation. We just circled the ring, rope-a-doping all the things we needed to talk about to fix what had broken between us—the push, the accident, Lane, Talisha. He would respond with infuriating emoticons, thumbs upping my attempts to repair the damage by reaching out.

I laid on the floor to binge watch a *Twilight Zone* marathon. I couldn't tilt my head to see the TV from my bed, so I laid on the bare carpet, always taking care to piss before I got onto the floor. Getting up wasn't easy. Hell, a turtle was more efficient at rolling over than me.

Right in the middle of a Rod Serling voiceover, Preston finally responded, five hours after my morning text: "Nothing."

Eventually, the casual texts would die. Preston and I grew apart as the expanders grew larger. The expanders in my neck had long surpassed softballs, but I didn't know what object to compare them to—perhaps robust grapefruit? Like, the massive ones that are obviously the result of some genetic food mutation?

They're the size of Lane's breasts.

I haven't heard from you in a while. Nice to see you're still around, you dick. Anyway, cantaloupes. My bubbles are the size of cantaloupes.

I can't believe she was leaving those lovely ladies buried under all those layers. What a shame. I hope she didn't carve those things up like she did her arms.

I bit my own inner cheek to shut me up.

We were slowing down the injections now that the expanders were approaching their maximum capacity. After that, it was a wait of about three weeks for the skin to fully grow and mature over the maxed-out bubbles, and then we could think about harvesting the useful tissue to cover up my scars sometime in the beginning of April.

My final operation would free me of my burns and mark an end to a year-long battle to rid myself of that stupid fucking boy who got me into all this in the first place. I fought him and those burns for the better part of six years, and I was determined to see them surrender first.

Just a couple more months, and I'd never be the same again. I closed my eyes and imagined myself in the hallways again, scar-free, just another high school kid on his way to class, a mundane day that everyone got to experience each and every morning.

Sure, the expanders sucked, the ache was awful, and I looked like a mutant, but it was a small price to pay for the same boring days as everyone else.

I hate to break it to you, but that's not all you've given up for this.

You again. Two times in one day?

You lost two seasons of basketball fucking around with your face. That's got to hurt more than the needles.

Shut up.

Sorry, did I hit a nerve?

I grimaced and struggled, but I got to my feet without incident. The basketball was resting on my desk, the Wilson logo looking at me through its cardboard frame.

I picked it up and tossed it into the upper shelf of my closet, then stacked some sweaters in front of it so I didn't have to see the orange grain peeking out at me every time I got out my morning clothes.

SPIRIT

After the holiday break, the hallways were scrubbed of all signs of Christmas and replaced with ornate pronouncements of school spirit.

First, it was just posters. Hand-drawn poster boards adorned the hallways, with the basketball players' uniform numbers made out of green glitter. The precision crafting was the work of cheerleaders, no doubt.

The pride continued to swell as my tissue expanders got even larger. As we neared the end of January, my bubbles were at seventy-five-percent capacity, the size of those dodgeballs you can easily hold with one hand, the ones that sting.

One morning I showed up and green streamers were taped to players' lockers. Another morning, I saw the cheerleaders had created dangly coils that hung from the drop-ceiling tiles, with player numbers twisting at the bottom.

Signs popped up in yards along my bus route. *Go Fighting Griffins! Herrick Pride!* If a player lived there? He got his own sign with his number and last name on it, as if living there increased the property value.

Soon, the cheerleading squad turned their crafting habit loose on themselves and had their own posters popping up in the gym—names and pictures, bullhorns and pom-poms, and the glitter-encrusted words *Ready! Set! Cheer!*

To top it all off, one morning, I walked into school and saw that the gym doors were completely plastered over with what appeared to be green and gold wrapping paper. The entire team's starting lineup, names, and numbers were hand-cut and glued onto the surface in artfully random ways. Just in case we forgot from all the other shit hanging everywhere else.

Theo's number was one. Of course. Luke's number was ten, kind of perfect, considering his sidekick relationship to Theo. The same number, but different. A tagalong number.

When I was a starter, I was thirty-three. Three was kind of my lucky number. I had no idea why. Maybe because I liked three-pointers and one day dreamed of scoring thirty-three, a goodish number for a high school player. I loved watching old Chicago Bulls videos, and Scottie Pippen was my favorite player—he was the glue guy on that team. The world can have its Michael Jordans—I'll take the underrated players who get the dirty rebounds and play lockdown defense. I even wore a wristband on my forearm like Scottie.

When I played, anyway.

The number thirty-three wasn't on that poster in sloppy, green glitter, and it wouldn't be showing up anytime soon. It all felt like advertisements for something wonderful I could never afford.

However, I finally did find my name in the hallways—that's when all of the blank space that hadn't been filled with basketball propaganda started getting smothered with prom stuff.

More glitter. They must have had a sale on the stuff. *Vote for Lane and Wilder!* Burgundy glitter on the lettering on plain white poster board. We seemed to have an underfunded campaign, while Theo seemed to have a Super PAC behind him. I checked the date—January twentieth—wondering how long our poster would stay up before some joker vandalized the sign with Lane's name on it.

At the end of Mrs. Thoman's class, she handed me a photocopied piece of paper.

"What's this?" I said, scanning the document. Dates. Times. And dear God, even worse than that—a graphic that said "box step" with footprints and arrows mapping out a ballroom dance.

"Don't worry," Mrs. Thoman said, placing her hand on my shoulder with a reassuring absence of pressure, "It's an easy dance."

We'd be practicing prom court in the cafeteria while the basketball team was in the gymnasium on most nights. On the nights closer to the dance, our practices were at 6:30 p.m. so that we could get a more accurate dry run in the gym itself.

Could I haul my bubble-anchored body around a box step waltz? Sure, it looked easy, but a couple weeks from now, at the ceremony, I'd be a sloshing whale with a modified tux. Could they even adjust a tux to fit me, or would I just need a super huge one that went over the expander in my arm? No collar in existence would close around the circumference of my bubbles without belonging to a shirt with so many X's before the L that it was downright pornographic.

Luckily, the dance did look easy and slow. Then it dawned on me that the faculty had conspired to select something slow and easy, something a broken boy like me could tolerate.

I envisioned a practice where some overbearing girl who had attended proms past, a Talisha-clone who was worried about nothing but her own court performance, would look at the dance and lament that this one was just too simple and not decadent enough. She'd wonder what had changed, then figure out that the lack of flourish and elegance was due to my damaged presence.

The bell rang, and I wandered into the hallway in a stupor. Prom didn't feel real until that exact moment.

We're doing this.

This is happening.

I don't mean to freak you out, but this is going to be a disaster.

Please, not now.

It's kind of my job. What kind of inner voice would I be without freaking you out? Look for the poster. That will make you feel better.

Shit. It's gone isn't it?

The gap on the wall still had a stray piece of double-sided tape left behind.

"I took it down," Lane said. I literally jumped, shaking the saline in my bubbles, a feeling that always made me feel like I was about to puke.

"Who needs that shit? Bait for the haters," she said.

"We can't win without campaign advertising," I said.

"The only thing worse than losing is winning," she said. "I swear to God, I'd spike the crown like a football. I've seen *Carrie*. I know a trap when I see one."

"Yet you still want to go?"

"Hello? I didn't want to go in the first place."

"I'm having second thoughts," I said.

"Don't," she said. "Now, I'm looking forward to it. Sort of."

We stared at the single patch of tape as if it were abstract art in a French gallery.

"That sign was low-budget anyway," I said. "What a dirty shade of red. We got the cheap glitter, for sure."

"The color of dried blood," she added.

"Or scar tissue."

"Our first practice is coming up," she said. "Don't go in there without me. Meet me outside the cafeteria. That way we don't have to go in alone."

She caught me touching my expanders. "Will a tux cover this up?" I asked. "How bad is it, really?"

"You're the cutest three-headed monster I've ever seen," she said. "I'd make out with all three of you."

The bell rang before I could respond. "Shit," she said, sprinting for her classroom door, but she still slowed down long enough to look back at me and smile.

Before our first prom practice, I loitered in the hallway near the vending machines, waiting for Lane.

As the students scurried out of school, Lane and a girl I'd never really talked to, Josie Pelker, were having a conversation at her locker.

I saw Preston leaving school, holding hands with Talisha. He glanced up at me and nodded once, jutting his chin out, a nonverbal "what's up." Talisha noticed the exchange and yanked him closer to her.

Preston and I didn't talk in the hallways anymore, unless you counted how he recited versions of "Sup, man," to which I'd respond some flavor of "Nothing much."

After a few weeks, the polite exchanges stopped, devolving into brief eye contact and the occasional nod. Each day, the gap felt wider, and when

I imagined the effort to close that gap, the bones of my mind ached.

As the rest of the students funneled out, I couldn't tolerate just standing in the hallway. You ever just stand somewhere, all alone? You don't know where to put your hands, how to stand, how to look busy. You don't want to seem like you're lame or just spaced out so you start doing something, no matter how mundane. For example, I was checking out the wares of the vending machine, even though I had them memorized.

Lane had lost the denim jacket, but now she wore long-sleeved blouses, sometimes even three-quarter sleeved shirts that ended a few inches above the wrist. In class, I looked at her arms when she rested her chin in her palm. The sleeve fell back even more, revealing the start of the white etchings that ran up to her elbow. I saw no red, no evidence of fresh cuts.

I'm sure people talked about us crushing on each other—that happened for everyone matched up at prom, but my "rescue" of her during the voting process cranked up the whispers. I'm sure Preston loved hearing those rumors.

I didn't feel compelled to go around stomping out rumors, especially when Lane seemed different lately. Her perpetual bedhead evolved into simple ponytails, and I saw more of her face around school, not only because her chaotic hair had been pulled back, but because she was looking at her feet less often.

Here she was, talking to Josie, and they had serious looks on their faces like they were discussing insurance premiums or interest rates. Was Josie making fun of her? Giving her some shit about prom? Making a crack about sleeping pills or hanging out with the walking, talking piece of bubble wrap known as Wilder Tate?

Then, Lane laughed. I heard it all the way down the hall, and it was only then that I realized I'd seen her smile plenty, but I hadn't heard her laugh nearly enough. To see her laughing along with another girl was like taking in some breathtaking scenery for the first time.

Josie was laughing, too. Eventually, they were the only two people in the hallway, and as they broke apart, Josie waved at her on her way out. I didn't know Josie, but I bet she had a responsible yet sporty Chevy Cruz with a list of prospective colleges sitting on her passenger seat to review later with her stable, loving parents.

"Hey, Wilder," Coach Ballard said, startling me. He'd come out of the cafeteria after helping Mrs. Thoman set up the practice.

"Hi, Coach," I said, thinking that would be the end of it. He put his hand on my shoulder.

"You doing okay?" he asked.

"Sure thing," I said. "Couple more months, max." Then, I added, "I'll be good to go junior year. As long as I learn to shoot left-handed, anyway."

"I don't doubt you for a second," he said. "Hey, you think you could peek in on practice tonight? Since you're around and all? The guys would love it."

"I don't know," I said.

"Just for a minute. Get them fired up."

"It's my first prom practice tonight," I said. "Box step. Intense stuff. Maybe some other time?"

"Door's always open," he said. "Maybe save it for a game, stop on in and say a few things to the guys before regionals? When we run into Mater Dei, we'll need all the help we can get."

By this time, Lane was doing her own awkward stall-dance in the hallway, staring into the trophy cases. A cut-down net was draped over a golden bowl—the 1989 regional championship, the last time Herrick won the tournament. Other than that trophy, it was pretty barren. Herrick was small, so the only organized sports were volleyball, basketball, and baseball, and trophies were hard to come by.

"I know about the stuff between you and Theo," Coach Ballard said. "I can safely say if what I heard is accurate, you're right to be upset. But I also know he's a solid kid and more mature this year than last year. He just wanted you on the team. We all did, and we all still do."

"Thanks," I said.

He started to walk away; I was glad it was over without things getting weird, but then he wheeled around and asked me the exact question I was hoping he wouldn't ask.

"Is there a reason you don't come to the games or the practices? Is it still just Theo?"

So right there, I was kind of screwed. At this point, even I could admit I was holding a grudge for an unreasonably long time, and when you drilled down to the molten core of it, it was something else entirely.

"I miss basketball too much," I said, the words coming out of my mouth before I could even think them. "If I watch them play, it'll just make me hurt even worse. I'll regret getting the procedure, and I don't want to do that, because I know how good it'll be for me in the long run."

He nodded, then he glanced over at Lane and said hello, then looked back at me as he headed into the gymnasium to dole out suicide runs and ball-trap drills.

"So?" she said.

"So what?" I said.

"You going to pull off an epic locker-room speech?"

"Maybe," I said. "I was thinking Al Pacino, *Any Given Sunday*. Do that one verbatim."

"Climb out of hell," she said, imitating Pacino—badly at that. "One inch at a time."

I laughed so hard my bubbles ached. "No way," I said, after collecting myself. "There's just no way you've seen *Any Given Sunday*. It's old and it's bad and it's not for girls."

"Umm, excuse me? It's old and it's fucking awesome and it's most definitely not for girls. It's for girls like me."

"Most definitely not for just any normal girl," I said. "Shit. Sorry. I didn't mean it—"

"Don't worry about it," she said. "Normal is just a word that means you're too scared to be anything else."

"I saw you talking to Josie," I said. "You guys friends? I didn't know."

"We're getting there," she said.

"Seeing you laugh . . . I don't mean to sound corny, but I like it. I'm not sure if I've ever seen you laugh like that before."

"That's because your sense of humor is fucking awful," she said and laughed again.

"I can't afford writers," I said, gesturing to the cafeteria doors. "Shall we?"

She took one step then stopped. "Wilder," she said, "does something feel different since we talked in my room that night?"

I swallowed hard. Every smartass comment lurking in my brain scattered for dark corners where I couldn't reach them.

"Yes," I said. "I don't know how, but yes."

"It's the jacket," she said. "Who would have thought? It's definitely the jacket."

She was blushing. I opened the door for her, and we headed to practice together.

PRACTICE

The entire first hour of practice was a Mrs. Thoman filibuster summarizing the importance of precision and timing at prom. She walked out the steps for each member of the court, emphasizing grace, while we were clustered together, listening.

Our prom worked different from the ones I'd seen in the movies. The school was small, so every class could attend, and anyone could win queen or king. The prom committee knew better than to try and book an off-site venue—fundraising in a largely low-income school was a hassle, and the nearest venue worth a damn was probably fifteen miles away, if not more.

Lots of proms are in May, but since ours wasn't senior-focused, we did it in April, when all the athletic seasons were over.

Six couples were on the court, three senior couples and one from each of the other classes. The rehearsal was thin that first night, with a few court members stuck in athletic practice. Theo and Ty were in basketball practice, with Jenna and Avery busy with the cheerleaders, who were doing a dry run of their sets just outside the principal's office with both gyms in use.

Avery was the odds-on favorite to win prom queen. She had no enemies, and every guy drooled over her. The source of her smoldering appeal was her perfect skin. Most girls battled a mountain range of pimples, choking them with flesh-colored makeup, but Avery had no such issues. Her arms were smooth and burnished with sunless tanner. Yeah, she was hot, but her hotness didn't impress me. Hotness wasn't beauty. Too many times, we just admired the lack of damage.

The only other contender was Jenna, another cheerleader, and her chances of victory hinged on the Theo effect, and the senior girls splitting the vote. Theo would undoubtedly be crowned king, and I suspected he'd be working overtime to make sure he had the queen of his choice. Then it would be yet another special thing he'd have given Jenna, and she'd probably thank him with her stunned, wet eyes and the dance and lean in and . . .

I shook my head, trying to physically derail my thoughts.

Mrs. Thoman illustrated the box step dance we'd be doing, slowing down the footwork as she waltzed with Miss Harrington. They were basically stalling for the sports kids to show up before we did anything close to a physical walk-through.

Jenna and Avery turned up first, still wearing sweats from cheerleading practice. Theo and Ty came in soon after, their hair shower-slick and patches of wetness spreading on their polo shirts. I knew that feeling— after practice, you were all hot and sweaty, and then you take a hot shower, and basically for about a half hour after that, you're still soaked, but you can't be sure if it's because you're still sweating or you just didn't get dry enough from the shower. You were in cleanliness limbo until your core temperature finally dropped back to normal.

Mrs. Thoman lined us up for the full walk-through. Kenny Zobrist, a pity nomination from the senior class, was nervously flirting with Kacey Garwood, who was as cute as you might expect from a Kacey-with-a-K. They were gloriously mismatched, with Kenny checking in at an uncoordinated six-foot-six, the tallest guy there, and Kacey being among the shortest. Lonnie Kuntz was the junior king candidate, another tall one but not quite Kenny's stature. I overheard him talking about how *The Walking Dead* was about other, more important things rather than zombies, but never quite drilling down to what those things actually were. He wore a bandanna and a tuxedo T-shirt, which he had purchased and changed into specifically for practice, tearing a page from the "trying-way-too-hard-to-be-funny-and-carefree" playbook.

Jenna, to her credit, listened to every word of Lonnie's *Walking Dead* analysis, and thoughtfully said, "I just can't get through all that grisly stuff to find out what it's really about, but it sounds cool." Peak Jenna.

Daityn Kistner was the freshman nominee, and she had a distinct laugh. I say distinct because I wasn't sure if it was cute, or if it was annoying. You can't really tell with such a small sample size. But she was laughing a lot. I didn't know Austyn Bertrand, her freshman counterpart, all that well, but he had her cracking up with mostly self-deprecating stories, from what I overheard. Those two were absolutely, positively going to date.

Mrs. Thoman cued up the music. Austyn locked arms with Daityn, and they started their walk. Mrs. Thoman admonished them for walking too fast.

Lane and I approached the launch area, a masking tape X along the cafeteria baseline. Once Austyn and Daityn were in place, Mrs. Thoman pointed at us, and we started walking.

"Wait, wait," she said. Miss Harrington cut the music. Mrs. Thoman came up to us, wanting to say something quietly.

"Can you lock arms?" she said, a small whisper. The whole sequence was predicated on the girl being on the right, the boy on the left. "If it's not comfortable, we can switch some things around if we need to," she said.

I shook my head. "It's okay."

She backed away, restarting the music. I stuck my elbow out, and Lane looped her arm through. I had one of those twenty-percent-more-nervous-than-normal moments. The girl who crashed into me with two tons of metal, breaking bones and eventually friendships, was on my arm during prom court practice. I concentrated on moving slowly, and Lane stayed with me, a lockstep pace.

"Looking jacked bro!" Lonnie exclaimed. The bubble on my right arm was positioned perfectly to make my arm look like a Schwarzenegger arm at the pinnacle of flexion. I know he meant it to be lighthearted, but it worked equally well as a sarcastic insult. I gave a thumbs up with my free hand.

We took our taped-off spots at the side of the cafeteria to make room for the next couple's walk.

"Perfect!" Mrs. Thoman clapped as if I were a puppy who finally went a day without pissing on the rug.

We had to wait for five more couples to make the slow walk, and then we'd have to work on addressing the crowd, doing the curtsey-bow combo thing. I relished the break, and it was then that I tried to bring my arm down, but Lane was clutching it, and she put her head on the top of my shoulder, a small oasis of normal terrain on my right side.

"Did you find a dress yet?" I asked.

"I got one from the counselor."

"Mrs. Ventura sells dresses?"

She sighed. "She has boxes of old crap—shirts for girls who are dressed too sexy for the dress code, pants in case someone shits themselves, I guess—and dresses for girls who can't afford them but want to go to the dances."

"That's good, though," I said. "Free is good."

"Free is also as ugly as paper-clip-scarred forearm flesh," she said. "But Mrs. Ventura is going to try to find me some of those long-ass gloves, the kind Aubrey Hepburn wore in *Breakfast at Tiffany's*."

"That is so Mrs. Ventura," I said.

"She's so sweet I think I got two cavities just talking to her," Lane said. "You ever see her office? It looks like a Pier 1 store had a child with an inspirational quote book."

Mrs. Thoman gave us her patented "shut up, I'm talking" glare. We piped down, and Lane leaned on my shoulder again, her arm looped through mine, and I found myself hoping she would stay that way until the end of practice.

She did.

SHOOTAROUND

Mom was parked right outside the main doors, her headlights simmering in the early dark.

She had agreed to give Lane a ride home from practice. When I asked her, she said "fine" in the tone moms reserve for when they know you want to do something stupid and they're powerless to stop you. A "fine" that reserves "I told you so" rights.

As we approached the vehicle, I didn't know how to arrange the seating in a way that was satisfactory to both my mother and Lane. If I sat in the front, I was putting Lane in the back by herself, and not being a gentleman. If both of us sat in the back together, Mom would think we were going out and pepper me with questions after we dropped her off.

The only safe option was to offer Lane the front seat. She said she didn't mind sitting in the back, so I opened the front door for her, straight-up gentleman-like, knowing she wouldn't turn down that invitation.

So the ladies sat up front, and I sat in the back, centered in the middle of the tight rear quarters of Mom's Corolla. During the ride, it was Mom who was being all awkward and non-chatty, which was the exact opposite of what I expected.

The silence was so agonizing that I brought up prom practice, describing the ease of the box step and the chattiness of Mrs. Thoman.

"Practice makes perfect," Mom said, a useless platitude, to no one in particular. We were at Lane's house in five minutes, even with Mom coming to complete stops at the most innocuous intersections, looking both ways with a point-making thoroughness.

When we pulled into Lane's driveway, another situation posed itself— do I get out and walk her to the door, or just say goodbye and get in the front seat?

I opted for the door walk.

"Sorry," I said.

"I wouldn't like me either if I were her," Lane said. "See you tomorrow?"

"Can't." I made a syringe injecting motion with my thumb and fingers against one of my neck bubbles.

"Don't go floating away on me," she said, smiling.

I fake-waltzed my way back to the car, and Lane laughed as she went inside.

"What was all that about?" I said getting in the car. "Talk about weird."

"I think it's nice, you and her," Mom said. "But there's a little more to it than you think."

"Such as?"

"Such as the fact she almost killed my only child?"

"Jesus Mom, don't be like Preston, okay? It was an accident."

"Yes, and as such, there is the matter of your medical bills and insurance. There are lawyers, and her father's insurance is fighting tooth and nail, and the fact that Preston didn't slow down much to avoid the accident doesn't help matters."

"I don't want to get involved in all that."

"You're not out of the woods just because you did your deposition," she said. "This goes to a trial and you may have to sit in front of lawyers, and maybe in front of an entire court, and talk about how the girl you have a crush on almost killed you and your friend."

"I can't even dissect all the things wrong with that sentence," I said. "Can't a guy just be nice to someone?"

"Of course," Mom said. "If it's not a crush, fine. I'm not accusing you. In fact, don't go working overtime to make it into one."

"Just don't make this weirder than it has to be," I said.

"If there's one thing I want, it's normal. Trust me," she said, backtracking the moment the words left her mouth.

"I'm sorry," she said. "Let's just forget about it, okay? How was school?"

School was a distant memory, but practice was intense, forcing me into a social crucible where I had no choice but to do rehearsed things in front of people.

And of course, Lane—I liked that she liked me, but I was so desire-starved I didn't know if I was making more out if it than actually existed. All the mess-ups and miscalculations and embarrassments with Jenna were fueling flames of utter terror. Did I like her as much as I did Jenna? Maybe I never did like Jenna and I just responded to my first dose of attention with an overreaction? Was I drawn to Lane because it would piss off Preston and Talisha? Was there more to this than I'd even admitted to myself?

It was a complicated equation, like the ones on Mr. Watkins's massive algebra whiteboard, and I wouldn't have a clear solution unless I worked that thing for days. My best option was to just go to bed and try to forget about it, but no boy in the history of the world had an easy time forgetting about any girls, let alone a girl who put her head on his shoulder for all of the prom court to see.

"Earth to Wilder?" Mom said.

"Sorry," I said. "What did you ask me again?"

"Oh dear," she said, half joking, and from then on I don't think I could tell her I didn't have a crush on Lane without her knowing I was totally full of shit.

———

I tried to get to bed early and kept thinking of Lane's head on my shoulder, her ponytail draped over my arm. I couldn't sleep. Once I gave up trying, I thought about my new basketball.

A new basketball was something you couldn't help but love, the pristine surface, the way the tackiness was still alive, forming a perfect bond with your hands.

Not the time for a new ball. Not yet. My Christmas-gifted ball remained buried in the closet.

I dug around in the laundry room closet for one of my old balls—a cheap, rubbery basketball with the nubs worn off from use.

I sat on the bed, holding it, shifting it into a shooting position.

With the ball slotted and ready to release, my missing half-finger wasn't much of an issue. In fact, it felt like I cradled the ball better, so I felt it more prominently on my remaining fingertips.

Some people said I shot a knuckleball, but that wasn't the case. Most shooters lined up so that their middle finger was somewhere close to the inflation hole, the grooves on the ball perpendicular to the crest of their fingers. The release turned the ball into an orange blur, the tried and true way that a ball was supposed to rotate.

I didn't shoot that way. Instead, I always instinctively put my shooting hand where all the rubber grooves met in a confluence, giving it a decidedly discordant look when it was spinning in the air. The ugliness of my shot was just an optical illusion.

Now, with half of that middle finger missing, it looked as though a black seam of the ball were coming out of my stumpy knuckle.

I shifted the ball into my left hand and cocked it into a shooting position. This would be starting from scratch, throwing away the tens of thousands of practice shots I'd launched with my previously complete right hand. No way I'd be any good from three-point range left-handed. Not only that, I'd be even more of a liability from the free throw line.

I don't know. You shoot pretty shitty from the line right-handed.

My asshole inner voice had a point, but there was only one way to find out.

I tucked the ball under my arm and went out to the basketball hoop. The first time I tried to dribble with my right hand, a familiar, fried-testicle ache exploded in my tissue expander, but my hand held up, giving me enough control and feel to cross over to a left-handed dribble.

The pain calmed down, and then I ventured a shot with my right hand, a baby jumper from about five feet away. Raising my right arm felt awkward, but I always kind of shot from the hip anyway. Without my middle finger to guide the spin, I pushed the ball off-target, barely grazing the rim as it went wide of the goal.

I picked up the ball and shot it again, this time left-handed. Airball.

Within minutes, I was sweating, and hadn't made a shot. I hadn't even decided if I was going to re-learn a right-handed shot, where my missing finger would make most of my shots drift off-target, or left-handed, where I needed a thousand reps just to get the depth and feel I needed to put the ball on plane.

I alternated between the options. When I finally drilled a lefty shot from the top of the key, my expanders were raging and sore, but man, how I missed that addictive, satisfying feeling of seeing a ball fall through the net.

The cold turned my breath into misty chuffs. The street light at the corner struggled against the shadows. On missed shots, I'd lose sight of the ball completely as it rolled into the darkness.

I found it again and again and kept shooting, staying lefty. My shot refused to adjust to my broken body. I made one out of every ten, and that's being generous. Not my typical success rate, but enough for me to fantasize again, whispering to myself how many seconds were left, counting back, letting the shots fly.

In those fantasies, I was typically a Bulls shooting guard drilling a game-winning three-pointer over LeBron James.

But on that night, my first time touching a ball for the better part of a year, I was stepping back on Robbie Imming and winning us the regional championship.

Once I was too tired to keep chasing the ball after misses, I practiced free throws. Left-handed, right-handed, it didn't matter—I was atrocious from either side. One miss planted hard off the back of the rim and came right back into my hands, a joyous little moment where you don't have to move to fetch the ball.

"If only free throws were truly free." Lane's voice. She was standing in the pocket of light provided by my corner streetlight. I thought I was hallucinating.

"Lane?"

"You're not supposed to be awake," she said. "And you're sure as hell not supposed to be outside shooting baskets."

She had a manila envelope in her hand.

"What's that?"

"Something I found for you," she said. "That's a cool basket, by the way. I've never seen one built by hand before."

"My dad made it when I was little," I said. "When we moved, I didn't want a new basketball goal, so we just put it on a new pole. Pretty sure the height is off."

"Pretty sure your shot is off," she said and punched my shoulder.

"So, what's in the envelope?"

"Please don't read this until I'm gone," she said, ignoring my question. "God, I'd die. Just promise me you'll wait until tomorrow?"

I took the envelope.

"You were going to leave this for me to find in the morning?"

"Great deduction, Sherlock," she said.

I pinched the clasp.

"Don't!" she said.

"Just kidding," I said.

"I guess I'll get going," she said.

"You walked?"

"Yup."

"Like three miles?"

"It's a decent night for a long walk," she answered. She picked up the basketball.

"Where's the free throw line?"

I pointed to a dent I'd made in the mud with my heel. She placed to toe of her shoe against it and dribbled the ball against the toughened ground.

"Let my mom drive you home."

"Pass," she said, dribbling the ball again.

"Let me rephrase that," I said. "Let me steal my mom's car and take you home."

"I don't want to get you in trouble."

"Tell you what," I said. "You make the shot, you get home however you want. You miss it, I take you home."

She winked at me then slammed the ball into the ground with two hands. She held it between her legs, standing upright, then softened her knees and flicked it at the goal underhanded.

The granny shot hit the front of the rim, then the back, then settled the side of the goal, teetering for a half-second before it fell through the net.

"Do you even know when you're getting hustled?" she said.

"Granny shots don't count," I said.

"What do you have against grannies?"

"Shaq once said that he'd rather shoot zero percent from the line than toss up a granny shot in a live game," I said.

"And what do you say?"

"I embarrass myself plenty from the line without shooting like a girl," I said.

"I think I want you to drive me home," she said. "But ask your mom for the keys. Don't get in trouble."

"What if she says no?"

"Tell her it was shooter's choice, and she shouldn't make her son into a welsher," she said.

———

My right arm was wound tight from the expanders, so I drove slow, putting most of the steering wheel's pressure in the palm of my left hand.

Thankfully, the road to Lane's house was mostly blacktop that only saw local traffic, flanked by farm fields and the occasional country house.

"So that thing I gave you, just really read it, okay? Read it close."

"Is it a letter?"

"Just read it close."

"Okay," I said then stopped talking. The silence gained momentum and weirdness, so I reached for the radio, a move that occurred in slow motion since I had to lean my whole expanded-ass body to get my outstretched hand that far.

Lane intercepted my hand, and for a moment, I thought she was going to hold it, that our fingers would interlock on the shifter and we'd get to her house in a melty, gooey state of Wondering What It All Meant. Instead, she just laid my hand on my thigh, not wanting the radio turned on.

"I'm pretty sure the envelope thing could be taken to mean that I like you," she said.

I didn't know what to say. I was convinced that *like* was a Rubik's cube of meaning that drove dudes insane. I didn't want to go into a thesis on how I hated the word *like* and how Jenna once told me she liked me.

"I guess that also means you're leaving open the possibility you don't like me?"

"I suppose," she said. "If you're a moron you could definitely reach that conclusion."

I knew we'd arrived at the part where I needed to volunteer just what level of like I harbored for Lane. So many to choose from, sort of like, kind of like, like you *but*, like you as a friend, like you too much, and I just said, "I suppose I'm not a moron."

"I suppose you are," she said. "Jesus. It's your turn. Say something about me. Something nice, preferably."

"I think you're cool and you're brave," I said.

"I tried to kill myself," she said. "That's the opposite of brave."

"But here you are," I said.

"Here I am," she said. More silence.

"I've heard every version of who you are and why you took the pills," I said. "Every version but yours."

"Jesus. Why can't you be like other guys? You could be saying you like me and pulling over in a cornfield, and we could just make out for an hour."

My face turned red enough to damn near glow in the dark.

"I'm joking, Wilder," she said. "Take a breath."

We were at the intersection where the blacktop ended. A right turn, and we'd be at her house within two minutes. She waited. I went straight, and she understood. I was giving her time.

"My uncle," she started, and then she stopped. She looked out the window, and I gave her time but heard her whimper, and only then did I know she was trying not to cry.

I pulled over by a cornfield and put the car in park. I made a fist and felt the absence of my middle finger. I reached over with my left hand to hold hers, but she pushed it away and interlocked her fingers into my injured hand instead.

"My uncle Carl abused me for a long time," she said. "I'll spare you the details, but he didn't hit me, so you know what kind of abuse I'm talking about. Jesus, I was five, six years old. I told my mom in the only ways I knew how to tell her. She didn't believe me; Carl was the golden child of her side of the family, and she adored him. He sold insurance, had a country club membership, the works—and helped us out when times were tough. Then, in sixth grade, my dad caught it happening. He spent a year in jail for how bad he hurt my uncle, my uncle did his time, and my mother struggled with the fact that she let it happen."

She sleeved away her tears and took a deep breath.

"You really need to hear more?"

"If it helps you to say it, to tell someone, I need to hear it."

"You shouldn't care. Not if you don't like me."

"I like you, Lane," I said. "I do. But like's a funny word, and I'm a twisted-up dude so I don't know if that means what you want it to mean."

Now she looked at me instead of the window. To look her in the eyes was rare, and to look anyone in the eyes for more than a few seconds was an experience neither one of us was comfortable or familiar with, but I think she needed eye contact to talk, and I needed it to see the pain she couldn't get across with words because she kept it fast and clipped, to get it out, wanting to shoo it away like some wild animal rattling around in her mind.

"My dad didn't forgive her, and they got divorced. She dipped into a dangerous place. I chose to live with my dad, but Mom lived across town in one of the old Hollenkamp apartments, and I went there to drop off some mail that came to our house for her. I had a key and went inside, and she had just hanged herself, and fucked that up like everything else in her life. Her feet were kicking, and she was struggling against the rope and twitching and instead of helping her right away I went to the kitchen counter and put her mail down and heard her choking. I wanted her to die for what happened but I didn't want her to die because she's my mom, so I grabbed her legs and held her up and screamed for help and in between screams she just kept saying, 'Let me go, I don't deserve you. Let me go. Let me go,' but I didn't let her go."

I squeezed Lane's hand.

"Now she's in a home and has a blend of brain damage and mental illness, and every day I think about that moment, about her brain cells dying while I put down her mail, about letting her go or not letting her go. I think about it until it feels like I don't even deserve my own existence."

I don't know if I breathed once while she talked, and when I swallowed, my mouth felt like it was full of sawdust.

"So I took the fucking pills," she said. "And then it was my father's turn to find someone dying. He didn't let me go."

"I'm glad," I said.

"I am, too," she said. "At least half the time."

We sat along the side of the road and held hands, hoping for the echoes of the past to fade, but echoes like that never do, no matter how long you wait.

"We should go," I said.

"Wait," she said, and her hand moved to my waist, tugging at my shirt, then moving to lift it.

I snatched her wrist, clutching it harder than I meant to, but she made no move to dislodge it.

"You can show me," she said.

I just shook my head and pushed her hand away. I tried to say "I can't," but my lungs were robbed of breath. The air felt thin, and black dots sprouted in my vision.

"Breathe," she said, and now her hand was on my thigh. "Breathe, Wilder. It's just me. You don't have to panic."

I collected myself and put my hands on the steering wheel. When my vision returned, I looked at her and said, "I can't. Not now."

"I told you everything," she said. "Showed you everything. If not now, when?"

"I'm not ready," I said.

She looked out the window again.

"Take me home," she said.

As I drove her home, she leaned against the window, her breath forming a patch of condensation on the glass. Her ponytail danced with each bump in the road. I already missed the feel of her hand on mine.

She left the car without saying goodbye.

ENVELOPE

Mom woke me up before dawn so I could get ready for my 9:00 a.m. hospital visit, a regularly scheduled inspection-and-injection. I wanted to stay on afternoons only, but taking a few morning appointments was the only way to stay on schedule.

I took some Aleve before we left to help with the pain and knocked back an impressive amount of scrambled eggs with hot sauce.

"How's the new basketball?" Mom said.

"I used an old one," I answered, shoveling a Tabasco-covered curd into my mouth. I waited for her to admonish me for exerting myself beyond the doctor-appropriated guidelines.

"Don't overexert yourself," she said. Thankfully, she didn't press it any further.

When we got into the car, I finally opened Lane's envelope. "Wilder" was on the front of it, in big, Sharpie-fied letters.

Inside, I found a newspaper clipping. Nothing else. No notes or context.

When I say newspaper clipping, I don't mean from an actual newspaper, either. She printed it out online. The *New York Times* headline was in bold: Black Holes Collide, Confirming Einstein's Theory.

"What's that?" Mom asked.

"Science experiment notes," I said.

A team of scientists announced on Thursday that they had heard and recorded the sound of two black holes colliding a billion light-years away, a fleeting chirp that finally confirmed Einstein's general theory of relativity.

I sifted through six pages of quotes from physicists and the journalist's attempt to simplify what they were talking about. I still had to read it twice before I even came close to grasping the concept.

One of the passages was highlighted by hand:

The collision created gravitational waves that are 50 times stronger than the output of all the stars in the universe combined. The bottomless gravitational pits from which not even light can escape, perhaps the most foreboding force in the universe, can combine to bend time and space itself, according to physicists.

Later, more highlights from Lane:

"The most unique and exotic things in the universe are indeed the most powerful: black holes, neutron stars, and the like. The early universe is waving hello," said Dr. Turner.

The last page of the packet was blank. The first time through, I thought it was just a blank page accidentally stapled onto the article. Printing from the internet is a fickle task.

After re-reading it, I noticed the blank page still had a footer, the URL from a Google Maps printout, and at the top, a clipped-off image of a map.

"Did Lane give you that?"

"Yeah," I said, and nothing else, figuring that would sufficiently end it. But no, she took her verbal shovel to the conversation one more time.

"Why? Is it really a homework assignment together, or something else?"

"Something else," I said. "I don't know what. Don't ask, okay?"

"Whatever you say, cranky-pants."

"It looks like I've got two grotesque planets orbiting around my head. I have a right to be cranky."

She gave me a pointed look and turned up the radio.

I wanted those expanders, so no, I didn't have a right to be cranky. The purple-hued spheres of flesh didn't happen by accident like all the rest of my scars and broken bones. I chose this and sometimes pretended like it was just another thing thrust upon me against my will, but I'd choose the expanders again, if given the chance. Losing the scars was worth it. I'd have plenty of basketball games to enjoy, all without the road crowd wondering what happened to the shooting guard's face and arm. I also owed this surgery to anyone who cared about me, now and in the future. A normal face would unburden my mother, and ensure any future girlfriend or wife was choosing me for who I was and not what happened to me.

I'd normally undercut your good vibes here and point out that you'll probably die alone, but I'm warming up to the idea of looking fresh-faced and getting a honey in our lives.

You're certainly chipper today.

You do realize this is a love letter, right? It's lame as hell, but still.

That didn't last long.

Neither will you when Lane—

Okay, that's enough. We're done here.

To pass the time, I pulled out the article again, plugging the long, messy URL of the Google Maps printout into the prehistoric browser of my Walmart phone. If Lane was planning on taking me somewhere after prom, as part of our denim-for-trip promise, perhaps this was a spoiler, but I wanted to know.

The location popped up. I stared at it, my whole body turning rigid.

"Wilder?" Mom said, turning down the radio. "You okay?"

I nodded. Barely.

"You turned pale so fast I could almost hear it."

"I'm fine," I said.

A part near the end of the black hole article mentioned a "ring down," where the combined mass of the two black holes colliding created a stronger black hole that was sixty-two times bigger than the mass of the sun.

Lane highlighted this passage. She thought magnified power was noble, as if it represented love itself. Yet the collision left a crater in the universe with waves that could shake down time and erase whole worlds from existence, as if all the light it ever touched never even existed at all.

PART THREE
WAVES

DISTANCE

Over the next few weeks, the prom practices became mind-numbing and redundant. I could do any part of the court, girl or boy, and I could do it moonwalking while blindfolded. We were less than a month away from the dance, going through one of the tiresome practices that were all about socializing now.

As predicted, Daityn and Austyn became a thing, Lonnie's act got stale enough for him to be just about as quiet as I was, and it was becoming clear to Avery that Jenna was a real contender. Everyone took a few turns learning the king and queen part of the court so that any one of us would be prepared after the winners were announced.

So far, I'd had one rehearsal as king, but the seniors got most of the practice. Theo took so many rehearsals at the king spot his election felt like a foregone conclusion. The other senior boys made it a point to joke about their looming defeat in a self-deprecating way, presumably to lessen the blow to their egos when they lost.

I never once mentioned to Lane that I read the contents of her envelope. I couldn't even think of that black hole article without getting upset, all because of the blank page she'd mistakenly left stapled onto the back of the package.

Lane was on my arm for most of the practices, as usual, but since the envelope, and my total lack of response to it, she'd dropped some of the more gushy elements, like putting her head on my shoulder. I sensed a change in her touch—not a coolness, just a layer of insulation that was safer for both of us.

Whatever gap she'd opened up between us, she had closed with other students. She walked with her head up in the hallways, and I caught her smiling a lot more than usual. She ate her lunches in the cafeteria now, mostly with Daityn, who had become one of her most trusted friends. Twyla and Josie ate with them a lot. The targeting reticle of high school assholes migrated to other people with more current mishaps to mock, like everyone talking about Marya Klostermann's belly. The joke was, "Too many Doritos or too many dicks?" The consensus was that she had a real shot of getting onto Maury Povich to sort out which upperclassman got the honors.

So while Lane and I faded from the current events of the school, we faded from each other. At lunchtime, instead of waiting for Lane in the library, I just chugged my Coke and took my lunch chips in two handfuls so I could escape to the gym before anyone came in and saw me.

Neither of us talked about the tension. Texts stayed flirty but only skimmed the surface. We smiled at each other but talked a lot less.

I knew she was mad at me for not showing her my scars after she told me about the shadows of her past, just as much as she was pissed about my non-reaction to her envelope gesture. What she didn't know is that I was livid with her because I figured out where she was planning on taking me after prom.

The Google Maps link she accidentally left in her black hole printout dropped on the address of the federal prison where Randy Meadows was serving a felony stretch for armed robbery.

She had the audacity to think a face-to-face with Randy could heal me when all that would do is freshen the wounds I'd worked so hard to close up. I just couldn't allow her to do that to me.

That night at prom practice, everyone seemed tired, probably just sick of doing the same walk, the same dance steps, hearing the same song over and over again. Even I was ready for prom to arrive, if only to put an end to the constant box step flashbacks I was getting while I tried to fall asleep.

Lane went for my hand, interlocking her fingers into mine. I allowed it for about five seconds, then pulled it away, faking an itch around the tissue expander in my face. Scratching with a non-existent finger looks obviously fake, so I switched tactics and tried to keep my right hand busy until we walked our rehearsal rounds. When we walked, she went to her old bag of tricks and laid her head on my shoulder when we settled into our positions.

"My shoulder hurts today," I said. "The expanders are almost full, and my arm is killing me. Can you let up?"

She obeyed.

When practice was about to wrap up, we filtered into the hallway. Mom was parked outside to drive us home.

"Hey, before we get to the car," Lane said, gently grabbing my arm, "can we talk a second?"

Everyone else filed out, while we hung back by the vending machines.

"Sure," I said.

"Did I do something?" she asked.

"I don't understand."

"Let's not play this game," she said. "I put myself on the line when I told you about my mom. You know all my secrets, so I just wanted to know all of yours. You recoiled in the car, and I get that. So I gave you space. But you're still recoiling. Why?"

"I haven't recoiled," I said. "Honest. I don't know what you're talking about."

"If that's true," she said, "then go on a date with me."

"A date?" I said. She'd cornered me. Either something was wrong and we needed to talk about it, or I could keep up the lie that everything was cool and go on a date with her.

"A real one. Pick me up. We'll go to the mall, watch a movie, share a bucket of popcorn. There's a great arcade. I'll kill you at air hockey because you're a gentleman and will let me win, and at the end of the night, we'll get near my house, and I'll tell you I don't have to be home for another twenty minutes and ask you to take us to the city park. I'll spare you the trouble once we're there. I'll make the first move, okay? I'll lean in and just kiss the nervousness right out of you, then you drop me off, and the next day you send me a text telling me you had a great time and you can't wait to do it again."

This was like the Jenna thing, right down to the air hockey, only it was somehow the exact opposite of that.

"I can't," I said, adding in the horrific cliché, "I'm only saying no for your own good."

The burned kid had done the rejecting for once, and she tried to hide how solidly that punch had landed, and something about doing the rejecting zapped me with a sort of buzz, a runner's high.

"You're saying no because you're scared," she said.

"Stop trying to convince me I'm scared," I said. "I'm just not worth the trouble, okay?"

"You will never be worth the trouble until you think you are. You look the way you look, and no amount of bubbles or surgeries will ever remove every trace of what happened."

"So maybe confronting Randy Meadows will help?" I said.

Lane scrunched her face, processing how I could have found out about her horrifically miscalculated gesture.

"You don't know shit," I continued. "You probably rehearse these little speeches a thousand times, and now I'm sitting here getting mortared. Total surprise attack. I couldn't even kiss you at the end of your stupid fantasy date. I don't think my face can get physically close enough to yours for our lips to actually touch with these things in my neck. It's the reverse of destiny."

Which was stupid—there was no reverse of destiny; it just was what it was.

"Try to kiss me, then," she said, and the sadness and confusion were gone. She tried to cut through all of it with her eyes, and every syllable rode a wave of genuine kindness.

I thought about it, I truly did, and maybe it was then that I knew I was wrong to be mad.

But then I saw prison glass and a phone, and a skinny man with a face that I hadn't seen in years picking it up, smiling at the visage of what I did to myself.

I stood pat. "I've given up too much to get past that day. You want to put me back to square one? To hurt me like that, all while you sit here and ask me to kiss you?"

Lane's trademark steel returned. Tears gathered in her eyes, but anger burned them away. None fell.

"You're a coward," she said. "Maybe you're right. Maybe I am dodging a bullet getting tangled up with you." She looked down at the tile, not wanting me to see her face. "I thought we were helping each other."

Now she was taking over the reins of rejection, and it stung. "We did help each other," I said. Heat roiled in my guts, begging for the cooling salve of retaliation. "I forgave you for the accident, and you made me feel normal, but not in that love story, inspiring kind of way. I'm screwed up, but I don't hold a candle to you. I was like a fat kid standing next to a fatter kid to look just a little more skinny."

She turned away before I could measure the damage. She caught up to Mrs. Thoman at the end of the hallway, who hugged her and glared at me so hard I felt a buzz in my ears. I retreated into the restroom and ran the faucet but never once acted on the stream of water. I just stooped over the sink and collected myself.

I went outside. My mother's Corolla idled by the curb, the last car standing except for Mrs. Thoman's van. Lane was in the front seat of the van, waiting for Mrs. Thoman to finish locking up the gym.

I slipped into Mom's car, trying not to catch Lane's gaze through the window.

"What happened, honey?" Mom asked. "Lane got in Mrs. Thoman's van. She's not riding?"

"I don't want to talk about it."

My mother leaned over and gave me a hug, careful not to squeeze too tight and hurt me. The bubbles were more tender than ever with less than two months to go before I could finally get them out. Then I could put the burns and Randy Meadows behind me once and for all, and on my own terms.

SOLO

The next day was an inflation day, so I didn't have to deal with school. I deserved the needles that day instead of pencils and whiteboards. I wanted the pain and the ache instead of the ring of bells and clang of lockers.

I slept on the way home, and Mom already had a meatloaf in the slow cooker, which tasted like equal parts rubber and tomato paste.

"I don't have to work tonight," she said. "Would you like to do something? Maybe go to the movies?"

The truth was, I did want to go to the movies—the latest superhero clash was screening for special Thursday night show times. I honestly wished I could just watch the thing at home where I could pause it to take a piss and refill my snacks and didn't have to worry about anyone recognizing me in the theater sitting with my mom.

"Maybe I can just borrow the car?" I said. I wanted to see Batman clashing with another impossible threat, but another part of me saw it as a fitting punishment to go through with the date that Lane had requested of me all by myself.

Mom agreed to let me go, and I could tell she was disappointed in that way moms are disappointed when their kids start to outgrow them.

At the theater, I sat in the parking lot listening to the radio while the showtime got closer. I was pathetically early. I had purchased my ticket online, so I didn't have to go through the box office line and ask a bored college student for a single ticket, which only rivaled asking for a table for one at a restaurant on the public-sadness scale.

I wore a heavier coat than the weather called for, hoping to pad my bubbles, and headed right for the ticket kiosk, printed my ticket, and snuck to the back row of the movie theater without being recognized.

Cheesy movie advertisements ran on a loop until I had them memorized. The theater filled to capacity. A dad and two sons sat next to me, with the youngest in the seat next to mine. A perfect draw—as he was so small, he didn't use the armrest, and as the previews rolled, I almost forgot he was sitting there until the straw in his Coke cup smacked against the empty bottom. The dad went for refills, annoyed, as the lights went another shade of glorious dark and the movie started.

In the movies, rich and beautiful people struggle, fail, and lose, over and over again, until they finally transform from what they are into what they must become, all within a couple of tidy hours. I was going on a year of torture. The end was closer than ever, my own, earned transformation waiting at the end of a scalpel. So I couldn't even follow the movie. I was the hero—a perfect face, a square jaw, and some ridiculously masculine stubble. A man Jenna would find irresistible. The kind of man that would make Lane eat her words, sorry that she ever doubted me, ashamed that she ever considered that she of all people would know what's best for me.

I spent two hours of running time with the handsome and heroic Wilder Tate, moving beyond the halls of Herrick Community High School and into the world, where my only burden was the cost of my secret heroics. I saved Jenna from street thugs. I rescued Lane from a pack of relentless bullies who threatened her physically. Preston and Talisha got mugged, and while Preston was powerless on his cane to fight back, I stepped in to save them, all despite the friction of our past. I was enlightened now, cleansed of scars, prepared to share the wisdom and bravery that is only earned through sacrifice and pain.

My own fantasy trumped the spell of the movie until the credits rolled. Only half the audience left, the other half waiting for a few more crumbs of movie after the credits were done. I waited for the lingering crowd to leave, hoping to be among the last people out of the theater to avoid the crowd. By the time I stood, the crew was already sweeping up popcorn and picking up trash. The lights came on, making my eyes ache.

"Have a nice night," a gum-chewing girl my age said, never looking at me. Perfect.

When I got into the lobby, the noise and light overwhelmed me. Massive lines were stacked up for the primetime show times. I pulled up my hood and started making my way to the door when I heard the plinking sound of an air hockey game.

I stopped. Could I really leave without looking? Just one loop through the arcade, where kids were pounding the joysticks on the classic *Streetfighter II* game and steering the wheels in the *Fast and Furious* gaming chamber. Still others shot baskets at a moving hoop or racked shotguns in the newest zombie-killing game. No one would notice.

When I peeked around the corner at the air hockey table, it was just competitive teenage guys bashing the absolute piss out of the yellow puck. They popped the disc off the table more than they scored goals.

Did I actually expect Lane to be there with another guy? Perhaps I even wanted her to be with another guy—at least then I'd know her pain wasn't real, and neither was anything she felt for me. Her hurt would have been fake and not my fault.

Jenna was another air hockey enthusiast, and I wouldn't have minded at least seeing her playing a game, smiling, pushing a stray strand of red hair behind her ear just before putting the disc in play. I let my movie fantasy get the best of me, letting the allure of seeing a beautiful girl bring me into a crowded arcade, where no hoodie in the world could cover my lumpiness.

"Wilder?"

The voice was muffled through my drawn-up hood, but when I turned, I saw a cane leaning against the *Teenage Mutant Ninja Turtles* game, where Preston was letting Leonardo get beaten by masked ninjas as he looked at me with the same stunned demeanor as a bystander seeing my blue-hued bubbles for the first time.

"What are you doing here?" Preston asked.

A stupid question just about any other time, but I wasn't the type to go out and see a movie, let alone go out and see one by myself, let alone go to the jam-packed arcade where the flashing lights spotlighted my peculiar shape.

Preston knew all of this because he knew me, and he knew me because he was my friend.

Whose fault was it that we weren't close anymore? I couldn't answer the question honestly. My shrugs could pass a lie detector test. It's not as simple as "his fault, he pushed me" or "Talisha is horrible." If that were the truth, was our friendship that weak all along?

"How's the ankle coming along?" I asked. By now, he didn't even need the cane to walk on most days. I saw him in the hallways without it, but his gait was off thanks to his weakened right leg. Yet he still took the cane everywhere, a crutch in more ways than one.

"Firming up," he said. "I think I may be all the way done with physical therapy from the bone graft by summer. What about your hand? You shoot a ball with that puppy yet?"

I held it up, making no effort to conceal the stump, deciding whether or not I should lie to him. Finally, I shook my head.

"Bullshit," he said. He smirked, and an ease we hadn't felt with each other in a long time finally returned.

"A little," I said.

"Not nearly enough," he answered.

We stood there, neither one of us sure what to say next. I took the leap. "Good to see you. Catch you around school."

"Wait," he said. "You seeing the new Batman movie?"

"Already saw it," I said.

"You want to see it again?"

"Isn't Talisha here?" I asked.

He nodded. "She's on the phone," he said. "Like always. Pacing the lobby like she's a stockbroker or some shit. We're going to miss half the movie if I have to wait for her to get off the stupid phone."

"I don't think she'd like me being a third wheel."

"She'd be the third wheel," he said. "Believe me on that one. Me and her being a thing ain't gonna be a thing much longer." He shook his head, knowing he was saying too much, saying it anyway, driving a nail into the coffin he'd assembled for their relationship over the course of the past few days. Hell, maybe the past few weeks. I couldn't know for sure.

"Sorry to hear that."

"The hell you are," he said, smiling. "Look, you were right about her, okay? She's not that nice. Like, at all. Except for whoever she's talking to on the phone."

"She is hot, though," I said, smirking, needing this conversation in the absolute worst of ways.

"Yeah, well, you show me a hot chick, and I'll show you a guy who's sick of putting up with her shit," he said. "But keep this on the down-low, okay?"

"Who the hell am I going to tell?"

"Just don't say anything. I may wait until after prom."

"Why?"

He shrugged, a meek little gesture that made me feel genuinely sorry for him. "I guess I don't want to not have a date at the prom dance."

"I don't have a date," I said.

"I didn't mean it like that," he said. "Besides, you got Lane."

"I don't have a date," I repeated, and he got the point.

"I'm sorry," he said.

"It's not like we broke up or anything," I said. "There wasn't anything to break up in the first place."

"Bones and dreams, man," he said. "That's all we break, you and me."

"Yeah man," I said. "Enjoy the movie. Batman dies at the end."

"Fucker," he said, laughing.

I started making my way out of the arcade, this time walking right by the air hockey table, brushing my fingers against the side bumper. The two players were too locked in to even notice.

"Holy shit, dude," a new voice said, not Preston's. "Wait up. Tate, right? Wilding Tate?"

I turned around, still buried in my hood, my hands in my pockets. I'd never seen the guy before in my life, but he was tall—every bit of six-eight.

"You're really you," he said. "By that I mean you're really real. Robbie, get a load of this!"

A couple guys were pounding the sticks on *Mortal Kombat* and joined their lanky friend. The shortest of them, I did recognize—Robbie Imming, Mater Dei's star shooting guard.

"This is that Wilding Tate," the tall kid said.

"Wilder," I corrected.

"That's even dumber," a third kid said, this one hovering behind Robbie. His face was a mask of acne, and he had red hair buzzed down to his pale scalp.

"Easy now," Robbie said. "Just chill. What's up, man? Robbie Imming. I heard about you."

He held out his hand. I shook it, and he leaned down, peering into my hood, not able to get a good look at my face.

"Can you take that hood down, maybe?" he said. "I heard about what happened. I don't want to upset you or anything, but I just want to see if what people say is true."

"What do people say?" I asked, knowing I was basically giving him permission to say whatever heinous thing he wanted to say about me. He didn't take the bait.

"Some not-nice things," he said. "But you look pretty normal to me."

"You shittin' me? Looks like he's wearing a midget as a necklace," zit-face said.

"How about you guys just fuck off, okay?" I said, turning away. A hand landed on my shoulder, stopping me cold. It was the tall kid, and he was strong.

"My friends might be assholes, but I'm being nice here," Robbie said. "I just want to see if you're for real; is that too much to ask?"

"Yeah, it is."

The tall kid yanked my hood down so hard that I heard some of the threading in the neck of the hoodie stretch and pop. The front of the zipped-up sweatshirt snapped hard against the expanders in my neck. A nebula of pain erupted, riding my nerve endings up into my temples. I groaned.

"Holy shit!" Robbie squealed. "Sounds like Frankenstein, looks like Igor."

By now, other kids were watching. I backed away, trying to put the hood back up as some laughed and others urged them to leave me alone.

I was surrounded by a blend of the two kinds of people I hated the most—those making fun of me and those who felt sorry for me. For too long, I'd invested equal amounts of wrath into each group, and for the first time that balance felt wrong.

I backed away, struggling with my hood, hearing Robbie say, "This is Herrick's secret weapon? He can't even put his fucking hood up!"

Robbie and his crew laughed, none harder than the tall kid—until a familiar cane cracked against the back of his head.

"Leave him alone!" Preston screamed as the tall kid stumbled forward, clutching the back of his skull. His hand came away bloody. Preston shoved the zit-faced kid, who was twice as thick as Preston was, and far stronger. He absorbed Preston's energy and then returned fire, pushing Preston away.

Preston backpedaled, struggling to keep his feet, but lost the battle. He fell, and his back smashed into the edge of the air hockey table.

The cry that came out of his mouth was a guttural riptide. I dropped to my knees. I knew that cry and the pain that came with it, and as Robbie and his crew scattered, I tried to comfort my friend.

Dozens of people were leaning in, asking if he was okay. "Back up!" I screamed at everyone, and being the Igor-looking motherfucker that I was, they listened.

"I'm okay," he said. I didn't believe him. We were never okay. We only broke two things—bones and dreams.

"Stupid fucking ankle," he said, his words riding on a weak, whine of a breath. "Help me up."

PROMISES

Once Preston got his cane firmly underneath him, I checked his back. A red crease ran across his spine where he smacked into the edge of the table.

"It's just sore," he insisted.

"Let me give you a lift home," I said. "Least I can do."

He considered the offer then hobbled over to Talisha. I watched across the lobby, her haughty gestures tipping off her objections. Finally, she turned away from him, making it a point to flip her hair as she shoved through the front door of the theater.

Preston made his way back to me. By then, I told the usher that everything was cool, and we were about to leave.

"She looks pissed," I said.

"Her natural state," he said. "Let's go, Wild Man." He hadn't called me that in a long time, and I missed it.

We didn't even pull out of the parking lot before he shut off the radio, and I knew the Big Talk was coming.

"How did you forgive Lane?" he asked.

The question was bitter on the surface, but I found an undercurrent to his tone, a curiosity that compelled me to give him an honest answer.

"You and I both know it was an accident," I said.

"I don't want to know why you forgave her," he said. "I want to know how. How did you do it?"

"I just said I forgive you. Works wonders."

"Did you mean it?"

"I did," I said. "I mean it even more now, because she's been punished. We got broken bones, but those heal, and we got the sympathy to match."

"Talisha shouldn't have done the shit with the note, I'll give you that," he said.

"I broke Lane's heart." Saying it out loud made it real. "I hurt her worse than Talisha ever did, and then she called me a coward."

"You're not a coward," Preston said.

"Sometimes I wonder about that," I said.

I turned the radio back up. We listened to classic rock until we pulled into Preston's driveway.

"Thank you," I said. "For standing up for me. You'd didn't have to do that."

"You're goddam right I didn't," he said. "But it's the things we do when we don't have to that makes them kind of cool. You know how sturdy that cane was? Still bent right across his skull."

"Bet he's sorer than you," I said.

"Probably too concussed to play the regionals," he said. "I should have whacked that little prick Robbie Imming."

"Yeah," I said, and both of us just shared our little moment of thinking about what a slimeball he was, letting his sidekicks lob the most jagged verbal stones while he sat there smiling.

"We can't beat them, but I hope someone does," Preston said. "I'll still be there when we play them. You can motherfuckin' guarantee it."

He waited for me to join him in that attendance pact, but I couldn't. I couldn't watch Robbie Imming fill up the net while he broke our team on our own court. Especially not after this. The thought of seeing him smiling, one step closer to cutting down the nets again, wasn't exactly appointment viewing for me—especially when the only person who stood between Robbie and victory was Theo Lang.

"Can you come inside for a little bit?" Preston asked. "There's something I need to tell you."

———

Mary and Dan were in the living room, glued to one of those Shonda Rhimes twist-fests.

I followed alongside Preston so they wouldn't see me. We planned this in advance. "If my Mom sees you, she'll talk your ear off," he had said. "Asks about you all the time."

Once in his room, Preston collapsed into his beanbag. I was used to him reaching for his PS4 controller soon after, but he just sank into the chair and let out a pained exhale, like he was trying to breathe away a headache.

I sat in his desk chair, the weight of my expanders pulling me into a hunched posture.

"Dad got a new job," he said. "We're moving."

"What? When did this happen?"

"I've known for a while now," he said.

"Did you tell Talisha?"

He shook his head. "You're the only person I've told."

"Why now?"

"I think we're about to be friends again," he said, "and I can't let that train leave the station. It's best for both of us."

"Don't speak for me," I said.

"I got to," he said. "You're not enough of an asshole to say it, but this whole being friends thing hasn't worked out too well for us. Bones and dreams, man. Busted hard."

"Add another one to the pile, I guess," I said. "How far away are you moving? Can I at least ask that?"

"Denver," he said.

"So that's it?" I said. He somehow sank even deeper into his beanbag.

"Yeah. That's it."

I stood up.

"I guess I never did apologize for shoving you into that whiteboard," he said. "I'm sorry, Wilder."

"I forgive you," I said. He looked away from me, and it was my time for a deep breath. The tension of the evening built a dull ache behind my eyes.

"I'm not Howie Malone," I said. "You don't have to do this." I reached out with a closed fist, ready for one of Preston Brenner's trademark bro-bumps. He reached out and gently pushed it away.

"You could do me one favor after I'm gone," he said. "Whatever college Robbie Imming goes to, don't go there. Go to one in his conference. Torture him for four years. Make his athletic life a living hell."

"Since we were friends once," I said, "I suppose that's a promise I can try to keep."

"Don't promise," he said. "A promise is just a lie on a timer. I'm just asking you to try."

Try? Easy. All I'd ever done is try.

You try, and you end up on fire.

You try, and a girl doesn't want your bracelet. A car crash breaks your neck. Your friend pushes you down, then stiff-arms the inevitable reconciliation.

You try, and you lose a year of your life, sitting there double your usual size, watching your teammates get beat and letting your only real friendship wither into nothing.

You try, and you hurt someone you care about, a girl who doesn't deserve to get hurt by the likes of you.

You try, and you fail, and you just can't help it because you're just a stupid black hole and you being what you are is just as blameless as the rain.

I left Preston's room, shuffling down the hallway, my bubbles sloshing in my neck, a new sensation with a new kind of pain.

Halfway down the hallway, the ache moved into my chest. I leaned against the wall to keep from falling.

"Wilder?" Mary Brenner peeked in from the kitchen, holding a glass of water. I looked up at her. That simple movement wrung new pain out of my expanders.

She scrambled to set down the water and help me into the living room.

"You okay?" Dan said.

Mary pulled down the collar of my sweatshirt. Her hands were fluent in tenderness, betraying the weathered lines that hardened her face.

"Can I try to press my finger on one of these?" she asked. I knew better than to nod, and whispered, "Yes."

She prodded at the expander, and the flesh sunk under her gentle impact. She prodded the other one, which was hard to the touch.

"Oh honey, I'm no doctor, but I think one of these is leaking," she said.

"Of course it is," I said, and no matter how hard it hurt, I couldn't help but laugh.

RUPTURE

Dan drove me home in my car, and Mary followed. Mom would be waiting at home, ready to take me to yet another trip to the emergency room.

"I've heard Denver is nice," I said.

"Ah, he told you," Dan said. "You should see for yourself over the summer. Our door's always open for you, my man."

If only Preston agreed.

As we drove past the school, we crossed the intersection where Lane crashed into Preston and me. I looked off into the darkened field, seeing the spot where I landed after getting tossed from Old Rusty. Two harvests later, the accident site had been turned over and buried, but not erased—dirt had a long memory, as long as you were willing to dig.

"Mr. Brenner," I said. "Do you mind if I borrow your metal detector sometime?"

Mom's hair was half-done, and she looked petrified to be out in public without makeup, but she didn't hesitate to pile into the car, thank Dan for driving me home, and shuttle me to the emergency room. The poor woman was expecting a quiet evening at home, and she was at the hospital with me. Again.

We sat in the exam room. I already explained in the car that I had tripped in the arcade on the way out of the movies and landed awkwardly, the probable cause for the rupture.

She wasn't buying it, sitting on the chair, her purse on her lap, tapping her heel nervously as we waited for the doctor.

"Are you going to tell me what really happened?" she asked, finally.

"We don't have time. The nurse is here."

Five seconds later, the door opened. The nurse ran through her basic examination and asked me what happened. I told her I fell. Even she was skeptical.

When she was gone, I pretended to read all the entries on the skin rash identification chart.

"I know when you're lying," Mom said.

I stared into the picture of rosacea as if it were an oracle.

"How did you know the nurse was coming in?" she asked.

"Footsteps," I said.

"I hear a lot of footsteps in the hallway."

"The nurses wear Danskos or Dickies or Skechers, but the soles are all basically the same," I said. "Just like that boom in the ceiling or this exam bed or that cabinet is bought from some supply catalog. So there's this little whine you can pick up when they're walking fast. Nurses always walk fast. It's not a squeak, really, just the way the rubber squishes against the tile."

She looked like she wanted to cry and laugh at the same time. "I wish this was your last hospital visit," she said.

"You know it's not. It's like I'll never be done with this."

"We," she said. "I'm in here with you. Every time."

She was reminding me, not complaining, but I was alone and didn't have the heart to tell her. She got to read magazines and sleep on pullouts and go outside. She didn't wear the neck brace. She didn't get the needles and the grafts.

The doctor came in before I could say something I regretted.

He explained that a ruptured expander didn't pose a significant threat unless it impacted your airway, and after examining me, he proclaimed that I wasn't at risk.

"You fell?" he asked. He wore thick glasses and was old enough to not give a single fuck about my cover story. So I didn't even bother.

"A group of assholes wanted to see my bubbles, and one of them yanked on the back of my sweatshirt."

"Pretty hard, I imagine," he said, tilting his head as he pressed his thumbs into the damaged mountain of skin.

"I guess so," I said. "Wasn't a big deal at the time. I didn't even notice I was hurt until like an hour ago."

"Tends to happen with kids as tough as you," he said, pulling out his well-rehearsed doctor's smile. "Just manage the pain until the surgeon can get you in and switch out the flat tire. I'll write you a prescription for hydrocodone."

"Don't bother," I said. "I don't like painkillers. Besides, I'm tough. Right?"

"Indeed," he said, giving me a real smile this time.

When we left the office, Mom didn't even stop to sign the paperwork. Maybe we had one of those punch cards that got you a free hospital visit for every ten you got billed for, like it was a Subway sandwich.

She didn't talk to me all the way home.

───────

When we got home, I just wanted to zone out to some television. As long as I didn't move around much, the ruptured expander didn't hurt. In fact, it was just the opposite—releasing the constant tension on the surface of my skin provided relief, at least until Doctor Iacabucci replaced my balloon and ratcheted up the tightness.

Mom set me up with extra pillows and started working in the kitchen. I heard the rattle of pots and the clink of utensils. After catching up with ESPN highlights for a while, I smelled chicken soup.

She didn't break her embargo of silence. Instead, she just drew a bowl of soup and started eating—I could hear her spoon hitting the bowl.

I was starving. By then, it was after eleven p.m., and I had skipped dinner. I didn't even snack at the movie theater because the line was too long, the lobby too full of people.

I walked into the kitchen. She ignored me, eating her soup the way moms do, pressing the spoon against the surface until it fills up with mostly broth, then balancing the load until she brought it up to her mouth.

My soup-eating habits were far more primitive. After ladling a massive serving into a mixing bowl, I stooped over it at the table, churning my spoon until the chicken pieces and noodles were gone. Then, I drank the remaining broth directly from the bowl before getting up for seconds.

The silence was off-putting, which was weird, since answering your mom's nosy questions over dinner was a drag—but here we were, totally quiet, and I was begging for a conversation to break up the sound of my slurping.

"Preston's moving," I said. "Colorado."

She nodded her head. "You two make up, finally?"

"He doesn't want to, since he's moving." I paddled at my soup. The worst of my hunger was gone, my belly swollen with broth that I ate too fast.

"That means you're his best friend," she said. I rolled my eyes, and she caught me with her peripheral vision, giving me a gentle scowl. "He's afraid it will hurt to move away from you."

She kept chipping away at the tiny serving in her bowl while I sat there, waiting for her to say more, to explain the world and all I didn't understand before her soup was gone.

I didn't move as she finished dinner. Then, she got up and started clearing our bowls out at the sink.

"I'll call the doctor's office tomorrow," she said. "I'm glad it isn't worse. I can't imagine this would set you back more than a few days, but I'm no doctor."

"I'm sorry I tried to lie to you," I said.

"I do know when you're lying," she said. "I'm sorry I got upset. You've had a long night."

I still couldn't bring myself to speak. I envisioned the lights of the operating table, heard myself counting down from ten into a hissing mask of anesthesia. I imagined my own flesh split open as the failed balloon was taken out. It wouldn't be starting from scratch. Mom was right—maybe an extra week or two tacked onto my timetable, max—but as the latex-gloved hands of Doctor Iacabucci slid the new expanders into the slack flesh of my open neck, I saw myself clearly.

By now, Mom had pulled up her chair beside me. She was stroking my hair, and I didn't even notice it, not until I looked up at her.

"What's the worst lie you've ever told?" I asked.

She took her hand away from me, sitting back in her chair, as if someone had physically struck her. She thought about it for a long time, and I knew she was actually going to answer me. She wasn't going to dodge the question.

"When your father died, I tried not to cry around you," she said. "Two weeks after the funeral, I had just gotten out of the shower. I was ready to put on my makeup, and the mirror in the bathroom was all steamed up. Your father used to shave in that mirror while I showered. Did you know that? He would wipe away the steam with his hand as he shaved, right there at the sink. So when I went in to put on my makeup, I saw the swirls in the glass, where the oils in his hands created permanent tracks in the mirror. I waited for the steam to clear naturally because if I wiped it away to do my makeup, eventually, I'd wipe him away, too. So I waited, and I started to cry. You woke up early, little devil that you are, and walked into the bathroom. You were five. You saw me crying, and of course, you knew why, so you asked me if Daddy being gone would ever stop hurting me so bad. Your exact words: 'Will Daddy being gone ever stop hurting you so bad, Mommy?' So I wiped away my tears, and I picked you up, and I hugged you, and I said yes, one day the hurting would stop."

Somehow, she hadn't begun to cry, staring mostly into the streaky grain of the fake-oak table.

"That was the worst lie I ever told," she said. She reached out and took my hand, then tried to pull me into a hug. I stopped her.

I didn't bother biting my cheek. If the tears wanted to come, let them come.

"You've known all along," I said. "You knew Randy didn't burn me."

She tried to hide the truth's frequency in the overpowering emotional noise of the memory she shared, but I felt it.

"What do I do, Mom?" The pleading tone of my voice was so pathetic, I had to fight the urge to slap myself.

"Whatever you need to do," she said. "And only you can answer that."

"I never meant for you to cover for me."

"I didn't," she said. "I chose to believe you. I don't regret that. I wanted you to get through it, and you did." She got up from the table and kissed me on the top of the head.

"No, I didn't," I said. "Not yet."

EMBERS

I snuck out of the house at dawn.

Mom already said she was calling off work that day, so taking the car wouldn't put her in a pinch, other than the massive amount of worry.

I couldn't risk the noise of a shower, so I got dressed by the light of my cellphone. Before I left, I parted the sea of socks in my top dresser drawer. My father's Timex was dead, the face cold and blank. Maybe I could try a new battery, or maybe it didn't keep on ticking after taking a licking, after all.

For what I had planned, I needed a piece of my father just as much as I needed a piece of the day I got burned.

I scribbled a note for Mom: "Took the car. Be back tonight. Please don't be mad, please don't call. I need to do something all by myself."

After an hour of driving south, I swung through a McDonald's in Metropolis and put it on my mother's credit card. Yes, Metropolis like Superman. In Illinois. They even have a huge Superman statue. I can't lie, I stopped to take a look.

While I was parked nearby crushing an Egg McMuffin, only then did I decide to research the logistics of my trip on my cellphone's crappy browser—the details necessary to visit an inmate.

The first bit of information I found wrecked my plans. My name had to be on Randy's approved visitors list, which had to be requested in advance. I couldn't request and visit same-day, even if he allowed my name to be posted.

Well, that's a relief. Better turn your ass around before it's too late.

Too late for what?

Maybe to avoid a traumatic confrontation with a fucking criminal, animal-torturing, evil asshole? I'm trying to preserve your sanity, here. Work with me.

And I'm trying to get rid of you.

I looked up the prison's number and dialed it. Twenty minutes later, I finally got connected with an administrator that could answer one, simple question—was I already on the visitors list for Randy Meadows?

Of course I was. Lane put me on the list months ago.

A guard named Danette processed me into visitation, a barrel-waisted woman with a ponytail so tight you just knew she didn't tolerate anyone's shit.

I put my cellphone in the bin. She looked at me, waiting, expecting something more.

"Are your pockets empty?"

I patted myself down, suddenly nervous, as if a wrong answer would land me in a cell of my own.

"I have my wallet, but there's no metal."

"You can only bring money for the vending machines. The wallet stays. So does your coat."

I took off my coat, and heard my keys jingle. As I fished them out, Danette said, "The keys stay."

"I promise I don't have any cell keys in here," I said, jingling them, hoping a joke might break the tension.

"Keys are potential weapons. They stay."

I dropped them in the bin and followed her. I expected a pane of glass and a telephone, some separation between myself and Randy Meadows, but instead, I was escorted to a commons area. Inmates in beige BOP shirts sat at circular tables chatting with their families.

She left to retrieve Randy. The compulsion to turn around and go home plagued me during the entire drive to Tennessee, but now that I was in the commons area, the fear and doubt I expected was silent.

The lights. The tile. Families upset, wishing their loved ones could come home. The smell of disinfectant, the clinical feel of the beige uniforms and shoes without laces. I was in a hospital, only every injury was self-inflicted, mistakes that couldn't be fixed with stitches and plastic surgery.

I sat down at an empty table and waited for Randy.

———

Randy was now every bit of six-foot-six, his tattooed flesh drawn tightly against his bones. He was thin enough to slide through the bars if he fancied an escape attempt.

He saw me, and no reaction flashed on his face. The scowl likely evolved after years of sharing a space with inmates, a nonverbal cue to keep his personal space protected.

He took his seat and put his hands on the chipped and dirty table, palms down.

His face remained a void, a mask that looked artificial until he blinked.

"Well, you look like shit," he said.

No one would believe he was only nineteen or twenty years old just by looking at him. His shoulders sagged, collapsing his posture, and each breath was audible and labored, as if he fought an intense gravity that afflicted only him.

"You drove all this way," he said, his voice having absorbed the southern twang of Tennessee. "Talk or walk."

His fierce eyes were buried in puffy flesh. The only thing that could sink eyes that deep was a steady stream of drugs made in trailer parks and long hours working in prison laundry rooms.

"The way I got burned . . . why didn't you tell anyone what really happened?"

He sat up in his chair and leaned closer. I tried to hold my ground, but eased away, keeping maximal distance between us.

"Why didn't you?" he said then slouched into his chair. "What's with the bubbles," he said, gesturing at my expanders, one of which was sagging from the rupture. "They supposed to fix you up?"

"Supposed to," I said.

"Supposed to, but not really," he said. "That's why you're here, right? To apologize? Get it off your chest?" He took a long breath, the exhale thickened by smoker's phlegm.

"I don't know," I said. "I think so."

"You always were a boy scout," he said. "No one would ever believe me over you in court."

"So that's why you never told anyone the truth?"

"You're such a selfish son of a bitch," he said. "You know the guys in here, they're trash. They steal 'cause they need the money, shoot up because they need the fix, beat some sorry some-bitch half to death because he needed the ass whoopin'. So in here, if you want to get your self-esteem up, you go after the rapists. The molesters. The murderers. It's like, if you just prove to yourself, 'I'm not as bad as them; I'm no killer,' then life is just dandy. You're a good person who's been victimized by bad things that needed your attention."

He leaned forward again then back. He shifted like a guy aching to light a cigarette.

"I left you to die," he said. The vacant look on his face was gone, his cheeks finally populated by blood, his eyes filled up with something that shined behind his murky irises. "You were on fire, dying right there in the dirt, and I just ran. I ran away, and I screamed the whole time—stop, drop, and roll, stop, drop, and roll—but those feet of mine kept moving, and I went home and watched TV thinking you were dead in your garage."

I nodded, and the deflated expanders allowed me enough motion to make the gesture visible. I nodded because I understood, and to invite him to keep going.

"I got a kid," he said. "A son. Jeremy. He turns one next month. I've seen him one time. That part of me that called out to you, that's what I want to give to him. That's going to help me get a diploma. That's gonna make sure that when I walk out those doors in two years, that I won't ever come back."

He scratched his neck. The inside of his arm was a minefield of splotches.

"But we both know that's bullshit," he says. "That little, best part of ourselves is a slippery fucker, isn't it? Hardest bit to hold on to."

"No," I said. "It's just hard to find."

"And you been lookin' a while, I take it," he said. "And you decided to take a look for it here, across from me."

He looked up at the clock, then down at his hands.

"You remember all the times we camped out in your backyard?" he asked, laughing at himself for even conjuring up that memory. "Before the times we got into fights? Your mom let us make up a little campfire out of flashlights and brought out all those snacks. Hell, I couldn't have been but nine or ten."

"I remember," I said.

He looked down at his arms. The tattoos danced as he closed his hands.

"She told me I was the older kid, so I had to keep an eye on you. She said if we wanted to do campouts, I had to promise to take care of you."

I nodded. He looked me in the eyes, all the slack gone from his face, each word becoming heavier as he lifted it.

"I sometimes wonder how life would be different if I just helped you that day," he said.

He looked away again, battling to maintain a hardness in his face, not wanting to show any of the other inmates visiting in the commons area weakness or emotion, but trying to hide pain is like poking at hot coals to put out a fire.

"I made that whole day someone else's fault," I said. "Another Wilder, stuck at the age of ten, always outside of that garage door. I think of him every day."

I felt sweat sprouting on my forehead, and my thudding heartbeat threatened to shake the droplets loose. Only when I tried to wipe my brow with the back of my hand did I realize how tightly my fists were clenched.

"I think I'm here because I don't hate that boy anymore," I said. "I think if I could go back to that day and talk to him, I'd take him by the hand. I'd tell him it's going to hurt, that it's not something we wanted or asked for, but that's me in there." I leaned forward, needing the eye contact with Randy. If I was lying to myself, I'd know it by the look on his face. "The only boy who exists is the one who walked through that door."

He brought a shaking hand to his forehead, leaving it there to cover his face.

"I'm sorry for what I did to you that day," I said.

He lowered his hand. He clenched his mouth to stop his chin from quivering, knowing the price of showing vulnerability in a place like this.

"For the longest time, I thought the 'stop, drop, and roll' came from my head," I said. "You saved my life, Randy. I don't care if you ran away."

He didn't try to speak, both of us knowing that if he did, the dam would break. He just looked me in the eyes long enough to nod.

I nodded back then stood up. He clasped his hands on the table, his head lowered, his shoulders even more hunched than before.

After a moment's hesitation, I headed for the exit. Danette stood there, her thumbs tucked into her tactical belt, ready to show me out.

I stopped. Randy was still slouched over his hands, afraid to show anyone his face. This was no hospital. Weakness was hidden. Vulnerability was stashed behind a wall of numbness. Healing was not required in order to leave—you only had to wait.

I did not wait and turned away from him. Danette led me out of the commons area. As she shut the door behind us, I did not look back.

MEATLOAF

When I got home, Mom was waiting at the dining room table, listening to the radio. I heard Fleetwood Mac and smelled meatloaf in the oven.

She stood up, the worry etched deep in her makeup-free face. She must have sat there all day after reading my note, waiting.

I hugged her. She didn't so much as hug me back as she did hold me. I was too tired to cry.

"Did you make the appointment to get my rupture fixed?" I asked.

"We meet with Doctor Iacabucci tomorrow at seven a.m.," she said. "I think he's planning on fixing it tomorrow as well. He said not to eat anything after six p.m., hence, the early meatloaf."

She finally saw my father's Timex on my wrist. She took my hand and held it up.

I took it off. "Can you have the battery replaced?"

She took the watch, rubbing her thumb over its scratch-hazed face. She nodded.

"Do you know where I went today?" I asked.

"You're back now, that's what matters," she said. "What do you say we eat before you're cut off?"

She turned to the kitchen cabinets, withdrawing two plates. Not even paper plates, so I knew she was serious about focusing on the feast and nothing else.

"Mom," I said. She froze. I reached out and took the plates from her, not wanting her to drop them. "Doctor Iacabucci isn't replacing anything tomorrow," I said. "I'm having him take the expanders out."

I braced for impact, having thought out all the objections on the way home. We only had two months to go, all my sacrifice and discomfort for minimal gain, a waste of money she'd taken years to save. I was ready.

She took the plates from me and placed them on the table.

"Like I said, you need to eat before you're cut off."

Mom's meatloaf never tasted better.

———

Doctor Iacabucci thought that dumping the expanders with just a couple months to go was a first-ballot entry into the bad medical decision hall of fame.

He didn't say that, of course. Doctors are great at saying things without actually saying them. Technical terms and big words are the perfect Trojan Horse.

You could wrap up "What the hell is this kid doing?" in words like "unnecessary difficulty" or "a lack of return on the investment of time and physical toll." You could hide "You're his mother; talk some sense to him, or are you stupid, too?" in "the margin for error on any visible repairs to the scar tissue is minuscule" and "the last few months of expansion are absolutely critical to a complete repair and long-term success."

The whole thing felt like a breakup. I know you can't shock a doctor easily, but he couldn't mask how he'd withdrawn from the conversation. His training was talking, not him. Gone were the smiles and witty jokes and the gentle, strategic touches on my shoulder he used to offer when inflating my expanders.

My mother stood her ground, supporting my decision, even when Iacabucci made a last-ditch effort to guilt me into changing my mind.

"Frankly, Wilder, if you insist on this course of action, you've not only wasted my time but your mother's time—and money. You both deserve a better result than what you would get by stopping now."

That was the Trojan Horse breaking apart—all of his judgment and frustration, now raw and naked, was on the attack.

"I've gotten exactly the result I was hoping for," Mom said. Polite but firm.

"I'm leaving for an extended vacation," he said. "Three weeks in Europe. If you still want to do this when I get back, so be it, but that's the best offer I can make."

"Bullshit," I said. "You've got an OR booked for my replacement procedure today. I'm fasted and ready. Take them all out."

"I'd like to give you time to consider the impact of this decision," he said.

"I considered it," I said. "They're coming out today, and if you won't do it, I've got an icepick at home that will do the job."

Iacabucci again considered his options, staring into his open manila folder.

"I'm not sure what you'll think you'll salvage," he said. "You don't want to have the expanders for a significant date, a big dance? You won't have the expanders anymore, sure, but you'll have staples holding the excess skin flaps to your face. We can't pinch them together without the additional length. Is it for sports? That's a nonstarter. I won't clear you for activity until those staples are out, and isn't basketball just about over?"

Regionals were in two weeks, right after our spring break. Even if they got the expanders out that day, even if I healed fast and got the staples out, even if I got a doctor's clearance, I'd be totally and utterly out of shape. I couldn't shoot until I perfected a left-handed release, which would take thousands of reps over the offseason. With flaps of new skin settling into the old pools of scar tissue, I needed time to learn how my body was going to move after all this, which could take God knows how long. I'd be back for the following season—I knew I could pull that off— but the regionals? The chances were slim, but they were not zero—and that was all I needed.

"It isn't for basketball," I repeated. "I'd just rather live with scars than regrets."

Doctor Iacabucci looked at my mother, giving her an almost imperceptible smile, but I caught it all the same.

"I'm gone for three weeks," he said, clicking his pen, on again, off again. "Switzerland. I'm looking forward to the hang gliding we have planned. I've done it before, in Colorado, but in the Alps? God, it's going to be beautiful." Click. Click.

"I'll refer you to my colleague, Doctor Palmer. She will oversee your post-surgery care," he said. "But that's with the understanding that only I can clear you for activity after a full examination when I return."

"That's fine," I said.

"Let me be a bit more clear," he said. "I don't want you doing something silly in the name of sports, so there is no possibility that I will clear you for activity before your basketball season is over."

"I thought I was pretty clear when I said that's fine," I said.

"Over the past three months, with all these appointments, I think I've seen you more often than I've seen my own family," he said. "So I'm comfortable telling you this is a colossally dumb decision, but I can't shake this weird feeling, a feeling I shouldn't have right now. I think it's pride. I think I'm proud of you for this. So maybe doctors are human after all."

"Maybe so," I said, "But can we perhaps save your weaknesses as a mere mortal until after the surgery?"

STAPLES

I woke up from the operation and saw my mother's black hair through the anesthetic film that coated my vision. I tried to blink it away as a familiar nausea rose in my guts.

Puking after a procedure was my signature move. Jordan let his tongue dangle, LeBron clapped chalk dust into the air before a game, and Wilder Tate barfed after surgery, always.

The pre-surgery fast made for dry, painful heaving, the kind where your eyeballs feel like they're about to pop free. The hard contractions irritated the new fault lines in my skin. The deep ache of the balloons was gone, but what was left was superficial and sharp. I felt each staple, and as I retched into the metal pan that my mother held, I thought they'd just start popping out from the rising pressure inside my body.

I caught my breath. Nurses helped me clean up. After the dribs and drabs of post-surgery vomit, there was still a lot of plumbing that needed to be cleaned up—nostrils into the back of the throat, multiple swishes of water before you think your mouth is finally clean of the bile, and even then it lingers, the burn of the acid imprinted on your teeth like an old memory.

I turned and looked at my mother. Since the balloons had reached a certain maturity, I could only aim my gaze with a creaky turn of the shoulders, but my flexibility had returned. I couldn't turn far before the stress was too much for the stapled wounds the balloons had left behind but damn it, I could turn my head.

"You got a mirror in your purse?"

"You're fresh out of surgery," Mom said. "Maybe just wait?"

I shook my head. A feeble move, but I shook it all the same. She gathered a cosmetic mirror out of her purse and handed it to me.

The balloons were gone, but they certainly didn't look cleanly removed—it seemed like the bastards had detonated. The flaps of skin they left behind were blue and purple, and each edge was held down by staples. Rows and rows of staples, metallic centipedes crawling across my face, down into my chest, looping up and around my upper arm.

The scar tissue itself looked irritated by all the roadwork being done in its proximity. Redder than usual, swelling angrily, trying to flex away any concealment perpetrated by the flaps.

The balloons were a weirder sort of disfigurement, a proportional anomaly. This was a little more traditional, but holy shit was it a mess. I'd gone from the Elephant Man into Freddy Krueger, a funhouse face transformed into Leatherface.

"The doctor says it will improve quickly," Mom said. The flaps would supposedly take hold and blot out at least some of the scar tissue. The staples would come out and leave clean holes to scab over.

I used to think some holy grail could cleanse me of all of the burns, and then things would get better. That always was kind of stupid, the same way us high schoolers think that if we just got into this one clique, we'd be happy. If we just made the cheerleading squad or the varsity basketball team, we'd be happy. If that report card were straight A's, we'd be happy.

Happy is one hungry motherfucker. It always wants another bite.

I handed Mom the mirror. "Trust me, it's already a lot better," I said.

The next morning, the discharge took forever. Prescriptions to prevent infection, medications for pain, how to care for the stapled areas, what to expect from the skin flaps, all the stuff I couldn't do, the challenges of bathing, the physical therapy exercises I needed to start at home.

Then, I got a note to keep me out of school for the next two weeks.

"That doesn't mean you can't go," Doctor Iacabucci said. "But if you don't feel up to going, you're covered."

He was flanked by Doctor Elizabeth Palmer. She was young, blonde, with a Kentucky accent. She'd introduced herself with a bubbly enthusiasm. I got the feeling she was faking it, treating me the way she thought doctors were supposed to talk to young patients. "I'd say take a couple of days to recuperate," she added. "Think of those skin flaps as plaster; you have to let them set up, you know? The way concrete hardens? Give it some time."

"Plaster and concrete are totally different," I said.

"You get the point," Doctor Iacabucci said, tearing off the note.

"What about P.E.?" I said.

"We can revisit your physical limitations once I'm back from vacation."

"How long until then?"

"Three weeks from tomorrow," he said. "Let me be clear. Staples are tricky, and your situation is unique. You can create new scarring if more staples are required since the edges of those flaps may migrate or not take. Doctor Palmer will take excellent care of you in my absence."

We thanked the doctors and headed home.

By the time I walked to the car, got out to have some McDonald's breakfast with my mother, then returned home, walked the driveway, and walked to my room, I was exhausted. I was ready for bed at approximately 9:50 a.m.

"Just lie down," she said. "I have a shift tonight, but I'm trying to get it moved."

"You don't have to," I said.

"I'm not leaving you here alone."

When I laid down in my bed, I saw my tuxedo. Mom must have picked it up during one of her errand runs. Regionals started in two weeks, and prom wasn't far behind.

I stared at that tux that was now too big for me—I was fitted with my balloons installed. I made a mental note to have it resized in time for the dance.

Mrs. Thoman repeatedly joked in practices that the boys were just window dressing, noting that the audience would be looking at the girls as they bowed. The boys would just be standing behind and to the side of them, folding at the waist, but the girls would be unleashing a regal, thoroughly rehearsed curtsey that would ignite the crowd. But I was the kid in the oversized tux with the horror movie face, and what girl would be curtseying beside me? Lane? A replacement? No one?

I teetered on the edge of sleep. Mom tapped on the frame of my bedroom door.

"I'm going to run to school and pick up your makeup work," she said.

"Can you do me a favor?" I asked. "Don't tell anyone at school I did this."

"You shouldn't have any regrets, honey," she said.

"I don't," I said. "At least, I think I don't, but I still have to figure out how I'm going to tell people. And show people. I'm not sure they can handle this new level of sexiness."

Mom laughed, then I followed suit, and for once it didn't hurt. The bubbles were gone.

R.A.K.

The next morning, getting out of bed was quite the chore. I had refused painkillers, so the unfiltered pain wrecked my sleep. My body felt tight all over—I was a snow globe, and every time I tilted or shifted, flakes of pain shook around, forcing me to stop until they settled.

I shuffled into the kitchen and ate a half a box of Cinnamon Toast Crunch from a mixing bowl. Then, I tried to do my physical therapy exercises, which took me until lunchtime.

The afternoon was better. I took a short walk, and with the blood flowing and a little more stretch to my body, my PT exercises were easier. Not splendid by any means, but I could slog through them

After a snack, I checked the calendar on the fridge.

It was Friday. The following week was spring break. The regional tournament would begin the following Tuesday, with games each night, culminating with the finals on Thursday. Two weeks after that, prom.

I counted out three weeks on the calendar. The earliest I could be cleared for any type of physical activity was long after the regionals had concluded, so the dream of coming back for a dramatic appearance at the regionals was limited to being a special guest benchwarmer to pump up the players and the crowd.

Mom finally went back to work that evening, and I had a date with makeup assignments. Thanks to my constant absences, every teacher had an efficient way to communicate the assignments to me. Each class had its own folder; the left pocket was background information, handouts, or context, and the right folder was quizzes, assignments, and notes from the teacher on how to complete them.

I racked and stacked my assignments, trying to go with the easier ones first—English—to gain some momentum for the math stuff. You couldn't pass calculus by watching *Calculus: The Movie*.

Tucked between the folders were some school update documents— lunch menus, event calendars, and the school newsletters. I typically skipped the newsletters, throwing them away with all the other junk stuff so I could focus on the classwork that actually mattered.

However, one of the school newsletters caught my eye. More specifically, it was a photo of Lane, an old one taken during picture day, her smile painfully forced, as if someone were pinching her off-camera. She wore that denim jacket I negotiated from her possession months ago.

She was the winner of the "Random Act of Kindness" Award for the month of February. The R.A.K. program was the brainchild of the counselor, Mrs. Ventura, and she was passionate about promoting it. Even Principal Turner reminded us each week about the program—nominate a fellow student if you see them perform a random act of kindness, and the counselor selects the winner at the end of the month. The winner gets prizes from local businesses. Local was a pretty loose definition—it was often ten-dollar gift cards from restaurants like McDonald's or Pizza Hut, and none of them were in Herrick.

The random acts were never described in much detail. Lane received hers for "helping a fellow student in a time of need." As surprising as it was to see Lane in the newsletter, I had to read the nominating student twice to believe it—Jenna Weaver.

Not that I thought Jenna wasn't nice enough to nominate her; it was just a weird cross-pollination of girls I liked in one newsletter entry. One of them broke my heart, and I did the same to the other one.

I scrapped the newsletters and tried to work on my English assignment. I needed to finish reading *Romeo & Juliet*, naturally, and answer a five-pack of essay questions about the play and Shakespeare in general.

Yet, I found myself reading entire pages with nothing registering in my mind. My eyes were moving, and I was staring at the book, but my consciousness was with the newsletter that was now buried in my wastebasket.

Finally, I gave up on the Montagues and Capulets and took the newsletter out of the trash. I read the entry again, then checked my phone.

I fought the urge to text Lane an apology. "I'm sorry" are words that need to be felt, not read. If I lobbed them from the safety of a text-message bunker, Lane would reject them. I knew her well enough to know that, but it wasn't Lane's number I was looking for—I was hoping I kept Jenna's phone number saved in my phone.

In the past, I had opened her contact more than once with the intention to delete it, back when the wounds of rejection were fresh. I never pulled the trigger, and here I was, dialing her up without the hesitation that plagued me back when I wanted her to be my girlfriend.

She answered after one ring.

"Wilder?"

"Hey," I said and got stuck. I took two breaths, false starts before she realized I wasn't myself.

"Are you okay?"

Another long breath, but I found Lane's eyes in the photo. Sure, it was just a pixelated picture in a photocopied newsletter, but it was enough.

"Yeah, actually," I said.

"I heard what those Mater Dei assholes pulled," she said. "Is it true? Did you break an expander?"

"Yes, they broke one of the two moons orbiting my neck."

"How bad is it? You haven't been to school, so people are talking."

"Jenna," I said and stood up from my desk. The reflex to pace when I talked had returned, now that the bubbles were gone. "I saw the newsletter in my makeup work. You nominated Lane for an R.A.K., right? What did she do?"

"It was so sweet," Jenna said. "Jackson was giving Ellie Herbstrom a hard time. I don't know what started it or how long it was going on, but he would hover behind her while she was at her locker, oinking."

Ellie wasn't even fat. She was more of the athletic type, just taller and thicker than most girls. Great frame to grab a rebound, and honestly, I thought she was cute.

"Lane just overpowers him with three words—'that's not funny.' That's all she said. All of a sudden, it was a scene. He stares at Lane, dumbfounded, as she puts her arm around Ellie. Puts her arm around her, Wilder, my God it was freaking heroic, and Lane walks her into the library. So I went up to Miss Harrington and told her what I saw, and when nominations came around, I visited Mrs. Ventura in person to let her know that Lane deserved it."

"She's something, isn't she?" I said.

Jenna didn't disagree. "What did you do to her?" Jenna asked. "At practice last night, Mrs. Thoman mixed up prom court. Lane's walking with Austyn, and you're walking with Daityn now."

"I hurt her," I said. "I don't deserve to walk with her."

"You really like her?"

"Yeah," I said not hesitating.

"How do you like her? Is it like finding a piece of leftover pie in the fridge you didn't know was there?" She gave herself a chuckle to loosen things up.

"I like her the way I used to like you," I said.

"That's sweet," she said.

"It says in the newsletter that the R.A.K. winners so far this year are getting recognized during the regional tournament," I said.

"Probably the first game, yeah," Jenna said. "I help organize the halftime stuff, and we don't want to jinx it. We might only have one regional game."

"We'll win by thirty in the first round," I said. "We got a good draw. Cakewalk to the finals."

"Then it's Mater Dei. Right?"

"Unless Robbie Imming gets hit by a bus, Mater Dei will make the finals," I said.

"What happens then?"

"They beat us," I said. "They're a bigger school. Robbie's all-state. There's no shame in losing to them. They're better."

"You should come, then," Jenna said. "Come to the final. Make a big, surprise appearance. Get the crowd pumped up, give the players a jolt. It would be awesome."

I looked at the basketball I got for Christmas, sitting in its cardboard sleeve, resting on the top shelf of my closet. A sliver of orange peeked out from where I tried to cover it with sweaters.

"Then you have to do me a favor, Jenna," I said. "Can you make sure the R.A.K. recognition happens in the final game?"

"Yes!" she said. "Shouldn't be hard at all."

"The catch is you can't tell anyone I'm coming," I said. "Don't even tell Mrs. Ventura. Honestly, I don't even care if you can't get the R.A.K. thing moved to the final. Great if you can, but just make sure Lane is there for that game. Can you do that?"

"I promise," she said.

"Promises are just lies on a timer."

My legs were already tired from pacing my bedroom. I slumped into my office chair.

"Does Preston go to the games?" I asked.

"He's on the team," she said, as if I should know. "The players that don't dress sit behind the bench during every home game."

On the team but hasn't played a single minute. Out for the season, but needs his number colored in glitter on the poster boards in the hallways, needs to say he's on the team, needs to feel like he's not forgotten. I couldn't blame him. Not anymore.

"I heard Talisha broke up with him today," she said.

Was that a preemptive strike on Talisha's part, or was Preston going to cling to a dying relationship so that he'd have a prom date?

"I figured something like that was coming," I said.

"I'm glad it's over," she said. "He deserves better."

I didn't leap to agree with her. Yeah, he probably did, but he was still a friend who stiff-armed our shot at reconciliation.

"Just please don't tell anyone I'm coming," I said. "I have doctors' appointments; I mean, I may not even be in school that much, if at all, right up until the day of the game."

"I promise—I mean I'll try my best—not to tell anyone."

"Fair enough," I said.

Just like that, we were out of easy things to say. I just sat there, looking at the newsletter, waiting for Jenna to get tired of the awkwardness and hang up.

"Wilder," she said, her voice easing into a tender space that reminded me of the nurses I liked the most, "I'm glad you felt like you could call me." A long breath. I waited. "I never meant to hurt you."

I knew now that she was telling the truth, that words and deeds can tumble out of us without intention—if that weren't true, then regret would be out of a job.

"I know," I said. "I was searching back then. Not for love, really. Something I didn't know I was looking for. A feeling. A forgetting. A way to not be the burned kid. I've been looking for that feeling everywhere."

I closed my eyes. I saw Randy's tattoos on his forearms, scars in their own right. I saw the cold, gray sky down close to me, when I was lying in that field after the car crash, thinking Preston was dead. The clouds were mottled. They looked like skin grafts.

"What did you find?" she said, thinking that my latest gap in conversation was me waiting for an invitation.

"Nothing," I said. "There was nothing to find. I'm the burned kid." I opened my eyes.

"I'll see you at the game, then?" Jenna said.

I glanced at my scissors, poking out of my desktop pencil cup. My miniature corkboard hung over my desk, totally blank, just three pushpins tucked into the corner, in case I ever had to post homework or hang handwritten notes to look at while I typed.

"You will," I said and hung up the phone.

I grabbed the scissors and cut out Lane's picture, leaving enough white space on top so I could tack it on my board without the red pushpin obscuring her face.

I headed to my closet and grabbed the basketball. The cardboard fell away when I pulled the tabs out of their slots. The leather grain bit into my hands, the tackiness of a new ball bonding with my fingertips.

Then, I went outside and started to shoot.

REBOUND

The next morning, I woke up early enough to use the car before Mom left for work, not to get anywhere, but to measure.

From the end of our dead-end road to my bus stop was point-one-five miles. Take that road all the way to the end of the block, and it's point-four-nine miles. Go around the block and back down the dead-end road, and it's one-point-two-two miles.

I parked the car, and she still wasn't awake. The sun had yet to rise, teasing the edge of the horizon, making the birds go wild.

I took a one-mile walk and got back before first light, walking as briskly as I could, making the distance in eighteen minutes and twenty-four seconds. Despite the cold, my stocking cap was soaked with perspiration. My hips felt tight at the end of the walk, and my lungs hurt from the frosty, outdoor air.

I slipped back into bed and waited for her to leave. She came in to kiss my forehead before she departed, thinking I was sleeping. Luckily, the sweating had died down, and she didn't detect anything out of the ordinary and left without hesitation.

I woke up and tried my hand at making eggs, trying for fried but ending up with impromptu scrambled after screwing it up. After scarfing them down, I walked another mile, trying to go ten strides farther than my first walk.

The accrued effort took a toll. The time was nineteen minutes.

The sun was out, but it was brutally cold overnight, leaving the mud around my basketball goal hardened by frost. So I set up a couple of empty milk cartons from the trash and dribbled around them while the ground was firm enough to ball-handle. After shattering the frost and turning the area around the hoop into a soupy mess, I set up for one-hundred left-handed free throws. I made nine of them.

Then, I worked through my old shooting drill I used in grade school, leaving my off-hand, now my injured right hand, away from the ball, shooting one-handed shots with my left from one foot away until I swished a basket.

I took a step back and repeated it until I nailed a swish. Then another step back, and another, until I was out to the top of the key. When I finally swished a three-pointer, I had taken roughly a million shots, and my face was a battleground where the sweat of immense effort pushed back at the bite of the frost.

I went inside and ate lunch, not even bothering to take off my jacket. My nose and cheeks warmed up, tingling in the heat of the kitchen, but they didn't thaw all the way before I went back out and worked the same drill from the corners.

I took a walk and then worked the drill from the wings.

I took a walk and then shot free throws.

I ate the dinner Mom had left me, a pasta bake, and finished off the entire casserole dish. During dinner, I forced myself to eat left-handed. I brushed my teeth left-handed. I wrote up my homework left-handed.

After an evening shower, with my muscles worked, warm, and relaxed, I went to my room and did double sets of my physical therapy exercises. I even dusted off some old ones I remembered from my burn rehab days.

Lie in bed, reach across and touch the wall with my hand. Lat stretches that challenged the flexibility of my shoulder. Head turns to stretch the flesh on my neck, head turns with tilts, touching my hands behind my back for shoulder flexibility.

The exercises gassed me, breaking open more sweat, so I drank water and took another shower. I tried to go to bed early but couldn't sleep. I saw Lane on my bulletin board then got up and went through a round of pregame basketball stretches, working from the bottom up—heel cord, calf, hamstrings, thighs, hips, groin.

I got back to bed and still couldn't sleep, so I went to the mental gym. I imagined myself ball-handling to the basket, taking shots that swished, and being low and fast on defense, beating my man to the spot as he tried to drive.

That man was always Robbie Imming, and when I drifted off to sleep, my soul stayed in that gym, practicing all night until my alarm went off before dawn.

I walked farther. More shots went down. The stretches were easier. Sleep came faster.

On Sunday, Mom didn't work. It was the Sunday before spring break, and she asked if I wanted to go shopping with her. I said no, but I wanted her to make meatloaves and pasta bakes, that I needed a lot of extra calories to recover from my surgery.

I did my walks and my shooting drills, not caring if she saw me from the kitchen window. This time, I felt good enough to get wide and low and do some defensive shuffling around the milk cartons.

She came outside to get in the car and asked me one more time if I needed anything.

"Get like three gallons of milk," I said. "And some multivitamins, maybe. Some of that stuff that keeps you from getting colds, you know?" She shook her head but didn't press me any further.

The next day, I took my walks with my backpack on, and one gallon of milk stuffed in the bag. My shooting percentages regressed a little, but progress isn't linear. I couldn't let it get me down. Instead, I punished myself for failure. If I didn't outshoot my previous round, I walked a suicide with the backpack on.

I logged ten miles with the backpack, and my endurance was returning, little by little. The stretches were going well. So on Monday, I dropped the resistance training and intentionally slowed down my walks. After three days of going as hardcore as I could go, I needed to recover. I split an entire meatloaf between lunch and dinner, this after a massive breakfast of whole milk and as much jellied toast as I could eat.

I kept my shooting regimen up and did double the stretches that day.

I got to bed before Mom came home from work, and when I woke up, there was a stack of orange cones by my dresser, straight from the sporting goods section of Walmart.

The next morning, I ran. I only did a half-mile, but I pushed myself and was delighted at the results. Six minutes flat, and the cold didn't bother my lungs. I intended to only run once that day and stick with my weighted walks, but instead, I did additional half-mile runs that day, logging five miles total.

I cut my shooting drills in half to work on defensive shuffling around my new cones and even set up some cones for suicides, so I could better regulate the distance. I found myself leaning into the corners a lot better, cutting a lot quicker.

I had made a promise with myself to not go 100 percent until I logged a full week of work, but I couldn't resist trying one suicide at top speed. For these, I wore my old baseball cleats, even though I hadn't played in years. They were a size too small, but I didn't want to slip.

The cuts were crisp, and my center of gravity was low. I had run a full suicide, full speed, and lived through it. I ditched the cleats before they could give me blisters.

Emboldened, I did double the shooting drills. Mom called me in for dinner, but I told her I'd come in when it was too dark. Without daylight savings kicking in yet, the night still came early, so I used up all the daylight I could and went inside to destroy some meatloaf.

After dinner, she cleaned up the kitchen table. I excused myself to do my stretches.

"Not tonight," she said. "Let's go to the store."

We went to Walmart. She said she just had a few things to pick up, but she lied. She took an empty cart to the sporting goods section.

"Is there anything here you might need?" she asked.

"How much money do we have?"

"I'll put it on the credit card," she said.

I threw some resistance bands in the cart, and a reaction ball—a bouncy ball with multiple contact points that you could throw off the garage door and never know where the hell it's going. I grabbed a stretch band, the kind of strap you use in yoga, and a new set of cleats that fit. All in all, fifty bucks. It wouldn't break the bank.

When I added my goodies to the cart, she told me to go warm the car up while she checked out, and she took so long to come out to the parking lot, I knew she had some surprise up her sleeve. I couldn't figure it out and forgot about it by bedtime.

The next morning, I was running when she left for work. I came home to a note that said: "Cody Logsdon is going to come by today and work on a little project for me, so offer him something to drink and let him warm up inside if he needs it. His payment is on the dryer."

Cody was a drunk that lived at the end of our street, but he was a nice one, the kind of guy that sat on his porch and waved to everyone. He was also a handyman who worked cheap. For a six-pack of Stag, he'd get elbow deep in a shit-stuffed toilet.

There were two cases of Stag on the dryer, so I figured she was having him build a castle.

After my afternoon run—the first mile I had logged in under ten minutes since I started rehabbing—the job he was working on was obvious. He was running wiring over a new hole in the siding above the garage, installing a spotlight. After lunch, I saw him mounting another spotlight on a new four-by-four post he was putting on the other side of my basketball goal.

That night, after dinner, my outdoor basketball court was sandwiched with light, and with a belly full of meatloaf, I went through my shooting drills under the spotlights until my legs were too tired to continue.

Doctor Palmer removed my staples, and while she was impressed with my range of motion, she adhered to the "No one can clear you but Doctor Iacabucci" rule. We measured my height, and I was three inches taller than my first appointment over a year ago. I made her measure again. She laughed. "Those bubbles finally let go of your neck, and what do you know, a growth spurt was hanging around in there all along, just ready to spring."

I looked at Mom. She sat in the corner chair as she always did, her purse on her lap.

"Did you notice I was getting taller?"

She shrugged. "I see you every single day, baby," she said. "But I'm glad. I always figured it would come along like this—your father was pretty tall."

"Six-six," I said. One of the few details she told me and I always remembered. Jordan was six-six. I was still well short of that, but I was officially a six-footer now—something else Lane had seen all along, and I didn't.

I turned to Doctor Palmer. "I was going to wait to beg, but you have to clear me for sports," I said. "You know what? Forget that. I'm begging. Please."

Palmer held fast. No release. I wasn't technically her patient. I still had one more appointment coming up, so I didn't fight too hard. I didn't want to discourage myself from what I had to do to be ready, just in case.

Spring break ended. I could run a seven-minute mile. I could walk five miles with three gallons of milk on my back. I could blast through a suicide with sharp cuts and acceleration that felt comforting and familiar. I went from sluggishly tracking down the reaction ball after missed attempts to shuffling into its path more times than not. Everything hurt in the best of ways, not that injured pain, but the pain that comes from effort, a sign of adaptation, of the pace I was putting myself through—I read once that the body is hard to get into shape, but that muscles have a long memory and getting back into shape goes a lot faster.

I was banking on it.

The new muscle-memory of a left-handed shot was going a lot rockier. I put my free throw percentage around a paltry 20 percent, based on my results per one hundred shots. Roughly half my three-point attempts were airballs, and of the ones that hit the rim, I'd say one out of ten went in. The only shot I could nail reliably with my left hand was one that I had practiced since grade school—a left-handed layup.

On Monday night, I cranked up Mom's radio in the kitchen and listened to the Herrick Fighting Griffins beat the holy hell out of the North Central Cougars in the first round of the South Central Illini Regional Tournament. Theo was a senior on a mission, dropping thirty-six points and six assists in the blowout.

While the team rested on Tuesday and Wednesday, I trained.

On Thursday, the team scored a rock-solid twelve-point win over the South Herrin Speedboys. Theo was more of a distributor, logging twelve assists as he drew a lot of defensive attention. I hated to admit it, but it was a sign of maturity, a team-first approach expected from a senior captain.

Mater Dei kept up their end of the bargain, logging a couple of blowouts on the way to the final. Robbie Imming scored forty-plus in each game, as the announcers salivated over his potential to play for a division-one college.

The championship would get settled on the following Monday, and I had every intention of playing. I had one more doctor's appointment on Friday morning to get the clearance I needed.

———

Doctor Palmer removed my staples and tested my range of motion again.

"Someone's definitely been doing their exercises," she said, jotting down notes.

"Getting back to basketball is a strong motivator," I said. "I need you to clear me to play."

"You need another week," she said.

"Regional championship is Monday," I said. "That's the only game I care about, and if you tell me no today, all the work I've put in these past couple weeks was for nothing."

She hesitated to answer. "I'll be honest, if it were up to me, I would say no. It just makes no sense to risk another setback. Any kind of hard contact could split you open. You might lose one of your hard-earned flaps in that case, plus there's the immunity risk. That's the primary reason

I've given you carte blanche to stay out of school."

"I've been taking a lot of vitamins, that effervescent stuff that keeps you from getting sick on airplanes," I said.

"So go back to school and attend your classes," she said.

"What if it does split me open?" I said. "So what? What's a scar on a scar?" I sat on that loud-ass, crinkly paper on the exam table, every nervous shift becoming an audible crunch. "I understand the risks," I said.

"Do you really?" she said.

"I understand them," Mom said. She sat on the office chair in the corner, observing with her purse resting on her lap. "All that we're asking is for you to speak with Doctor Iacabucci. We're not asking for much."

"Perhaps your definition of vacation isn't the same as mine," Doctor Palmer said.

"As long as doctors have patients in their care, they are never truly on vacation," Mom said.

"I'm just looking out for your son."

"Which I appreciate. You know what's best for his body, but I know what's best for my son."

Palmer glanced at me, then Mom, then back to me again, tapping her pen against the clipboard.

"I will call him today. I'll bring up this situation, offer my feedback, and respect his recommendation," Doctor Palmer said. "I'll relay that recommendation to you this afternoon, and that's only if I can get in touch with him. He's not expecting me to bother him with non-emergency issues such as this. Best I can do."

Mom nodded and stood up. "I'll accept it for now, but don't tell me for one moment that's the best you can do." She thanked the doctor and led me out of the office.

Once we were in the car, the reality hit me. I destroyed myself to get ready for a game I'd never play. "It was worth trying," I said to Mom as she pulled onto the interstate. "It was dumb and irresponsible, but at least you let me try. So, thanks."

"Does this mean you'll still attend the game? Even if you can't play?" she asked.

Lane's picture was still on my bulletin board, and the R.A.K. winners were being honored at halftime of the regional final. Jenna came through, so Monday, I was coming back. I was just coming back as a student and not an athlete. I'd still get a standing ovation. I'd still get to see Lane, and she'd see me, and maybe then, without the expanders, she'd understand. She wanted me to show her, and since the day I confronted Randy Meadows, I was trying to do just that.

"I'll go back Monday," I said. "I'll go to the game."

"Don't get down yet," she said. "Maybe Doctor Palmer will come through."

Doctor Palmer did not come through. That afternoon, I was running through my shooting drills after a half-hearted two-mile run and Mom came out to the porch, wrapped in her coat. When I saw her, I pinned the ball to my hip and waited. She just shook her head, the tightness in her face letting me know just how much she hated telling me no.

When the sun went down, I didn't use the spotlights to keep shooting. I went inside and ate meatloaf.

"She blew me off," Mom said, breaking what was up until then a silent and kind of depressing meal. "She said she interrupted his breakfast to discuss the matter and that he said 'under absolutely no circumstances is Wilder to be cleared without an examination from me,' but I think it's bullshit."

Mom didn't swear all that often, so she had my attention.

"He's in Switzerland. They're seven hours ahead of us. He wasn't eating breakfast."

"Don't let it get you mad," I said. "Maybe she lied, but she's right. He's not clearing me from a Swiss hotel."

"I just wish I could give you this one thing," she said. "I know how much you care. I saw your bulletin board."

Mom was just moving the food around on her plate by now, eating nothing.

"Your father's watch is broken," she said. "I had two jewelers look at it. It's an old Timex. The only repair is replacing it."

"I'll still need it for prom," I said, smiling at her. "That way you can't blame me when I break curfew."

She smiled back. "How about after dinner, I bundle up and sit outside a while? Show me that new left-handed shot of yours."

So as I had after so many meals during my lifetime, I finished a meal and then grabbed a basketball to shoot around, but unlike most of those times, I didn't do it alone.

———

The next morning, I dragged myself out of bed. I had no choice, putting my alarm all the way across my bedroom to guard against the temptation of the snooze button. Even though I didn't have to run or train anymore, I had one more day of work ahead of me.

Preston's parents would be home early on a Saturday morning, but they wouldn't be awake—so I had called Mr. Brenner the night before. He had no problem when I finally called to cash in a favor I had asked for weeks ago and left his metal detector behind the bushes at their front porch for me to pick up. The instruction booklet was taped to the handle in case I needed it.

I drove to the field where Old Rusty launched me, broken-necked, into the dirt. The cultivated rows of soil were crusted with frost, and the sun hadn't risen high enough to loosen its grip.

I slung the metal detector into position and started scanning. Ten seconds into the job, the beep alerted me of metal. Chewing through the crust with a spade was hard work with my bum hand, and it took me fifteen minutes to locate a random strand of rusted steel.

The task wouldn't be easy—the remains of Old Rusty had been turned over during farming seasons, and they were everywhere. I couldn't go five steps without a beep.

Ball bearings. A piece of a brake pad. An old wrench thrown from the truck's toolbox.

My head steamed as I drove the spade into the field. The fingers of my gloves were smothered with mud and half-frozen from sifting through the dirt, uncovering the bones of Old Rusty.

The full sun never arrived. One hour became two, and the murky sky did nothing to loosen the frost. I kept working.

Three hours later, the beeps were less frequent. I stripped the field of almost all the false leads, and now, the detector stayed quiet for minutes at a time.

I expanded my search, but I needed to get back soon for my doctor's appointment.

Maybe it's buried too deep.

Don't say that.

Could be that it was lost along the highway, where the truck first turned over. Some vagrant probably found it already.

No. It's in the field. Everything is in the field.

You sound different. I'm not used to you encouraging me.

It's an adjustment for me, too. So don't be a dick about it. Just keep looking.

I kept looking.

An hour later, the detector chirped, and I started to dig. The spade bit through the veneer of frost. I peeled away the ice-chunked surface and ran the detector over the fleshy earth underneath. The chirping was louder.

I sifted with my fingers until I plucked the charm bracelet from its frozen grave.

GAME DAY

On Monday, the day of the regional final, I had every intention of going back to school. I'd held back the secret of my premature expander removal for two weeks hoping to unveil it at the game, but without being able to play, I figured I'd get an early start on letting everyone get used to the new Wilder. Everyone would ask me why I got them out early, and if I was coming to the basketball game. I didn't figure out a good answer for the first question, at least not one most random classmates could understand, so I'd just emphasize that I was going to the game and keep the conversations focused on basketball.

I woke up to bright sunlight filling my bedroom, a feeling I hadn't experienced in weeks. My alarm clock and cellphone were gone.

I stumbled out of my bedroom, still trying to shake off the newly woken haze, and Mom was sitting at the kitchen table. The clock on the stove read 8:30—I had missed the bus by a solid hour. A plate and fork were at my seat, and I smelled eggs and bacon. My cellphone was next to the silverware, and the alarm clock, unplugged, with the cord wrapped around it, was on top of the fridge.

"What's going on?"

"Sit," she said. "Eat."

She loaded my plate, a mountain of eggs and a half-pig's worth of bacon.

"I overslept."

"You deserved it," she said.

The bacon made me salivate, but I was too confused to eat.

"Maybe this will wake up your appetite," she said, handing me a piece of paper.

The letterhead was from the Alpina Gstaad Hotel in Switzerland, and the handwriting was the familiar scrawl of Doctor Iacabucci: "Cleared for P.E. and sports," the note read, with his oversized signature bigger than the note itself.

"It's game day," she said. "Better eat up."

"How?" I said, the only word I could form into human language.

"I spent most of the weekend calling upscale hotels in Switzerland, and when I found his, I started leaving urgent notes at the front desk every hour until he called me back."

I traced my fingers over the handwriting on the note, half-expecting it to dissolve in my hands as I woke from what had to be a dream.

"He says good luck at the game," she added.

"Why'd you keep me home?"

"I had every intention of sending you to school today, but when I called Coach Ballard last night to share this news with him, he seemed pretty open to your original intentions."

"What intentions?"

"Wilder, please. I'm your mother. You were going to skip school and make your big comeback without anyone seeing you. For once in your life, you wanted to make an entrance."

I struggled to talk, stuck on the note, marveling at its existence. "I don't know how you did this," I said, folding the note to get it away from the blast radius of the grease from the bacon I was about to devour.

"After tonight, a lot of people are going to ask you the same thing," she said.

———

Coach Ballard wanted to meet with me two hours before tip-off and had told my mother he'd leave the side door directly to the gymnasium open for me.

When she dropped me off, the door was propped open with a rack of basketballs. I went inside dressed in sweats, my duffel bag over my shoulder. The gym lights were quivering and dim, having just been turned on. As they warmed up, I heard the sound of a single basketball dribbling against the hardwood. Coach Ballard was shooting free throws, even though he was wearing slacks and a polo shirt.

When he noticed me, his smile was wide enough to see from across the gym. He walked over, the ball pinned to his hip.

"Go ahead and say it," I said.

"Say what?"

"I told you so? I remember our talk. You were right."

He turned around and shot a deep three. The ball smashed off the back of the rim and hopped into the bleachers.

"I said you wouldn't regret those bubble things until you were older and married," Coach said. "You figured yourself out a hell of a lot sooner, kid. Congrats."

No one ever figures themselves out, not the way Coach was saying. We just look for who we are, all the time. We look for the answer in other people, and that's where it always goes wrong.

"Wilder?" Theo's voice. I turned around, and he was in the doorway, wearing a heavy coat and basketball shorts. He stripped off the coat, and he was wearing his Fighting Griffins warmup shirt.

"Holy shit." He dropped and commenced pumping out ten pushups without Coach even telling him to pay the fine for swearing aloud in practice. Coach Ballard strutted over to the bleachers to fetch the stray basketball. Theo got to his feet, examining my face with such an intensity that I couldn't tell if he was just fucking with me.

"They're all gone?" he asked.

"Jenna didn't tell you?"

"Jenna knew?" Theo might have duped the shit out of me in the past with his Jenna-centric master plan, but he was still bad at lying in general, and I could tell that Jenna had kept my secret.

"I can't believe she didn't tell you," I said.

"If you asked her not to say anything, and she didn't, that's cool with me," he said. "You look . . . " He trailed off, wanting to compliment the way I looked but still wary of sounding gay. We were in small-town, mostly white, highly closeted Southern Illinois, so it was more of a reflex than a deep-seated bias.

"Deflated?" I said, finishing the sentence for him, relieving the pressure.

"You look like a Fighting Griffin," he said.

Coach Ballard bounced the ball over. I caught it.

"It's one thing to psyche the crowd up with a surprise return," Coach said, "But we're here on business, boys. Wilder, you may be cleared to play, but that doesn't mean you're ready to come back and play well. I've got five starters that gave us a 22-6 season. Five starters that got us to the finals. They worked hard. So don't even think for a second I can start you tonight. However, we could use some defense and shooting off the bench. What's your condition right now, percentage-wise? Be honest."

"Seventy-five," I said, without hesitation. "That's if you roll me through drills or set out cones or ask me to do suicides. And that percentage is only my legs and lungs. I shoot left-handed now, so free throws, I'm at like twenty percent. I can't dependably hit the three anymore. But I didn't come back to score. I came back to do what you need me to do—I'm here to stop Robbie Imming."

Coach nodded his head, digging the message, keeping his smirk pushed off to one side of his mouth. He always had a boner for competitiveness.

"Dress out, then," he said. "Let's see what you've got on a suicide and some defensive slides. I want to see you at seventy-five percent."

I gestured with the ball toward Theo. "Forget the drills," I said. "Let Theo try to score on me. That should tell us what we need to know."

I chucked the ball to Theo at the top of the key, and he tried to out-quick me with his off-hand, dribbling left without pausing, hoping to take me by surprise.

I cut him off near the elbow, shuffling to the spot before he got there. He bumped into me, and I could already tell that in my time away, Theo had gotten stronger, more physical. I'd heard he was better around the basket, too, relying less on his give-up fadeaway jumpers that plagued him during his sophomore season.

He dribbled into me three times, but I didn't give ground. On the third try, I jabbed at the ball—his dribble had been sloppy in the post—and I grazed the leather, but he maintained control. He used it to spin away from me and took two long strides to the basket, going airborne for what would be an easy layup.

I pushed hard off my right foot, regaining my balance, tracking him from behind. He had me beat, but I could still meet him at the destination—the backboard. I jumped as he went to lay the ball off the glass, and I just kept floating into the air until the ball was within reach. I slapped it off the glass, a rare shot block. I never blocked shots. I couldn't jump like that. Could I?

No one was more surprised than me. As the blocked shot trickled toward the wing, Theo hesitated, trying to process what just happened.

I never trained my vertical, having given up on adding inches to it a long time ago, but I was still a teenager—even while I wasn't working out, my type-II muscle fibers were ripening on the vine. It didn't hurt that I was taller and longer than I'd been my freshman year, although hardly anyone noticed thanks to the expanders.

Theo tracked down the loose ball, ready to come at me again. I sensed him pulling up to shoot from the wing, and I closed ground. He gave a head fake and tried to drive again, but I drop-stepped, cutting him off. He had no choice but to back me down again. He tried to spin, picking up his dribble, but I beat him to the spot, closing off his angle.

If he tried to shoot, I'd swat him, so he went back to his Old Faithful, fading away as I leaped forward, trying to block it. The shot went softly over my outstretched hands, arcing high over my defense. The ball swished into the basket from twelve feet.

Coach blew the whistle, but Theo didn't let him talk.

"No one could defend that shot," Theo said. "You gotta play him."

"At seventy-five percent? Over our regulars? Who do you want me to squeeze out of the rotation?"

"Seventy-five percent of Wilder Tate may not be much," Theo said, "But seventy-five percent of the Doberman? He's better than any defender we've got."

"I'll give him some minutes on Imming, and we'll see how it goes," Coach said. "Off the bench," he added, with emphasis.

"You put him on the bench, and the first time Imming hits a bucket, the crowd is going to freak out and wonder why he's not in the game," Theo said. "The signs in the hallway are all about being loud tonight, packing the place. You were talking about the home court advantage at the pep rally. They'll get frustrated and quiet. That's not what you want."

"What are you saying?" Coach asked.

Theo looked at me. "Did you pack your undershirt?"

My gold, dri-fit undershirt was a staple of my game-day uniform. A long-sleeve shirt that I'd cut down with scissors to end at my elbow, I wore it under my jersey, covering up all of the scar tissue that would've been visible on my right arm. I knew what Theo was really asking, and the truth was, I didn't even remember to pack it in my duffel bag. I shook my head.

"I've got an idea," Theo said. "If you're both willing to listen, I think it would be fucking amazing."

Theo dropped to do his pushups, but when he was done, we listened.

DOBERMAN

I spent the hour before tip-off in Coach Ballard's office, the blinds drawn, the door locked. Only Coach and Theo knew I was inside. Even though I couldn't hear the thrum of the crowd that had packed Herrick's gymnasium, I could feel it, a reverberation in the base of my stomach. Either that or I just had the urge to puke.

The team was gathered in the locker room. I walked to the window, where I could just hear Coach, imagining him pacing in front of his whiteboard, marker in hand.

"You know what Mater Dei is all about," he said. "It's Imning and a tough, zone defense. But you know what? I'm not sure Mater Dei knows what we're all about."

The marker squeaked on the board. I didn't need to be there to know the word he was writing.

"Competitiveness," he said, letting the word linger. "From the tryouts of your freshman year to the regional championship game in your senior year, competitiveness. From conditioning week through the holiday tournament and conference play all the way up to this moment, competitiveness. Mater Dei might very well beat us tonight, and no one but God knows the outcome, but what I do know is that we will compete with them. They'll know they were in a fight, because competitiveness is the only thing we can control, and I can guaran-damn-tee we're going to bring it tonight."

The team cried out in agreement, clapping, high-fiving.

"That's why tonight, I'm doing something a little different. I'm going to let everyone know the bar has been raised. I'm having competitiveness announced tonight as our fifth starter. And if we don't deliver maximum effort, I don't care what the score says, I'll be just a little embarrassed that we didn't deliver on our promise to compete at the highest level we can reach, and I bet you guys will be, too."

Silence. Playing hard sounds good in theory, but when your legs ache and your lungs are on fire and your self-preservation instinct is begging you to just lie down and chug some water, it's a different story.

"So, who's going to give up their starting spot tonight? Who's ready to put competitiveness before himself?"

Theo had told Coach and I that he wouldn't raise his hand immediately, that he wanted all the starters to see him hesitate before he put his hand up.

"That's a captain, right there," Coach said, so I assumed Theo finally raised his hand. The other starters would follow suit, but who would be the last one to raise his hand, if he raised it at all? Theo had a guess, and he was right.

"Ty, you put your hand up last. You're off the bench tonight," Coach said. "Now, bring it in."

Sneakers wailed against finished concrete as they packed in tight and recited a loud and unified "One-two-three-COMPETITIVENESS."

The team poured into the gym, receiving an ovation that echoed in the empty locker room. I finished double-knotting my sneakers and tucking in my number thirty-three jersey. I left Coach's office. Music bumped in the gym as the players warmed up. I stepped in front of the mirror. Without the shirt, my arm looked detestable, with the undersized skin-flap stuck in a sea of red tissue, the edges dented from the healed-over staple holes.

My nerves had my blood pumping, which increased the redness in the scars on my face. The flaps hung over the damage, trying to touch, but they didn't have the length to cover it up. Squint a little, and the whole works looked like an angry, red eyeball was trying to open up along my right jawline. The tightness of the repair had my right eye drooping by the corner, pulled down into the epic wasteland of my abominable face.

I looked horrific. I looked worse than I did before the expander operation, and it would stay that way for weeks. I looked creepy and intimidating and unnerving.

I looked like a badass. I looked ready to go to war.

I looked like a Fighting Griffin.

The music fell away, and I lingered near the entrance to the locker room, leaning out just enough to see every inch of the bleachers packed. The side behind the benches was a sea of green and gold, and our crowd spilled into the other side of the gym, where Mater Dei's crowd struggled to compete with our sheer numbers. Perhaps the inevitability of Mater Dei winning regional championships had damaged the turnout, or maybe they were just stuck in the hallway, standing room only, scrambling to get a decent vantage point from the doorways.

Preston and the jayvee players had a roped-off VIP section right behind the player bench. Jenna and the cheerleaders were on the court, whipping everyone into a frenzy.

I couldn't find Lane, but I did see another roped-off VIP section behind the Mater Dei bench, and I recognized the Random Acts of Kindness winners I remembered from earlier in the year. Lane wasn't in their reserved section.

The PA announcer was Mr. Baldridge, the ag teacher. He tried to bring that old-school, Jordan-era Bulls energy to announcing the starting lineups, which everyone loved. He even deadpanned announcing the opponents, draining their intros of anything resembling excitement.

He did that now, and when Robbie Imming was announced, I heard a smattering of boos. I'm sure some of our fans knew about the events at the arcade, but the great majority of them were hesitant to poke the beast who could destroy their beloved Fighting Griffins.

On our bench, four starters waited to get announced. The rest of the team had lined up to high-five them as the starters met near mid-court, a scene that played out in every basketball game across the country since pretty much the beginning of time.

In anticipation of our starters, the crowd rose. They clapped in unison. I eased back into the locker room as my stomach dropped. The current of nervousness coursing through me turned hot enough to burn the color right out of my blood.

"At forward, number twelve, Pete Novak!"

The crowd screamed. I closed my eyes and took two deep breaths.

"At forward, number forty-four, Bryan Holmes!"

I tried to pause at the top of the breaths, hoping to lower my heart rate.

"The man in the middle . . . at center, number ten, Luke Conant!"

Each heartbeat crashed into my ribcage. I felt my pulse in my toes.

"At point guard, the captain, number one, Theooooooo Lang!"

Theo was always announced last, so the crowd was programmed to jump up a few decimal levels and then slow down for the tip-off. They popped as he high-fived our guys and joined the other three starters, then the noise dropped to a murmur. Maybe by now, they were wondering why there were only four starters. Mr. Baldridge's voice lowered, his tone turning formal and measured.

I opened my eyes. I smiled. To this day, I don't know why. I was in a state of utter terror, but I smiled.

He ramped up his vocal energy, each syllable riding a rasp into the rafters of the gym. His excitement crested so high, his voice cracked and broke when he finally said my name.

"At shooting guard . . . number thirty-threeeeeeeeee. . . . Wilderrrrr Taaaaaaate!"

Before he was finished drawing out my first name, the gym became a thunderdome. The lockers chattered as I left them behind. I walked out, and the light hurt my eyes, and I'm sure people mistook my squinting for tears. At least, I hope they did, because when the team crashed into me, greeting me by becoming one voice of unbridled joy, shielding me from the light and noise by surrounding me, I choked up hard.

We were a single thing, a tangle of arms and jubilant, senseless swearing, the roars showering down on us, never letting up, but still I waited, fighting to keep my game face locked in, waiting for the noise to die down so I could speak to them.

The crowd didn't die down, transitioning from shock into a tight, loud drumbeat of my name being chanted. So I screamed over the crowd noise and told the team what I had come to tell them.

"I'll never quit on your guys ever again." If they didn't hear it, they felt it, and we would have stayed there forever if the referees didn't realize this was never going to end. They broke up the mob under our basket, and the crowd finally died down, saving their energy for the long game ahead.

I got to take a long, slow walk across the court to the bench, and that's when I looked over at our opponents. The Mater Dei starters were waiting near center court, and four of them were clapping politely. Robbie wasn't. He raised his hand, giving me a "bring it" gesture.

Coach wanted to gather us into a quick pre-tip huddle. When I got to the bench, the crowd was close enough to touch, and they roared again.

Preston was in the front row, on his feet like everyone else, looking almost punch-drunk. His mouth was open, and as I shifted one of the folding chairs to greet him face-to-face, his mouth moved, but no words came out.

"I just want you to know," I said. "Colorado isn't too far for me, as long as it's not too far for you."

I gave him time to respond, but the game was about to start. His mouth continued to quiver, but I'd said my piece. I headed back to the huddle.

Coach Ballard was on a knee. No whiteboard. He left it on the bench.

"You guys ready to have some fun?" he said.

"Hell yeah," Luke said, his deeper register drowning out everyone else's enthusiastic reply.

"You may not believe this," Coach said, "But we're going to play a box-and-one. You know the drill. Wilder's on Imming. He needs help, you help. Make someone else beat us."

Theo reached his hand into the center of the huddle. "Doberman on three!" he cried.

He counted us down, and we broke the huddle on "Doberman." I turned around to get a cone of water before gathering at center court for the tip and saw Preston standing right behind the bench. He had something to say, after all.

"That day on the bus, a long time ago, I told you friendship was weak . . . " He trailed off, looking for words, not finding them. Then, he just smiled and held out his fist.

We had tapped knuckles a thousand times before, but that was the fist-bump I'll always remember.

———

Robbie was a point guard and took the ball up the court. Playing denial defense was impossible when he already had the ball. Coach had us packed around the three-point line, on our defensive heels by design, and I was picking up Robbie around the top of the key or the wing. I kept forgetting he was a lefty, and in some of my defensive postures was actually inviting him to the basket with his strong hand. He took those invitations, and I quickly learned he was even faster than Theo.

His shot was better than Theo's as well, the release quick, the range deep. Late in the first quarter, I was waiting at the three-point line to meet him, and he pulled up beyond NBA range and buried a trey.

I had trained hard, but I wasn't in game-shape. Adrenaline fueled me through the first quarter, but adrenaline only stretches so far. Soon, lactic acid assaulted my muscles during even small bursts of defensive activity. I took extra breaks by stalling with my shoelaces (I had to tie them, slowly, about five times) or haphazardly rolling the ball to where the referee had to give me a few extra seconds as he retrieved it for an inbounds play.

Despite the exhaustion and Robbie's talent, I didn't relent. He crossed half court, possession after possession, and I put him through the fires of hell, doing my best to make him earn his space on the hardwood, inch by grueling inch.

I jammed my finger-stump into the ball trying to swat it away, sending a charge of pain up my forearm. I got floor burns chasing the basketball whenever I loosened it from his grip, and I'm sure every adult in the gym cringed whenever they heard the squeak of hardwood smearing my flesh.

Floor burns were never worse than first degree. I could handle them.

The team matched my energy, and the crowd pushed us beyond the human limits of exhaustion, full-throated with every stoppage in play. We flew out to an early six-point lead, but Mater Dei fought back. They took a five-point lead. We went on a run where Theo hit a couple of deep threes, and I logged a steal when the Knights' center tried to shovel the ball to Robbie on the wing.

We led by two after the first quarter. I choked down three cones of water, barely hearing Coach going through offensive sets. Mater Dei was still guarding me at the three-point line—they hadn't figured out I wasn't the shooter they expected in their scouting report. So I had two easy roles that required no coaching—stopper and decoy.

I drank water. Preston stepped away from the bleachers to talk to me. "Robbie's lazy without the ball," he said.

"I know," I said, shocked at how out of breath I was. "Hard to play denial defense when he takes the ball up the court."

"He doesn't take the ball out of bounds, does he?" Preston said. He was hinting at playing denial defense for the entire length of the court, trying to prevent the inbounds pass from coming in to him. Preston had a point, but even in my best condition, maintaining that kind of pace and intensity was almost impossible. Not if Robbie worked hard to get the ball, scraping me off of screens.

As I returned to the huddle, I glanced over at the R.A.K. section. Lane still wasn't among them.

"Hey," Preston said. I turned around. "Dairyn ran out of here during the first quarter. Someone had to have called Lane about your Willis Reed moment. I bet she's going to pick her up."

"Wilder, you playing or mingling?" Coach Ballard barked. The second quarter was starting. I ran out to join my teammates.

In the second quarter, I had a plan for the next time Robbie beat me off the dribble, which was inevitable with Robbie's quickness and skill. I left him space to slide by me on a left-handed dribble, then I met him at the basket and crushed him with a clean, hard, foul, clotheslining his forearm, sending him crashing onto the floor. The referee gave me a polite warning, and I knew I'd used up all of my "burned kid guts out playing a big game" capital with him.

As Robbie lined up to shoot free throws, I walked by him and said, "All day." I wanted him to know if he got to the basket, he'd pay the price as long as I had fouls to give.

The foul dampened his aggression for a few possessions, and we put them through a scoring drought, stretching our lead to ten. However, the problem with using grit instead of talent to build a big lead is that it's exhausting, and when you finally have some breathing room, you use it to breathe. I loafed on a couple of plays, and Robbie made me pay. Luke's clunky hands cost us a couple of possessions when he fumbled sure layups out of bounds. Theo took a few ill-fated "heat check" shots that had Coach Ballard stomping in frustration.

With four seconds left in the half, we were up by two points. Robbie pulled up just past half court and banked in a three at the buzzer. He left his hand up where I could see it, showboating as he strutted to the locker room with a one-point lead.

Our crowd greeted our effort with more loud praise, showing no signs of tiring out. They stood during the entire first half, and I imagined plenty of folks were cheering through palms bruised from applause and throats shredded by constant screaming.

A team that was supposed to beat our asses was only up by one point, and they knew they were in for a fight. We had already locked down a moral victory, and we had two more quarters to turn that into a real one.

As the team jogged into the locker room, I walked. Every step threatened to induce a cramp. We had a fifteen-minute break, and I'd need every second of it to stretch and hydrate. Just before going into the tunnel, I turned around and looked for Lane. She was nowhere to be found.

———

The starters gathered around Coach Ballard, who was diagramming at the whiteboard. I saw the fatigue in their rounded shoulders. Pools of sweat gathered underneath them, shimmering on the concrete, fed by a steady drip from the tips of their downcast noses. Towels laid limp around their necks. They didn't bother lifting their arms to use them.

I sat in the back of the locker room behind everyone, even the bench players who hadn't even logged a minute in the game, their jerseys crisp and dry. Coach was leaving his best players on the court until they fouled out or collapsed.

Coach was running through some tweaks to our offensive sets, but I couldn't focus. I heard Mr. Baldridge's voice echoing in the gymnasium as the Random Act of Kindness winners were announced.

I stood up and leaned out of the tunnel so I could hear better, my attention divided between Coach Ballard and the names being announced.

Then, I heard her name.

"The winner for February, Lane McKenzie," Mr. Baldridge said, to polite applause. Everyone was busy getting popcorn or lining up at the restrooms, and the ones that stayed behind in the bleachers needed their own rest after a raucous first half.

"As for defense," Coach said, writing the word COMPETITIVE-NESS on the whiteboard, in all caps, and then underlining it. "Change nothing. Go as hard as you can as long as you can."

I was leaning into the doorway even more. The students were lined up in front of the scorer's table, and Mrs. Ventura was handing out certificates.

Lane was out there, facing the crowd, her back to the locker-room entrance. I couldn't see her face, but I imagined her smiling.

I wanted to look at her so badly that I almost stepped out into the gym in that very moment, ready to ignore Coach Ballard and the team to tell her I was sorry and how much I cared about her.

I could say all I wanted, but it wouldn't mean anything. I heard Lane's voice from what felt like a lifetime ago—*show me*.

Show me your secrets. Show me what you don't show anyone else. Show me that you trust me, that you care about me, that all the things that matter are the things we cannot see.

"Wilder?" Coach said. I snapped to attention. The entire team was looking at me, wondering why I'd drifted away from them.

I drifted back. Coach had once said that the only world that existed was between the lines of the court. I understood that he meant to teach me that distraction could damage my play, but tonight, I wouldn't just blur the lines—I'd erase them. Those boundaries are what was protecting Mater Dei and Robbie Imming from the rabid avalanche of our crowd's energy, and the faces that channeled that energy into a broken body that had no business keeping up with conditioned, high school athletes.

Lane. Mom. Preston. Jenna.

"I'm going full-court on Imming," I said. "After every made basket, after every rebound they get, I'm going to stick him and make sure they can't pass him the ball."

Coach looked at me, dumbfounded. "You'll wear out in two minutes if you go that hard," he said.

"No," I said, "I won't."

"Let him try, Coach," Theo said. "I bet Imming starts loafing before the Doberman does."

Coach shook his head, not to say no—he just couldn't believe what the hell he was about to do.

"Well if Wilder's going to stick Imming full-court for an entire half, you guys can handle a half-court trap, right?"

The agreement was loud and unanimous. He drew up the trap layout on the whiteboard. We had our plan.

He held out his hand. "Coaching's over, boys," he said. "I'll do the pushups later, but go kick some ass!" We stacked our hands onto his and counted down to a cry of COMPETITIVENESS! as we broke the huddle.

As we walked to into the gym for the second half tip, Mater Dei was already out there, shooting around on their side of the court.

Robbie Imming smiled at me. He had no idea what I was about to unleash.

———

We broke one final huddle on the sideline and headed to mid-court for the tip-off. Lane was in the reserved section, right behind the scorer's table.

She saw me for the first time since the expanders were removed. I angled my body so she could see all of my bad side. She put her hand over her mouth, stifling a gasp. Tears boiled out of her eyes so quickly I started to mist up myself. The certificate in her left hand trembled. When she removed her hand from her mouth, she was smiling. I smiled back. Then, she looked up at the scoreboard. I followed her gaze. We looked at each other one more time as the ref loaded up the ball for the tip. I wanted to wink, or nod, or give her a sign that she was the reason I was at the game, but before I could do anything clever or memorable, the referee blew his whistle and the ball was in the air.

I had work to do.

Luke won the tip. Theo brought the ball up, and on our first possession, he passed it to me on the wing. Mater Dei was playing a zone defense, and they collapsed on the interior when I caught the pass. It took them half the game to figure it out, but I wasn't taking open shots with my injured right hand, so they were going to pack in their defense and allow me to shoot.

With the space they offered, I drove to the basket. Two Knights stepped up to cut me off, one of them holding his arms over his waist, hoping to absorb the impact and draw an offensive foul. I jump-stopped and threaded a bounce pass in to Luke, who had his defender sealed off with his hip.

He caught the pass clean, laid the ball into the basket, and we had a one-point lead. Everyone scampered back to the other side of the court, but not Robbie, who stayed behind to take the inbounds pass.

I stayed with him, matching his every step. The denial defense took them by surprise, and there was no one around to set a screen for him. Their center ran the baseline, trying to find an opening, hoping to avoid a five-second call, which would turn the ball over to us if he couldn't inbound it in time.

After a few seconds, he lobbed the inbounds pass over the top of me as Robbie ran toward mid-court. I jumped, selling out to try and deflect the pass, grazing the leather with my index and middle fingers just enough to slow it down. The loose ball hit the hardwood. Robbie turned back to pick it up, and I dove into the ball, the gym floor squealing as it rubbed more floor burns into the skin on my knees.

With both of us wrestling for the ball, the referee called for a jump ball. The possession arrow was in our favor, so we got the ball back. Theo hit a three from the deep wing, and the crowd popped.

This time, the Knights left a screener back to help Robbie get the ball. I anticipated the pick play, sliding away from the screener, staying between Robbie and the ball. The lob attempt was deeper this time, but

Theo was at half court, ready to trap. He saw an opportunity and ran down the lob, intercepting it, giving us another possession.

Theo missed a jumper, but Luke tapped the rebound in. We were suddenly up by six. The bleachers shook—our fans weren't just cheering but jumping, stressing the joints of the wooden planks.

Mater Dei called a time-out. I spent the break sitting at the end of our bench, trying to catch my breath and rest my legs.

I looked into the crowd. Lane was clapping, and she smiled at me. Mom was in the back row of the bleachers with some other mothers. She looked happy and proud, dancing along with the cheerleaders. Jenna was leading the cheer squad, drumming up a FIGHT-ING GRIFF-INS chant. Preston saw me taking it all in and flexed his arm, pointing to his bicep, a reminder that I was strong enough to go the distance.

The time-out ended. This time, the Knights ran a double screen on me, but it was a decoy, and the shooting guard took the inbounds pass. Robbie ran off the screens, and I slammed into the second pick, not expecting the impact. I dropped to the floor as Robbie got the pass from his teammate.

I sprung to my feet, pleased at how much effort and focus Mater Dei needed just to get Robbie the ball seventy feet away from our basket.

After the chaos had cleared, Robbie had the ball, but I was ready to meet him at half court. I crouched into my defensive stance and slapped the floor the way a Spartan might beat on his shield. Robbie dribbled into enemy territory. Every nuance of his body language screamed out "not again," and I knew the game was over.

With a minute to go in the game, the Herrick Fighting Griffins were up by eleven points. After a furious possession that took more than thirty seconds, Robbie hit a deep three to cut the lead to eight.

Coach Ballard called time-out, let us catch our breath, then knelt in the huddle. With so little time left, we could just run out the clock unless Mater Dei fouled us on purpose, hoping we'd miss the free throws and give them the ball back with time to make a comeback. Our team had struggled all night at the free throw line, and that was with me taking zero foul shots to drag down our percentage even further.

Coach drew up a play, thinking that Mater Dei would trap Theo with full-court pressure, hoping to get a clean steal before finally fouling. He was diagramming a way to get someone open for Theo to touch pass it down the court before they could trap.

"Ty, you're in for Wilder," Coach said then went back to reminding us on our options if one of us got trapped.

I hadn't come out the entire game, but at this point, with less than a minute left, I had to agree substituting made sense. Anyone would be a better foul shooter than me, and Ty especially was a smart replacement. He had one of the team's best free throw percentages.

Theo wasn't having it. "No way, Coach," he said. "This is the ultimate Doberman game, and he's gonna be on the floor when the buzzer sounds and we win this thing."

"We need free throw shooting," Coach said. "I'll get him back in once it's locked up."

"It's locked up," Theo answered.

"Wilder will hit the free throws, Coach," Luke said.

"We don't need Robbie getting loose with just a minute left," Ty added. I didn't know if he was too scared to guard Robbie for a possession or two with the game iced, or if he just picked up on the fact that everyone was rallying around me, and he didn't want to be the outlier.

Coach looked at his whiteboard and started wiping away the diagram. We didn't need much of a play if I was on the court. Mater Dei would be delighted to have me shooting free throws.

"Here's my official coaching strategy," Coach said. "Make your free throws, and then we celebrate."

As we walked onto the court, we stacked up to run the inbounds play. Robbie got close enough for his chest to touch my shoulder. They were setting up pressure defense, desperate to deny the ball to everyone but me.

"Let's see you ice the game, Igor," he grunted. When the referee blew the whistle, he ran away from me, double-teaming Theo as Luke monitored his inbounds options. Five guys were guarding four, and I was left all alone at half court. Luke threw it to me, and Robbie followed the ball in flight, making sure to foul me the moment I caught it. I started walking to the free throw line, trying to calm myself down. Even with a decent lead and time running out, the crowd was nervous—but nowhere near as nervous as me.

Robbie walked right alongside me. "No pressure," he said.

Theo nudged him away, walking me to the line. "You got this," he said.

I positioned myself on the line and took the pass from the referee, staring at the center eyelet of the rim. I took three dribbles and cocked the ball to shoot left-handed. The home crowd got quiet. I hesitated. Then I felt the nerves too acutely and started dribbling the ball again.

"Let's go, thirty-three," the ref said, tucking his whistle into his mouth.

I glanced over at the R.A.K. section, where Lane and the rest of the students in the front row had locked arms, uniting to will the ball into the basket. The weight of the prayers in that gym was a tangible thing, and I felt that kind of pressure on my shoulders in games past, but not tonight.

I winked at Lane and returned my focus to the rim. I spun the ball and held it loosely between my palms, dangling it between my knees. I unleashed a classic granny shot, flipping it at the basket underhanded, and swished the free throw.

The crowd went wild. The Mater Dei players struggled to come up with trash talk since the shot went in, opting instead to shake their heads in disbelief. If they didn't know it already, they knew it now—this was not their night.

The second shot touched the rim, then the backboard, then teetered on the side of the rim one more time, then fell through the hoop. We had a ten-point lead with forty-five seconds to play.

The Knights pushed the ball down the court and missed a frantic shot by their small forward from the top of the key. Robbie should have taken it, but I was draped on him, denying him on the deep wing, and his will to fight himself open was gone.

When we got the ball back, their coach barked out, "Don't foul." Twenty seconds left. Theo dribbled out the clock, but with four seconds to play, he bounced it over to me. I held it at center court as the buzzer went off, then I threw the ball into the air as the students poured onto the court.

We won, and even though we had the game wrapped up for most of the second half, I still didn't believe it until that moment. My body returned from that transcendent place where fatigue and pain didn't exist. I collapsed onto the hardwood, laughing the entire time.

When I went down, the crowd packed around me backed off. Someone asked if I was okay, and I just kept laughing. Preston fought through the density of celebrating students and reached out his hand to help me up. I took it, and he curled me up to my feet. I put my arm around him, my legs rubbery, shaking from effort.

"Damn son, you drunk again?" he said.

The ladder was already out, getting unfolded underneath the basket. Players would take turns stepping up to the top and snipping off a piece of the net, a moment every high school basketball player dreams about.

"I don't think I can make it up the ladder," I said. "Your ankle good enough for you to get up there? Snip off two pieces for us?"

I let him go. My legs held firm.

"Yeah, dude," he said. "You sure you don't want to do it? It's your moment."

I saw Lane by the baseline, away from the thickest part of the crowd.

"It's a moment worth sharing," I told him.

I pushed through the crowd. Lane stood there, arms crossed, one of her hips cutely jutted out to one side, not just waiting for me but expecting me.

When I was close enough, her arms parted, and we embraced. My legs were strong again, and I lifted her up, spinning us around while hugging her. We just laughed.

"Come with me," I said. I pulled her away from the chaos of the gym into the hallway, where disappointed Mater Dei fans were filtering out. I held Lane's hand, taking her through the hallways and into the library. Our library.

"The game just ended, and you want to study?" Lane said.

"I wanted to show you something," I said. I untucked my jersey and rolled up the front, prepared to take it off and finally show her.

She touched my forearm, stopping me.

"No," she whispered. "You've shown me enough."

Her eyes were wet with tears yet to fall, shining with the reflection of the library lights. She looked like a constellation.

"I'm sorry," I said. "I was just scared. I shouldn't have hurt you like that."

"I broke your neck," she said. "I think we're just about even."

She reached out, placing her fingertips on the side of my face, then tracing the line of the remaining scars down to my neck. I lacked the nerve endings to feel it, but somehow, I felt it all the same.

"I can't believe they're gone," she said.

"They were in the way," I said and kissed her. I didn't know the kiss was happening until my lips were on hers, but she didn't share my surprise, tilting her head as if she were ready all along.

I never felt anything so warm and incredible in my life, and I couldn't tell you if we spent days or hours or minutes in that kiss. Time didn't stop—it stretched and twisted and snapped back into place only when the kiss was over.

"You won the big game and got the girl," she whispered. "What's next for Wilder Tate?"

"Everything," I said, and then we kissed again.

PART FOUR
GRAVITY

PROM

After the coronation of Theo and Jenna as the prom king and queen, after the prom court's box step dance, after the parents had gone home and the night finally belonged solely to the students of Herrick Community High School, I lingered in the hallway all by myself, away from the party.

Our regional championship trophy was in the glass cases that lined the hallway, and in the school days that followed our win, I often found myself checking that it was still there, as if the whole thing were imagined and could be yanked away if I just woke up.

The DJ was kicking off the party with dance music. The subwoofers made the glass chatter in its frame, sending ripples through my reflection.

"I thought I'd find you here," Lane said.

I saw her slender arm bent in the softened light of the hallway, as she adjusted an elegant choker that laid against the plain of her upper chest. The dress was blue with sequin and crystal as if the sky and stars had melted together. She wore formal gloves up to her elbows, a distinct accessory none of the other girls wore.

Her dark hair was gathered into a gem-encrusted bun. Her earrings flickered as she turned her head, and her bare shoulders shimmered with a body powder spiked with glitter.

When she looked me in the eyes, I didn't care about one thing that happened to me in my scorched, bone-breaking life—I'd laid eyes on Lane McKenzie on the night of prom, and only a few hundred living souls would be able to share in that accomplishment.

"There's some old guy with a strand of basketball net pinned to his bulletin board," I said. "He sees it, and he remembers the janitor getting the ladder out as the fans roared, waiting his turn to climb up and snip it off the basket. It's a piece of this net, right here."

She stood beside me, and I pointed not to our trophy, but the last one Herrick won in 1989.

"Look at how old that trophy looks." Our 2017 trophy was gilded with only the finest fake gold spray, crowned with a net as bright and new and white as a young bride's dress on a spring day. "I think it's just a reminder to enjoy it. Time can be an asshole."

"I don't think your trophy is going to tarnish for quite a while," she said, taking my hand.

"That's your trophy, too," I said. "I don't think we'd have it without you."

"Maybe you're right. You only scored two more points than me that night, superstar." She kissed my cheek. The bad one. "Your girl wants to dance with you. You coming?"

I took the charm bracelet from my pocket and pressed it into her hand. I paid a jeweler fifteen bucks to professionally clean it, so now all the mud was gone from the links, and he told me all the scratches or marks on the surface was just burnishment, a sign of a well-worn, well-loved piece of sterling silver jewelry.

"Is this?" she said, not finishing the question.

"It is," I said. "I was going to trade it in for a brand-new one, just for you. One without a history."

"Don't you dare," she said, running her thumb over the links.

"I don't have any charms," I said. "I was thinking we could figure that part out together."

Lane peeled off her gloves. Self-inflicted cutting grooves covered her arm, but I was overjoyed to see the whiteness of healed scars and no fresh wounds.

She rolled up the gloves and gave them to me. "I guess I have something for you, too."

"They'll look great with that denim jacket," I said.

She playfully slapped my chest then held up her hand as she slid the bracelet onto her wrist.

I took her by the hand, and we returned to the gym. We eased into a dance, her hands on my shoulders, my hands on her jewel-studded waist, and in that moment, all the things that once happened to us were firmly underfoot, and the only thing left to do was climb.

ACKNOWLEDGMENTS

The day that I signed the contract to publish this book, I clicked send on the document and then left to go to my mother's visitation. I lost her in January, 2019, after a long battle with cancer, and I tried to honor her strength and resourcefulness in this novel, which is why Wilder's mother shares her name, JoAnn. Thank you for everything, Mom.

The book wouldn't have existed in the first place without the patience and steady hand of Kirby Kim, who inspired me to try and turn an essay about the injuries and heartbreak of my teenage years into a full-blown, dramatic work of fiction.

I owe the team at Turner a huge debt of gratitude for taking a chance on me and on this book—thank you Stephanie Beard, Heather Howell, Kathleen Timberlakew, and Todd Bottorff. I appreciate Ashley Strosnider taking my thoughts and words in this novel and making them cleaner and better.

I dedicated the novel to my wife, Krissy, and my daughter, Noelle. A love story is hard to write without a great love, and Krissy has always been that for me. She sacrifices so I can have time to write, listens to every crazy idea, and keeps me grounded during the ups and downs of the writing life.

Noelle is six years old as I write this, and I can't think of anyone more inspiring, more full of joy and energy and creativity, more kind and generous, than my baby girl. (I love you, Noelle!)

A story so deeply tied to my childhood requires a thank-you to many of the friends who helped me survive and have been at my side for decades. I can't possibly name everyone, but Bucky Miller has proven to me that family doesn't require blood—we are brothers, plain and simple, and our stories would require a book all its own (possibly more than one volume). Glenn Reynolds and Kevin Thompson were there for me since my days in Vernon, and along with Bucky, they carried my mother when she needed carried one last time.

A round of thank-yous that will get me in trouble for the people I'll inevitably miss:

To Ballard and Renfro, for the times when we aren't joking around, when I needed you, and you were there.

To Mitch Cain, one of the hardest-working men I know, for enduring long and meandering phone calls and tolerating me long enough to build a real estate business.

To Michael Nye, for so much . . . you are the Tango to my Cash.

To my sister, Megan, for your strength and humor.

To my niece, Josie, for being like a sister to Noelle.

To the early readers of this novel, who braved the early drafts and helped turn it into the (hopefully) polished product you just finished (hopefully) enjoying: Talisha, Jenna, Cassie, Kurt, Brandon, Kristy.

To Chuck Palahniuk—you were right.

To Dan Loflin, for the inspiration, for listening to my ideas and helping me shape them, for being at the center of my cool LA stories, for being my sometimes-therapist, and for the excellent brisket.

To everyone in my life who was there for me when I was broken and helped put me back together, over and over again.

And to anyone who thinks all is lost, who has lost someone, who has been stomped on and forgotten, who has been broken or bullied . . . remember the words of Hemingway: the world breaks us all, but afterward many are strong at the broken places.

We call those places scars. Wear them with pride.

FRED VENTURINI
April 15, 2019

For a personal thank-you gift
from the author, please visit

FREDVENTURINI.COM/THANKS

CPSIA information can be obtained
at www.ICGtesting.com
Printed in the USA
BVHW031030031019
560137BV00006B/32/P